Autumn Wind and Other Stories

Lane Dunlop has won several awards for translation, including the Japan–US Friendship Award for Literary Translation for both *A Late Chrysanthemum* and *Twenty-four Stories from the Japanese*, and the American Academy of Arts and Letters Academy Award in Literature. He is co-translator of Yasunari's Kawabata *Palm-of-the-Hand Stories* and the translator of numerous Japanese novels, including Kafu Nagai's *During the Rains & Flowers in the Shade: Two Novellas*.

Lane Dunlop

Autumn Wind and Other Stories

Translated by
Lane Dunlop

TUTTLE PUBLISHING
Tokyo • Rutland, Vermont • Singapore

For Ce Roser

Acknowledgments are due to the editors of the following magazines, in which these stories first appeared in slightly different form: *Translation* for "The Fox", "Mount Hiei", "Autumn Wind", "Bamboo Flowers" and "Borneo Diamond"; *The Literary Review* for "Flash Storm", "Along the Mountain Ridge", and "Ivy Gates"; *Prairie Schooner* for "The Garden", *New England Review* for "One Woman and the War" and "Grass"; *Mississippi Review* for "The Titmouse" and "Ugly Demons"; *Michigan Quarterly Review* for "Invitation to Suicide."

Kitsune ©1909 by Nagai Kafu, 1959 Nagai Nagamitsu; *Niwaka are* ©1916 by Satomi Ton, 1983 Yamauchi Shizuo; *Heizan* ©1935 by Yokomitsu Riichi, 1947 Yokomitsu Shozo; *Akikaze* ©1939 by Nakayama Gishu, 1969 Nakayama Himeko; *Higara* ©1940 by Kawabata Yasunari, 1972 Kawabata Hite; *Senso to hitori no onna* ©1946 by Hayashi Fumiko, 1951 Hayashi Fukue; *Iwa one nite* ©1956 by Kita Morio; *Shumatachi* ©1965 by Kurahashi Yumiko; *Take no hana* ©1970 by Mizukami Tsutomu; *Jisatsu no susume* ©1969 by Watanabe Jun'ichi

Published by Tuttle Publishing, an imprint of Periplus Editions (HK) Ltd., with editorial offices at 364 Innovation Drive, North Clarendon, Vermont 05759 U.S.A. and 130 Joo Seng Road #06-01, Singapore 368357.

LCC Card No. 94-60314
ISBN-10: 4-8053-0850-8
ISBN-13: 978-4-8053-0850-9

Distributed by:

North America, Latin America & Europe
Tuttle Publishing
364 Innovation Drive, North Clarendon, VT 05759-9436 U.S.A.
Tel: 1 (802) 773-8930 Fax: 1 (802) 773-6993
info@tuttlepublishing.com
www.tuttlepublishing.com

Japan
Tuttle Publishing
Yaekari Building, 3rd Floor, 5-4-12 Osaki, Shinagawa-ku, Tokyo 141-0032
Tel: (81) 3 5437-017 Fax: (81) 3 5437-0755
tuttle-sales@gol.com

Asia Pacific
Berkeley Books Pte Ltd
130 Joo Seng Road #06-01, Singapore 368357
Tel: (65) 6280-1330 Fax: (65) 6280-6290
inquiries@periplus.com.sg
www.periplus.com

07 09 11 12 10 08
1 3 5 6 4 2

Printed in Singapore

Contents

Translator's Preface

These stories span sixty years of twentieth-century Japanese literature. Between the bittersweet, nostalgic evocation of childhood in Nagai Kafu's "The Fox," set against a background of a still largely traditional Japan, and the alienated, thoroughly modern world of Watanabe Jun'ichi's "Invitation to Suicide" is a development comparable in range and scope to that of any world-class literature. During these years Japan, after centuries of seclusion, adjusted to its full-scale entry into the world, to the successive traumatic shocks of the Great Earthquake of 1923 and the catastrophic defeat of World War II, and to the phoenix-like revival of its economy.

Most of the writers represented in this selection are what might be called standard authors. Their work, all or some of it, continues to be in print decade after decade. Kawabata Yasunari, Japan's only Nobel Prize winner for literature, needs almost no introduction to Western readers; on the other hand, Juichiya Gisaburo, who is perhaps remembered for the one story included in this selection, must be all but unknown even to Japanese. The anthology includes the famous and the unfamiliar, writers known to English readers and others whose work has not been translated previously. Most of the stories themselves are new to English. Those that are not exist only in translations that have been out of print for so long as to be well nigh inaccessible to all but the most devoted student.

It may be said that the dominant tone of Japanese writing is one of characteristically understated sobriety. Whether this is due to the nature of the language, the Japanese temperament, or the realistic mode that has prevailed in the literature is beyond the ambition of this preface. But having once noted it, one must also note the variety of modulations this voice is capable of. In this selection alone are the poignant yearning for the past of Nakayama Gishu's "Autumn Wind," the buoyant cynicism of Sakaguchi Ango's "One Woman and the War," the sexual knowledgeability of Kurahashi Yumiko's "Ugly Demons"—perhaps as many variations as there are writers. It is the translator's sincere hope that some of the pleasure afforded him by the perusal and translation of these stories will be conveyed to, and shared with, the reader.

AUTUMN
WIND
and
Other Stories

The Fox

永井荷風

NAGAI KAFU

The sound of dry leaves racing through the garden, the sound of wind rattling the paper doors.

One afternoon in my winter study, by a dim little window, as if in memory of the autumn-evening field where I'd parted from my lover some years ago, I was leaning lonelily against a brazier and reading a biography of Turgenev.

One summer evening, when he was still a child without knowledge of things, Turgenev wandered through his father's garden, densely overgrown with trees and shrubs. By the weedy edge of an old pond, he came upon the miserable sight of a frog and a snake trying to devour each other. In his innocent, childish heart, Turgenev had immediately doubted the goodness of God . . . As I read this passage, for some reason I remembered the frightening old garden of my father's house in Koishikawa, where I was born. In those days, already more than thirty years ago, the canal of the Suido district flowed through fields of spiderwort like a rural stream.

At that time the vacant residences of vassals and lower-grade retainers of the old shogunate were coming on the market here and there. Buying up a group of them, my father built a spacious new mansion, while leaving the old groves and gardens intact. By the time I was born, the ornamental alcove posts of the new house had already acquired some of the soft luster of the polishing cloth. On the stones of the garden, which was just as it had always been, the moss grew deeper and deeper, and the shade of the trees and shrubs grew darker and darker. Far back, in the darkest part of those groves, there were two old wells, said to be vestiges of the original households. One of them, during a period of five or six years from before my birth, had been gradually filled in by our gardener, Yasukichi, with all the garden trash, such as dead pine needles, broken-off cryptomeria branches, and fallen cherry leaves. One evening at the beginning of winter, when I had just turned four, I watched Yasu at work. Having finished the job of getting the pines, palms, and bananas ready for the frost, he broke down the sides of the well, which were covered all over with mushrooms dried white like mold. This is one of my many frightening memories of the garden. Ants, millipedes, centipedes, galley worms, earthworms, small snakes, grubs, earwigs, and various other insects that had been asleep in their winter home, crawling out from between the rotten boards in great numbers, began to squirm and writhe slipperily in the cold, wintry gale. Many of them, turning up their dingy white undersides, died on the spot. With a helper whom he'd brought along, Yasu gathered the day's fallen leaves and dead branches together with the chopped-up boards of the well and set it all on fire. Raking in with a bamboo broom the insects and wriggling snakes that had begun to crawl away, he burned them alive. The fire made sharp, crackling noises. There was no flame, only a damp whitish smoke, which as it climbed through the high tops of the old trees, gave off an indescribably bad smell. The wintry wind, howling desolately in those old treetops, seemed to blow down dark night all through the garden. From the direction of the invisible house, the voice of the wet nurse was calling loudly for me. Abruptly bursting into tears, I was led by the hand by Yasu back to the house.

Yasu neatly leveled the ground over the plugged-up old well, but during the spring rains, evening showers, stormy days, and other spells of heavy rain the surface of the ground would subside a foot or two. Afterward the area was roped off and no one allowed to go near it. I remember being told with a special sternness by both my parents to stay away from there. As for the other old well, it indeed is the most terrifying memory I have of that period, which I could not forget even if I tried to. The well seemed to be extraordinarily deep, so that even Yasu did not attempt to fill it up. I don't know what kind of house now stands on that property, but no doubt the well, with the old tree alongside it, is still there in a corner of the grounds.

All around in back of the well, like the precinct of a shrine that's said to be haunted, a grove of cedars stood in dense, dark quietude both summer and winter. It made that part of the garden all the more frightening. Behind the grove there was a black wooden fence with sharp-pointed stakes atop it. On the other side there was, on one hand, the unfrequented thoroughfare of Kongo Temple at the top of a slope and, on the other, a shantytown that my father had always disliked, saying, "If they would only pull that place down . . . "

My father had bought up what originally had been three small estates. It was all our property now, but the old well was on a patch of wasteland at the base of a cliff that, since it was far down the slope from where the house had been built, was almost forgotten about by the people of the household. My mother often asked my father why he'd bought that useless piece of land. My father's reply was that if he hadn't, a slum would have gone up at the foot of the hill. We'd have had to look at dirty tile roofs and laundry drying in the sun. By buying it up and leaving it the same, he kept it nice and quiet down there. Probably for my father, the sinister forms of the old trees that howled in the wind, wept in the rain, and held the night in their arms were not frightening at all. There were even times when my father's formal, angular face seemed more vaguely alarming than the wen-shaped knot of a pine.

One night a thief got into the house and stole a padded silk garment of my mother's. The next morning our regular fireman, the foreman of the carpenters, and a detective from the police station came by. As they went along examining the footprints by the edge of the veranda outside my father's sitting room, they found more prints in the trodden and crushed frost that led clear through the midwinter garden. It became evident that the thief had sneaked onto the grounds from the black wooden fence in back of the old well. In front of the well, there was a dirty old towel that he must have dropped in his getaway. Taken by the hand by the chief carpenter, Seigoro, who in feudal days had served the house of Mito, for the first time in my life I walked around this old well off in a corner of the old garden. A solitary willow tree stood by the side of the well. Half-rotten, the trunk had become hollowed and many sad-looking dead branches hung down from it. Struck by an indescribable eeriness, I didn't so much as think of trying to peer down to the bottom of this well that was too deep to fill up even if one had wanted to.

It was not only myself who was afraid. After the robbery, that part of the garden at the base of the cliff and around the old well became a place of dread for everyone in the family except my father. The Satsuma Rebellion had just ended, and the world was full of stories of conspirators, assassins, armed burglars, and bloodthirsty cruelty. Dark, paranoid suspicions hovered everywhere in the air. One could not tell when, under cover of night, lurking under the veranda of the stately gated house of a well-to-do person or of a merchant with a big storehouse, listening for the sleeping breath of the master, a terrorist or assassin would thrust his sword up through the tatami mat. At our house, without the proposal coming from my father or mother, it was decided to have the regular fireman make a watchman's rounds at night. Night after cold night, as I lay in my wet nurse's arms, I heard the clacking of his wooden clapper sound out loud and clear all through the sleeping house.

There was nothing so unpleasant and frightening as the night. After having a Beniya bean-jam wafer from a shop on Ando Slope as my snack, I would have just started playing house with my mother when the yellow evening sunlight on the translucent paper sliding door would fade away even as I looked. The wind rattled drearily through the bare-branched trees and shrubs. It started getting dark first by the black walls of the ornamental alcove in the parlor. When my mother, saying that she was going to wash her hands, stood up and slid open the door, it was dusky all through the garden to the base of the cliff, where it was completely dark. Of anywhere on the grounds, the place where it became night earliest was at the base of the cliff, where that old well was. But wasn't it from the bottomless depth of that old well that the night welled up? Such feelings did not leave me until long afterward.

Even after I had begun to go to grade school, along with the tale of O-Kiki of the Plate House advertised on the notices for peep shows on temple festival days and the picture book *Mysterious Lights on the Sea* from which my wet nurse read to me, not merely the old well but the ancient, half-decayed willow tree alongside it took on the force of a natural spell. I could not tell how many times they had frightened me in dreams. I wanted to see the frightening thing itself. But when I timidly asked about it, the wet nurse snipped off the buds of my young awareness with the scissors of superstition. As for my father, when he scolded me for disobedience one of his worst threats was that he would drive me out of the house and tie me up to the willow tree by the well. Ah, what terrible memories of childhood. Even when I was twelve or thirteen, I was afraid to go to the bathroom by myself at night. But I dare say I was not alone in this among the children who grew up in that period.

My father was a government official. In those days the cabinet was called the Great Hall of Government, and a minister was addressed as My Lord. At one time my father had been passionately devoted to horsemanship. Four or five years later, when that enthusiasm had died down, he suddenly took up archery. Every morning, before going to the office, he would place a target halfway up the cliff. Standing by the side of the well with his back to the willow tree, he twanged the bowstring in the cool morning breezes of summer. Soon, however, autumn came around. One chilly morning my father, who practiced with one shoulder bare, having excitedly dashed up the cliff path and back down with the bow still in his hand, called out in a loud, hoarse voice, "Tazaki! Tazaki! Come quickly. There's a fox in the garden."

Tazaki was a youth of sixteen or seventeen who, by virtue of being from my father's native village, was living at our house as a student-houseboy. Because of an imposing physique and a way of throwing back his shoulders and giving loud harangues larded with many Chinese words, he seemed to me like a pompous adult.

"What is the matter, sir?"

"Damned nuisance. There's a fox in this garden. It was startled by the sound of my bow and jumped out of the beargrass at the foot of the cliff. It must have a hole around there."

Together with his rickshaw man, Kisuke, and Tazaki, my father searched the dense growth of low, striped bamboo from around halfway down the cliff. But soon it was time to go to the office.

"Tazaki, search this place thoroughly."

"Yes, sir. I will do so."

Tazaki prostrated himself in the entryway as my father's rickshaw, with a crunching sound over the gravel, went out through the front gate. The minute it was gone, he tucked up his formal divided skirt and with a shoulder pole in one hand stepped out into the garden. When I think of the student-houseboys of those days, it all comes back—the laughable distinctions observed between master and servant, just as in the old feudal days.

My mother, who was gentle and kind to everyone, seeing the preparations of Tazaki, said to him, "It's dangerous. The fox might well bite you, and then what would you do? Please don't go."

"Madam. Are you suggesting that I'm not a match for a fox? There's nothing to it. I'll beat it to death and have it ready to show the master when he gets back."

Squaring his shoulders in that way of his, Tazaki put on a blustering front. Later this man was to become an army officer, and in the Sino-Japanese War achieved a bloody death in the field. Perhaps he felt a natural affinity for slaughter. Our cook, O-Etsu, who was not on good terms with Tazaki and who was a country-bred person full of superstitions, paled and explained to him that it would be bad luck for the house if he killed the fox-god. Tazaki rejected this point-blank, saying it was not for the likes of a rice cook to poke her nose in where the master's orders were concerned. O-Etsu, puffing out her full red cheeks as she talked, and my wet nurse then told me all about fox possession and fox curses, instances of people being bewitched by foxes and of the miracles of the fox-god, Takezo Inari, whose shrine was in back of Denzu Temple. Although thinking uneasily of such things like the much talked-about method of divination called table-turning, I halfway sided with Tazaki's bravado and wanted to go with him on his fox conquest. But half of me doubted, wondering if there was anything in the world as strange as this.

Tazaki, thrashing about in the beargrass thickets until he was called back for lunch, his shins scratched and bleeding from the raspy-edged bamboo blades and thorns, his face all covered with cobwebs for nothing, came back without having found anything that even looked like a fox hole. In the evening my father returned, followed by an old man called Yodoi. Yodoi, who was my father's chess and drinking companion almost every night, was a lower-grade civil official who did some money-lending on the side, an underling from my father's office who made the maids cry because he stayed so long. He drew pictures for me of the horse-drawn trolley cars downtown that were coming into use at that time, and for my mother he had stories of such heroes as Tasuku Hikosaburo and Tanosuke. Accompanied by Yodoi as Tazaki led the way with a paper lantern, my father searched all around the garden twice. In the late evening air, the noise of myriads of insects sounded like falling rain. It was my first discovery of the purity, coldness, and pallor of an autumn night.

My mother told a story of having been awakened in the small hours that same night—it was no dream—by an unmistakable wailing sound in the garden. From the next day on the maids would not set foot outside the house after dark no matter what. Our devotedly loyal O-Etsu, believing that bad luck was in store for us, caught a cold from sprinkling well water over herself at daybreak and praying to the god of fire. Hearing about this, Tazaki secretly reported it to my father, and the upshot was that poor O-Etsu was harshly scolded and told that there was a limit even to making a fool of oneself. My wet nurse, after talking it over with my mother, just happened to get a dog from our regular fish dealer, Iroha. In addition, she now and then left out scraps of fried bean curd in the beargrass thickets at the base of the cliff.

Early each morning, paying no mind to the chill that deepened day by day, my father went out to the rear of the garden by the old well and practiced his archery. But the fox did not show itself again. Once an emaciated stray dog that had wandered in from somewhere had its ear bitten off by our dog, who set on it savagely as it was eating the fried bean curd. By slow degrees, a mood of relief had spread through the household. Perhaps the fox had escaped to somewhere. Or it hadn't been a fox at all, but some other stray dog. Already it was winter.

"Isn't there anyone to clean out the brazier in this cold weather? All the servants in this house are blockheads." One morning, these chiding words of my father's were heard all through the house.

Throughout the house the storm shutters, the paper sliding doors, and the openwork panels over lintels banged and rattled. At the edge of the veranda, like water poured out on the ground, the lonely sound of the wind in the shrubbery was suddenly heard and as suddenly not. When it was time to go to school, my mother, saying that I should wear a scarf, pulled out the drawers of the clothes chest. In the chill, empty air of the big parlor, the smell of camphor seemed to spread through my whole body. But it was still warm in the afternoons. When my mother, the wet nurse, and I went out onto a sunny part of the porch, the appearance of the garden, compared with the time of excitement about the fox, was as changed as if it were another world. I took it strangely to heart. The branches of the plum tree and the blue paulownia were bare and barren. The luxuriant growth of fall plants, such as the rose mallow and the chickenhead clover, had all faded away and died. Unfiltered by leafage, the brilliant sunlight fell full on the ground. From the filled-in well, where Yasu had burnt alive the small snakes and grubs, to the dark, scary grove of cedars at the base of the cliff, you could see everywhere in the garden through the wintry skeletons of the treetops. As for the maples among the pines on the lower slope of the cliff, their scarlet autumn foliage had turned into dirty old leaves that pell-mell flew and scattered in the wind. In the bonsai landscape tray, set out on a stepping stone at the edge of the veranda, one or two solitary leaves, dyed red as blood, were left on the miniature waxtree. Outside the circular window of my father's study, the leaves of the *yatsude* were blacker than any ink, and its jewel-like flowers pallidly glittered. By the water basin, where the fruit of the nandin was still green, the low twittering of the bush warbler was always to be heard. On the roof, under the eaves, about the windows, and everywhere in the garden, the chirruping voice of the sparrow seemed almost noisy.

I did not think that the garden in early winter was either lonely or sad. At least I did not feel that it was any more frightening than on a slightly overcast day of autumn. On the contrary, it was a pleasure to tread underfoot the carpet of fallen leaves, to walk about amid its crackling noise. But from the time that Yasukichi, wearing his livery coat dyed with the family crest, came with his helper to make the pines and banana trees ready for winter as he always did, it was not long before the first morning frost did not melt until the afternoon. After that, there was no setting foot in the garden anymore.

Before we were aware of it, our house dog had vanished somewhere. Various explanations were given, such as that he had been done in by the dogcatcher or that he was a valuable dog so somebody had stolen him. I begged my father to let us have another dog. But saying that if he did so, other strange dogs would hang around when it was in heat, breaking down the hedges and laying waste to the garden, my father refused to allow another dog in the household. Some time before this, a small poultry yard had been built by the well outside the kitchen. I used to love to feed the chickens every day when I got back from school. For that reason I didn't complain very much about not having a dog. It was the happy, peaceful season of midwinter seclusion. As for the mysterious affair of the fox, it faded out of the fancies of the maidservants and the other people of the house. There was no dog now to bark at the footsteps of a person going by late in the night. In the sound of the wind that swayed the tall trees of the garden, there was only the thin, distant peal of the temple bell of Denzuin. Sitting at the warm, sunken hearth with my mother and the wet nurse, I turned and spread out the pages of storybooks and of woodblock color prints under the quiet lamplight. My father, with his subordinate and crony, Yodoi, played go with a crisp, clinking sound of the stones behind the six-leafed screen that had been drawn around them in the inner hall. Sometimes he would clap his hands and shout at the maid for her faulty way of pouring the saké. My mother, saying that such things could not be left to the servants, would get up and go through the cold dark of the house to the kitchen. In my child's heart, I almost hated my father for his lack of consideration.

It drew near the end of the year. A man who had been a palanquin-bearer in the old days, lately reduced to making frames for paper lanterns in the slum at the foot of the hill, hung himself. At the top of Ando Slope, not far from us, a gang of five thieves broke into a pawn-shop and killed a sixteen-year-old girl. An arsonist set fire to a secondary temple in the precinct of the Denzuin. A restaurant called the Tatsumiya, which had flour-ished on Tomi Slope in the days of Lord Mito, went bankrupt. We heard these stories in turn from such people as Kyusai, the family masseur, the fish dealer Kichi, and the fireman Seigoro, who frequented our back door, but they left hardly any impression on me. All I wanted was to attach a humming string to my nine-crested dragon kite with the old man Kansaburo, who was a porter at my father's office and who came to visit us only on New Year's Day. I thought only of such things as whether the wind would be blowing that day. At some point or other, however, the family greengrocer, Shunko, and our parlormaid, O-Tama, had become secret lovers. One night, hand in hand and carrying their clothes on their backs, they tried to elope. Tazaki nabbed them as they were going over the wooden fence by the back gate. The ensuing household uproar and the decision to send O-Tama back to her parents' house in Sumiyoshi, although I did not understand what was happening, seemed terrible to me. The sight of O-Tama's retreating figure, in tears as she was dragged through the back gate by her white-haired mother, seemed sad even in my eyes. After this, I felt that there was something grim and hateful about Tazaki. My father was well pleased with him, but my mother and the rest of us could not abide him. He was a lowdown person who had done a bad thing.

All of New Year's Day I did nothing but fly my kite. On Sundays, when there was no school, I would get up especially early to play. I begrudged the fact that the winter sun went down so soon. But before long it was February, and then came a Sunday when it was no use getting up early: there was snow. Out by the back door, where my father almost never went, there was the sound of his thick, husky voice. With him was Tazaki, doing most of the talking. There was also the voice of my father's rickshaw man, Kisuke, who'd come by as he did every morning. Not listening to the wet nurse, who was trying to change my sleeping kimono, I ran toward their voices. When I saw my mother, standing on the threshold with her back to me and her arms folded, a sort of sad happiness filled me. Clinging to her soft sleeve, I wept.

"What are you crying about so early in the morning?" My father's voice was sharp. But my mother, taking out one hand from her bosom, gently stroked my head.

"The fox has come back. He's eaten one of Mune-chan's favorite chickens. Isn't that terrible? Be a good boy, now."

The snow was blowing in fitful gusts through the back door into the dirt-floored entryway. Half-melted lumps of snow that had been tracked in under everybody's high clogs quickly made mud of the floor.

The cook, O-Etsu, the new parlormaid, one other maid-servant, and my wet nurse, all aflutter over their master's unexpected appearance at the back door and shivering with cold, sat as if glued to the floorboards of the raised part of the kitchen.

My father, putting on the snow clogs that Tazaki set out for him and taking the paper umbrella that Kisuke held over his head, started on a tour of inspection out in back of the house and around the chicken yard by the well.

"Mother, I want to go too."

"No. I can't have you catching cold. Please don't ask."

Just then the wicket of the back gate was opened and Seigoro, the head fireman, came in, saying, "It's been quite a heavy snowfall." Dressed in his firefighting outfit of quilted hood, livery coat, and old-fashioned Japanese gloves, he was making the rounds of the neighborhood on his initial snow inspection.

"What's that? Oh, how terrible. A fox took one of your chickens, you say? Why, it's the most exciting thing to happen since the Restoration. Just like the samurais, the fox-god was deprived of his stipend. And he couldn't smell the fried bean curd under all that snow. So he wandered over to your chicken house. It's no great matter. Your folks will catch him for sure."

Seigoro kindly carried me on his back to the side of the chicken yard.

Apparently that morning at daybreak the fox had craftily stolen with rapid strides across the accumulated snowdrifts, dug a hole under the bamboo fence, and crawled through it into the yard. Snow and dirt were scattered all about where he had scratched and scrabbled his way through. Inside the bamboo enclosure, on the snow that had blown into it, not only were chicken feathers mercilessly tossed about but a drop or two of bright red blood was to be seen.

"It'll be no trouble this morning. There are prints all over the snow. 'If you follow my tracks, you'll soon find me in the Shinoda woods,' as the old line goes. Eh—it's been living in the cliff in your garden since last year?"

Just as Seigoro said, a trail of fox prints was found that led from the garden down the cliff and vanished at the base of a pine tree. My father at their head, the band of trackers raised a spontaneous cry of triumph. When Tazaki and the rickshaw man scraped away the snow with a spade and a long-handled hoe, the fox's lair, that all the last year had been searched for without success, was nakedly exposed in a thicket of beargrass that grew densely even in winter. At length a consultation began on the best method of killing the fox.

Kisuke held that if they smoked it out with red pepper, the fox, unable to bear the pungent smoke, would come yelping out of its hole, and they then could dispatch it. Tazaki, saying that it would be a shame if the fox got away, was for setting a snare at the mouth of the hole or, failing that, gunpowder. But then Seigoro, unfolding his arms and tilting his head to one side, broached a difficult matter.

"Foxes usually have more than one hole. There's bound to be an exit somewhere. If we only stop up the entrance, we'll look like real fools when the fox sneaks out the back door."

This started everybody thinking again. To find the back hole, however, in all this heavy snow, would not just be very difficult but almost impossible. Finally, after another conference that lasted so long that everyone began to shudder with the cold, it was decided that all they could do was to smoke out the hole at this end with sulfur. Tazaki made ready for firing a gun from the house. My father laid an arrow on the string of his great bow. Kisuke with a shoulder pole, Seigoro with a fire axe, and the gardener, Yasu, who just then had come by a trifle belatedly to shovel snow and was pressed into service, also with a shoulder pole, were ready for action.

My father returned briefly to the house to change into some old Western clothes. Tazaki went to the apothecary's in front of Denzuin to buy sulfur and gunpowder. The others noisily whiled away the interval with a two-quart keg of saké, from which they drank with teacups. What with one delay and another, it was almost noon by the time they finally began smoking out the mouth of the hole. I said I wanted to watch the subjugation of the fox with all the others but I was sternly kept indoors by my mother. With her and the wet nurse, I turned over and spread out as usual the pages of a storybook at the sunken hearth. Unable to stay still, however, I got up and sat down again and again. The only sound of a gun that we heard was the muffled *dun* of the noonday cannon at Marunouchi. Although so far away, it surprised us on clear days by rattling even the translucent paper sliding doors of our parlor. And yet the sharp report of the gun, shooting the fox dead right at the base of the cliff, would have split both my ears, I thought. The women in the house were as agitated as myself. Wouldn't somebody get bitten by the fox? Wouldn't the fox-god come rampaging into the house? Some of the women were even intoning Buddhist prayers and putting on amulets. My mother, however, gave detailed instructions for the saké treat to be served to all the people of the house.

From time to time I went out onto the veranda but not a sound came up from the bottom of the cliff. It was as if nobody was down there. There was no sign of any smoke. There was only the lonely sound of the accumulated snow slipping off from the nearby shrubbery. Although the dark sky hung low over the tops of the groves, which were shrouded by a cloudlike mist, in the snow, scattered about or lying piled in silvery, gleaming drifts, the garden was everywhere a shadowy brightness that was more than mere twilight. After I had lunch with my mother, another short while went by. I was slightly tired of waiting, and also starting to feel a sort of heartweariness. All of a sudden, there was an indescribably piteous shriek, followed by a triumphant shout of many people. Almost kicking down the paper doors, everyone rushed from the house onto the veranda. From what I heard later, the fox, suffocated by the smoking sulfur, had timorously stuck its head out at the mouth of the hole. Seigoro, waiting for it with his axe, had struck the animal a single blow. It was a lucky hit. The blade had split the fox's head right between the eyes, and the fox had dropped dead on the spot. My portly father in the vanguard, carrying his great bow, then Tazaki and Kisuke between them shouldering the long pole from which the dead fox dangled by its paws, and Seigoro and Yasukichi bringing up the rear, an orderly procession appeared at the top of the cliff. As it tramped through the snowdrifts, I was reminded of the long file of warriors, the Treasury of Loyal Retainers, which I'd seen in my picture book. How manly and heroic they all looked, I thought. Tazaki, the intrepid student-houseboy, advanced toward me and in his usual high-flown, classical manner announced, "Young master. Thus it goes. Heaven's net is wide and slow, but lets none escape." With that, he thrust the fox right under our noses. When I saw the axe-cleft skull, the muddy drops of life's blood that dripped from between the clenched fangs onto the snow, I had to hide my face behind my mother's soft sleeve.

It was decided to hold a great saké banquet in the house that afternoon. Because the heavy snowfall had prevented the fish dealer from laying in supplies, my father resolved to regale the servants and regular trades-people with some of our freshly killed chickens. Everyone was in a great good humor. In the little yard where the fox had crept in by stealth, they grabbed two chickens and openly dispatched them. The previous fall, those two black-and-white mottled hens, chicks then, had chirped to me each day as I set out for school and when I got back. Their bodies had been enfolded in fluffy golden wings like cotton puffs. Tossing them feed and giving them small plants to eat, I'd cherished them. By now they had grown into splendidly plump mother birds. Both of them, alas, with the same pathetic squawk, had their necks wrung by the hands of Tazaki. Their feathers were plucked by the hands of Kisuke, their stomachs were cut open and the guts pulled out by the hands of Yasu. The flushed faces of the feasters, who sat up until late at night drinking saké and licking and smacking their lips, seemed to me like those of the goblins that I'd seen in my picture book.

In bed that night, I thought, Why did those people hate the fox so? Saying it was because it had killed the chicken, they had killed the fox and two more chickens besides.

From the struggle of the snake and the frog, Turgenev in his child's heart had doubted the benevolence of God. As soon as I'd begun to read literature, I doubted the meaning of the words "trial" and "punishment," as they are used in the world. Perhaps it was that killing of the fox in the distant past. Perhaps those memories had, without my knowing it, become the source of my doubt.

俄
あ
れ

Flash Storm

里見　弴
SATOMI TON

The light, at about two o'clock in the July afternoon, bore down intensely everywhere on the wide parade grounds. Along the earthen outer wall of a barracks that stood at the western edge of the grounds ran an uneven road. Like the dried up, irregular channels of a stream bed, in several places it had been pounded into two or three ruts by wagon wheels, horses' hooves, and men's feet, in other places flowing together into one. If you stood there and looked east, far away in the gently undulant landscape the tops of a dark forest faintly appeared and disappeared. They were like the eastern edge of the enormous grounds. To the north and south also, large groves of tall and short trees stood in lines that, shimmering in the heat, linked up with the forest on the remote eastern side. Within these borders, aside from the summer grasses that, barely surviving the hobnailed boots of soldiers, grew here and there in islands of lifeless green, there were hardly any trees. The blue sky, saturated with the blazing light, trembling with its fever, glared down at the red dirt grounds wherever you looked. They were like two faces, each growing angry at the other's obduracy, each browbeating the other with swollen, sullen grimaces. There was not a breath of air. Unless something came between them and made peace, there would be war between these two any minute now . . . no small birds, of course, but not even big birds dared to fly across the sky. Instead the cicadas, an insect kind relying on its numbers, from the deep, leafy shade of the surrounding groves, drew out their long, monotonous song of the hot, stuffy smell of grass, the irritable, heat-mirage ague of summer, a song with a touch of mockery. Even the blue-tail lizard, as if its pride and joy, the tail that gleamed blue and then green, were too much for it, left it limply extended as it stuck its head under the meager shade of the grass, its silvery white belly pulsing as if out of breath. Some very energetic ants, lugging around the body of a dragonfly left half-uneaten by a praying mantis on their black, shiny, little backs, were hard at work even in this heat. As for human beings, there were none to be seen anywhere. But no, there was just one, the arsenal sentry standing guard on the wall of the barracks. Of course, even though he was a man, anything like human mental activity had come to a halt in him. His brain simmering steadily like gray soup, he stood bolt upright. Even if the arson of the sun, like a red-hot iron, had touched off a tremendous explosion in the arsenal, surely he would not have budged an inch . . .

Just then a certain young man, on his way to see a friend who lived on the far side of the parade grounds, took off his hat in the suburban trolley and let the warm wind that fitfully blew in at the window fan and tease his soft crew cut. His business being somewhat urgent, he had braved the blazing heat, but he dreaded the long walk across the parade grounds.

Suddenly at the southeast corner of the grounds, a cloud of reddish-brown smoke or dust arose. As he looked, it fanned out and hid all the view behind it. Quickly spreading across the field, it created patterns of light and shadow, spiraled about like a tornado and rushed this way like a tidal wave. In less than a minute it had swept across the parade grounds and invaded the grove on the north side. Hit head on, the trees, waving their heads and soughing in wavelike rhythms, were simultaneously deluged with red dust. At the same instant the attacking dust storm was thrown back by the earth wall on the west side, somersaulting as it danced up into the air. Caught by another blast of wind, it whirled crazily and was hurled against the barracks.

Just then the young man, having gotten off the trolley, happened by. Coming up against this wall of dust at the corner where he'd meant to turn onto the grounds, he instantly clamped down his hat and spun right around so that his back faced the wind. His summer kimono and *haori* over it were plastered to his body so that his rear outline down to the knot of his obi was clearly shown. Any looseness in his clothes was at once blown out streaming and flapping in front of him. His body was bent from the waist in the shape of a bow. But while leaning back into the wind, he was trying hard to straighten up again. (In a print by Hokusai, a man in a strong wind is also bent over like a bow. But that is a pictorial exaggeration.)

"Puh. It's too much." Just as he thought this, he was blown downwind two or three steps. The next moment, made fun of by the wind he'd been leaning against, he staggered backward. As it reversed itself, the wind flung dust and sand in his face. Self-defensively he'd shut his eyes tight. Even so . . . "This is awful!"

After listening intently to the sound of the wind's retreat, he slowly turned around and looked out over the parade grounds. Often while crossing this field, he had run into little dust flurries, but never before this kind of hurricane-force gale. He felt a curiosity, as if now he would be able to see something absolutely new to him. Like ripplets that rise in the wake of a surge, small, whispering afterwaves of the wind blew here and there and any which way, swirling up the dust. Then in the distance, a second wall of dust, densely expanding as he looked at it, began heading his way full tilt. Although thinking "I can't take any more of this," he gazed at it now, rather with a feeling of awe-struck excitement . . . before he knew it, from the eastern horizon a low, black cloud had closed in on him until it was almost overhead. Up to then he'd thought that the sudden dusk all around him was due simply to the clouds of dust that were blowing across the sun. Aston-ished by this theatrically abrupt change in the weather, he thought, "Here it comes!" Trying to decide if he should retreat to the trolley stop or make a run for it to his friend's house, he calculated the distance in both directions and, by the look of the sky, how soon the rain would start coming down. He made up his mind to go forward. Letting the second gale sweep past him, he deftly tucked up the skirt of his kimono in back and, lowering his head, began to charge. In the wind that

now came at him from the side, his feet, in white *tabi*
that in a few seconds had been dyed yellowish-brown,
raced along alternately beneath his narrowed eyes. By
degrees a sad, gloomy darkness completely unlike the
calm darkness of night, a mysterious darkness that in
old times had made men dread the unusual phenom-
ena of heaven and earth, fell over all. It was like looking
through a yellow glass. Everything lost its own colors.
With the blurred contours of a volcanic region that has
been showered with ashes, the scene turned a sad and
dreary hue. Five or six times the wind went by, with an
eerie echo that crawled along the ground. Each time
the young man struck the same haughty, gallant attitude . . .

For as far as he could see, he was the only man in the
field. In the intervals of the wind, from the groves near
and far, like the sand and pebbles drawn after a retreating wave, a chafing, uniform sound of a going, a long
sighing and soughing, followed from the tops of the
trees. During such lulls, piercing the thunderheads that
blackly piled up in the east, lavender flashes of lightning sprinted hither and yon. Just as he thought, "Don't
thunder!" a wave of thunder broke with a roar. Duck-
ing despite himself, he felt an unease as if the thunder
were reverberating in his gut. Yet he also felt a deep
pleasure, somehow as if he had stood up inside himself.
(This kind of extraordinary scene is often accompanied
by a sublime extravagance that draws men to it.) Anyway, he was already halfway across the parade grounds.
That isolated cottage on the far side of the field was his
friend's place.

Just when the first drops of rain like glass pellets had
begun to pelt against his straw hat, the young man slid

open the lattice door of his friend's house. He was welcomed by his friend's wife, who said her husband had gone for a swim in the nearby river but would soon be back. The young guest, somehow proud of himself like a boy who has gotten himself all muddy in a war game or nicked himself on his fingertip, showed off his yellowish-brown stained *tabi* and the traces of rain-streaked dust smeared on his sweaty shins. Almost boastfully he told her about the bursts of thunder and gusts of wind that he'd met with on the way. Drawn into the spirit of the thing, the wife became lively and gay. Busying herself, she drew some water for him in a bucket.

By the time the guest, his bare feet not quite wiped dry, stepped up into the house proper and damply padded into the parlor, it had got even darker outside. Only the rain, pallidly gleaming as it came down like a Niagara, seemed to keep it from getting as dark as midnight. The guest and the wife, dumbfounded by this torrential downpour—it really was like a vertically plunging river—stood on the veranda and vaguely stared out at it awhile. As it often is in such storms, the rain did nothing to diminish the force of the wind. On the contrary, it was now blowing harder than ever. The shrubs planted around the outhouse were easily blown almost flat against the ground. No sooner had they lifted up their heads than, swaying and shuddering as if there was no willpower or fight left in them, they were pounded down again. Even the big oaks and cedars that towered up along the east side of the garden attached to this house, even they, which most of the time stood quietly steadfast like old giants whom nothing could move, shaking their great heads in a fine trembling apart of masses of foliage, raised an alarming shriek in the wind and rain. In the trees whose leaves had pale undersides, here and there among the leaf clusters patches of grayish-white flowed together and vanished and flowed together again. As the thick branches that they'd trusted to for safety were terribly shaken, small birds were all but blown out of the trees. In a panic, madly beating their wings, with frantic-sounding chirps that seemed to bode ill, the birds all tried to hide themselves deeper within the foliage. From the lofty treetops that one had to crane one's neck to look at, leaves and even snapped-off twigs went flying off into the distance like green sparks. The thunder, as if it were beside itself by now, pealed in a continual fury. A lightning bolt zigzagged as if to earth itself right in front of the veranda. Without a second's letup the rain came down in cataracts. The smooth garden lawn, almost instantly flooded under several inches of water, was like a rice paddy. The rodlike lines of rain, bouncing off its surface with the force of flung pebbles, shattered in spray. Uttering only an amazed "Yaaaa," the young man looked on spellbound. As with many people who are possessed of a powerful curiosity, he had a nature that derived an obscure thrill from this kind of unusual scene. Once during a summer flood in Tokyo, wading about knee deep in such neighborhoods as Shitaya, Asakusa, and Mukojima, he had stayed away from home for three days.

"My, did you ever see such a storm!"

These were the wife's words when she came out on the porch again after having gone to make preparations for tea. The guest had observed for himself that the wind was blowing the spray not only onto the porch but, according to their exposure, into the rooms. The tatami mats were turning a damp yellow. "This won't do at all."

Having looked all around him, the guest suddenly stood up on his tiptoes. With the wife he went about closing all the rain shutters in the house. Like a trolley car that as it races along the rails sends flying the muddy water that has collected in the grooves, the rain shutters ran swiftly along their slots as they sliced through the accumulated water. The guest, his skirts tucked up, had as much fun as a boy as he slid the doors shut with bangs that echoed throughout the house. He had worked his way around to the kitchen in back. There, at that moment, the wife was trying to shut the water gate. Never in good order, it was stuck fast now. The eaves being shallow on this side of the house that also faced the wind, the big raindrops splashed against the wife's impatiently frowning face and stylish Western coiffure. She was about to get soaked to the skin. Already the translucent paper of the high-paneled sliding doors was being blown to tatters.

"Here, let me try."

Saying this, the guest stepped down into the garden by the wife's side. But his efforts didn't go too well either. Constantly bucking himself up with cries of "Yo!" and "Umm!" he put his back into it. Nervously wringing her hands, the wife muttered, "This gate always gets stuck. I can't do anything with it." She put out a hand to help. Her cold, wet hand touched the guest's hand. Standing back, he let her try again. Under his eyes, on the wife's perspiring nape, the muscles stood out roundly with the force of her effort or relaxed to their former rounded smoothness. From her soaking-wet clothes, from her skin, the scent of a woman was especially strong . . . at last the gate slid to. Thinking to do so before it got pitch-dark, the guest made his way back through the almost completely shuttered and darkened house to the parlor. Stumbling over the tea things, he'd seated himself tailor-style in what seemed to be the middle of the room when he heard the heavy, thudding beat of his heart. He thought back to that moment when, looking up at the sky over the parade grounds, he'd decided to go on. He now regretted that he hadn't turned back then and there. And as he did so, he listened hard to the mighty thunderstorm outside. Inside, in the shut-up house, drumming in torrents on the roof, the eaves, and all around, the rain sounded as if it had lost any outlet. It resonated eerily, as if it were falling indoors. The guest, in this isolated house surrounded and cut off by the storm, was very much bothered by his consciousness that he was alone with his friend's wife. In the darkness there floated up a picture of O-Shichi in the tale by Saikaku, as she lay inside the mosquito net on a night of thunder and rain, murmuring to herself, "Oh dear, the master will scold me for this." On a pilgrimage she had taken refuge in a wayside shrine. The illustration from an old-fashioned storybook of O-Shichi being grabbed by the hand by the *rōnin* in his stage wig of a warrior's shaven head drew itself in the guest's mind. The round muscles of the wife's nape worked smoothly in his mind's eye . . .

"Even though you're easily swayed by the emotions of a situation, to let yourself act like those characters in old stories who forget themselves because they're alone with a young woman in a dark house in a thunderstorm—it's rating yourself too cheap." The guest tried to upbraid himself. But in the dark a series of sensual apparitions passed before him. As if it was stamped there, he felt the touch of the woman's cold, wet palm on the back of his right hand.

About ten feet away from the main part of the house the twenty-one-year-old houseboy crouched in the servant's room. Afraid of the thunder, he had blushed scarlet with shame when, at intervals in the storm, he'd heard the rain shutters being slid shut across the way. (In this house it was the custom to employ a young male student rather than a maid.) Starting to his feet, he bounded at two strides into the entryway.

"Takebe-san, have you been cowering in your room all this time?"

In the dark corridor, looking startled and ready to flee, the wife was caught in the pallid light that just reached her from the entryway. Dripping wet, her sleeves were rolled up all the way to her shoulders, like those of the villain Sadakuro in the puppet play *The Treasury of Loyal Retainers*. Her white, plump arms hung limply at her sides. The inner front skirt of her summer kimono, pulled high up on her thighs and tucked into her half-width obi, revealed a slightly damp-looking white muslin slip and, beneath it, her bare feet to clear above her ankles. The houseboy, who'd literally taken a leap in the dark, stood as if fixed to the spot when he saw the wife before his eyes in a state of undress.

The pale face, dimly afloat in the half light, gave a casual laugh and asked again, "You have been, haven't you?"

"..."

The houseboy's answer, drowned out by the sound of the rain, did not reach the wife's ears. But that does not matter much. What's more interesting is that the houseboy himself had no memory of how he'd replied. He knew that the husband had gone for a swim. But he did not at all know that the guest had dashed into the house just before the downpour began. That was how mesmerized he had been by the thunder. The thought now took hold in him that he was alone with the wife in the darkened house. Until that moment when, working himself up with a desire to do his duty, he had rushed inside the main house, he'd been as good as ignorant of this fact. But now that he stood face to face with his mistress, it flashed through his mind like a lightning bolt. His knowledge of it at once took on a weird clarity that clung around his heart. From here on he would follow a psychological path that was more or less the same as that described for the guest. He too heard the thudding of his heart. He too regretted having come into the house. And in listening hard to the storm outside as he did so, he was also like the guest. That the wife, with a levity unusual for her, had teased him this way went far to stir up a certain thought in him. In the darkness before his eyes, he repeatedly visualized and erased the wife's face that had just now sunken into them. Thanks to that "certain thought," this houseboy who was even younger than the guest was finely trembling. There was a tightness in his chest, as if his breath was coming and going only in his mouth.

When he heard the wife's voice from over toward the entryway, the guest, his heart beating harder than ever, stood up to go to that part of the house. He thought he'd heard her say "Kato-san, will you please help me" or words like these. Then he heard a man's voice, mumbling what sounded like an apology. When only now he

realized that it was the houseboy, he tried to feel relieved. But that was not at all what he really felt. At once
the sallow face of the houseboy came back to him. Even
more than before, it seemed the face of someone who
belonged to the lower classes. It irked him extremely
that the vulgar houseboy should make his appearance
in what up until now had been a splendid pantomime.
But when he guessed at the passions that even in the
oafish servant must be making his heart pound with
exactly the same temptation as his own, he felt an
almost unbearable self-contempt. "This hackneyed role
is just right for him. It's quite clear that he's not the
leading man. As for the woman's part . . . h'm, I'll let
you have it. Here it is. Eat." As if tossing a piece of
tainted meat to a dog, the guest did his best to hold
aloof from the scene. Just then he heard the wife's
footsteps coming his way.

The wife was not at all concerned about her husband's
whereabouts. A very good friend of his lived on the
bank of the river where he'd gone for a swim. He
always invited this man to join him, so it was almost
certain that having encountered this sudden storm her
easygoing husband was enjoying himself at his friend's
house. He was not one to come home if it meant charg-
ing through wind and rain.

When, having changed out of her wet kimono, she
came into the eight-mat guest room, this fact floated
across the wife's heart with a strange clarity. But unlike
the two men (the guest and the houseboy) she did not at
all feel bothered and menaced by her awareness of it.
Like most women, as she considered a fact that she had
placed center stage in her consciousness, if she felt it
was an inconvenient fact that might make for trouble in

a given situation, she at once and skillfully pushed it back down under the threshold of her thoughts, using sensitivity, guile, timidity, and wisdom to make sure it didn't raise its head again. This is a characteristic of women that might well be called intelligent foolishness. It gives a lot of men difficulty.

"My, my . . . it's pitch-dark. Where are you?"

"Shall I open one of the shutters a little? It's too dark."

From the darkness came the guest's voice, tinged with a faint trembling and heavy, as if he were sighing. "But it's still teeming."

The wife was the same age of twenty-eight as the guest. But she had always tended to treat this young man, who was much younger than her husband, as if he were a child. In fact, this young bachelor who as the child of a good family had known no hardship, was quite often startled and hurt by her sharp-tongued way with him. The wife, liking to watch the look on the young man's face at such times and enjoying herself often so, had decided that he was easily manipulated, a man whose strings she could pull as she pleased. However, this belief of hers was mistaken, in that she observed only his momentary expression and not the movements of his heart afterward. It was not that she had the bad nature to flaunt her superiority and torment the young man. On the contrary, at ease in her superiority, she did not grudge him her special loving friendship. Now when the wife heard the young man's voice, she was immediately able to picture to herself his rigid attitude in the dark. Lured by the usual pleasure of her superiority, an utterly female playfulness reared its head in her.

"My word, it was simply awful out there. I was absolutely soaked . . . oh, and you too, surely? You must have gotten all wet. Why don't you change? I'll give you some of my husband's clothes . . . if it won't make you feel odd."

"No, it's all right. I'm fine this way."

"Really, though, do change. You'll catch your death of cold. You must have been drenched."

"No, not all that much." As he said this, the guest patted his clothes here and there.

Wouldn't the wife's hand, any second now, reach out to feel how wet his clothes were and happen to touch his hand? It was this fear that made him say "No, not all that much" and move his hand around on his clothes. But in the dark where the wife's voice had come from, there was only silence. He did not know how to interpret it. A fear arose in him that it would be broken by the wife's all-too-innocent surprise attack. Against the dusky light that leaked through cracks and knotholes in the shutters, opening his eyes wide, the guest studied even the faint tremors of air. Suddenly a flash of lightning shone into the room. As he saw her at that instant, the wife's figure had a calmness about it that disappointed him. Leaning on her left hand planted on the tatami behind her, her half-opened right hand lightly resting palm upward on her relaxed, slightly sideways lap, she sat at an angle across from him. His fear had been like a sumo wrestler grappling with himself. And yet the space between their knees was much smaller than he'd thought. Pushing himself back a little, he said, "That brightened it up a lot." No sooner had he spoken than an earsplitting peal of thunder broke with a shattering roar that seemed right outside the room. It rattled the glass panes in the sliding doors. The guest felt as if his blood had leapt all at once into his head.

"That was a big one."

He spoke these words to himself to quell his uneasiness. The next moment, however, he already felt somewhat free of his unease.

"It really came down that time. And it seemed rather nearby."

Even when he spoke out loud to her, from where the wife sat in darkness there was neither an answer nor the sound of any slight movement of her body. Because of this, how the wife looked and what she was feeling at a moment that had struck fear even into him were completely beyond the guest. Unless the wife didn't have a nerve in her body for thunderstorms, an intense emotion must have been roiled up in her that was stronger than any fear for her life. Unable to relax, the guest felt a disquiet that would not be dispelled until he'd gotten a word, any word, out of the wife.

"The thunder doesn't bother you?"

Even to this, there was no reply. Beginning to feel slightly forlorn, he mumbled as if to himself, "It's coming down like a waterfall . . . there's some more thunder."

"Don't you like it?"

Coming as abruptly as they did, the wife's words seemed to explode in his ears.

"What . . .?" The guest leaned forward despite himself. He deliberately left an interval in which a certain meaning of these words, which could be taken in two ways, might be broached, either by what the wife said or did (if she was going to make an overture). But soon becoming unable to endure that interval, the pressure of its silence, he asked again, "The thunder?" If this conversation had taken place in a bright room, he would not even have had to ask "What?" Now brusquely, he flung out the words that were appropriate to the other meaning (an extremely ordinary one), words that should have been said right away. At the same time, aware of his satisfaction in having warded off a danger and not waiting for what the wife would, of course, reply, he went on, "It's not that I particularly dislike it. But that last one was a bit too close for comfort. Anyone would have . . ."

Covering his words, the wife said, "I don't mind it at all myself."

"Not again!" the guest thought. It was getting ridiculous. He felt as if he were being told the same joke many times. The "snake," as long as one was afraid of it, was like a real snake. But if one deftly parried its lunge, it was nothing but a rotten straw rope that was starting to unravel. Not to have grabbed that rope and tossed it in a ditch was going too easy on the perpetrator of the prank. And for her to twirl the old rope around yet again! "This sort of woman is anathema in Soseki's stories," the guest muttered to himself. This time, for his own part, he took up the passive defense of "the silence of darkness." After a while the wife said, "What a scaredy-cat you are." But he obstinately held his tongue.

The silence went on and on. Meanwhile, the guest sobered up from the delicious saké of superiority. Had he been wrestling himself again? If the wife's words had only the ordinary, apparent meaning of the like or dislike of thunder and held no hidden message, had he run on a little too far ahead? Yet mulling over once more their affected simplicity and their context, he did not think he was mistaken.

"But if from the start she meant that other thing, and wasn't talking about the thunder at all . . . how banal. What does she take me for?" The guest began to grow angry.

"It's all because of this darkness. I wish I could open the rain shutters right now. These silly thoughts would vanish with the dark."

This was suddenly called out by the wife in a loud voice. It startled the guest. Only now he remembered the houseboy. What had the oaf been doing with himself all this while?

"Takebe-san."

The wife raised her voice again, louder this time. She had seen some leaks in the ceiling of her husband's study and had sent the houseboy in with an empty bucket, but now thinking there might be other leaks, she wanted him to look around the rest of the house. She too wondered where he'd been in the interval. Much to her surprise the houseboy answered her from the next room, the morning room. Realizing at once that their conversation had been overheard in its entirety, she and the guest felt some displeasure. But the wife hesitated to show hers openly. Instead, in a pleasant voice, she said, "Are you all right? After that great big thunderbolt? Shall I put up the mosquito netting for you?"

From the next room came a laugh that was completely lacking in mirth.

"Takebe-san." This time the guest spoke. "I'm sorry to bother you, but will you bring some matches and a tobacco tray?"

"Oh, forgive me. I was so distracted by this uproar that I forgot all about them."

Getting to her feet, the wife went into the breakfast room. "Oh dear. The fire has gone out."

"Do you want me to light it?"

"No, it doesn't matter. Now, where are they? They were around here somewhere. How about the utility charcoal? You don't know?"

"I think it's in that cupboard." There was a sound of sticky, padding footsteps as the houseboy went to fetch it.

"Ouch!"

"Oh, excuse me."

"You hurt me. Where? At the bottom?"

"That's where it was last time."

There was a clattering sound. In the parlor the guest started to get exasperated. "Just matches will be fine. Matches."

"It was here somewhere . . . isn't it in this box?"

"Yes, that's right. Probably in there."

"And the matches . . . ?" Then a moment later, "What are you doing?"

In his gradually heightened state of carnal desire, from this kind of talk the guest could see it all—the small space between the wife's body and the houseboy's, their contact, the wife's damp, fragrant hair, the houseboy's thudding heart and trembling body—much more vividly than if he were looking at it in a well-lighted room. And he could feel it all—the subtle inner excitement that he could not have perceived with his eyes. Once again a jealousy that was without reason raised its serpent's head in him.

From the morning room there was the sound of a

match being struck and a little while afterward the wife's voice.

"Takebe-san. You're pale."

"It's nothing. It's the candle."

"Are you quite sure?"

Presently the wife, the tobacco tray in one hand and a candlestick in the other, came back into the room. By then the guest had noticed that the rain had tapered off to a drizzle.

"We no longer need a light. Probably we can open the shutters now." Saying this, he got to his feet and opened two or three himself. The pale, whitish light abruptly shone in. The darkness was gone.

The wife of his friend was standing at his side. Wonderingly he looked at her. She was his friend's wife, and nothing else.

"Why are you staring at me so?"

"Because somehow it's as if I'd met you again after a long time."

"Why, you're right! For a while there I could only hear your voice. I *haven't* seen you in a long time."

"Good afternoon. How have you been?"

"Fine, thank you. And you?"

The storm, as in its onset, was rapid in its ending. Each minute the raindrops were finer and farther apart. The wind died away. The sky kept on getting brighter. After twenty minutes or so the rain had completely stopped. Already patches of blue sky appeared here and there in the upper cloud cover. In the lower sky clouds like white cotton puffs still sailed before the wind at a fairish speed. Heaven and earth, in the explosion of their magnificent quarrel, the electrical enmity that each had harbored against the other until it couldn't be held back, had bared their hearts to each other. Now both were cool and refreshed, as if they'd revived. The cicadas also, which had been struck dumb by the thunder, took heart again and started up their raucous, sultry cry in chorus. The rooster, which when sky and earth had closed with each other in darkness had flown up in a panic to the perch hung from a rafter in the shed, now came down and, getting its bearings, gave a loud war cry.

From far across the rice paddies there was a brave answering cry. The dog, as wet as any drowned rat, its head hanging low, entered the garden shaking off the muddy water in a spray of droplets. When it saw the wife and guest, a fond, friendly look came over its face. Licking its jaws, it propped its chin on the edge of the porch and whined emptily. Chided for that, it gave itself a violent shake that sent the spray flying every which way. Sitting back on its legs, its forepaws exactly side by side, it swiveled its head around and began licking its shoulders.

Even those plants and trees that had gotten the worst of the storm, now green and dripping, washed and clean again, respired the faint, fresh scent of earth. It was as if everything, breathing through its pores a life deep in lively freshness, aware only now of the full authority and the benevolence of nature, steeped itself single-mindedly in its own happiness.

Moving their cushions to the veranda edge of the room, the wife and guest lost themselves in the lovely scene, which even in the dullest person alive must have distilled a drop of its charm and touched his heart. In the guest's heart also there was a happy contentment. Beyond the moral, negative satisfaction of not having slept with his friend's wife, he felt a pleasure approaching arrogance in the fact that today, of all days, he had attentively, intimately, honestly, and stringently, as if holding a baby in his hands, steadily, from beginning to end, looked at his heart, the heart that usually was so difficult to grasp, and especially that while doing so, he had nakedly exposed that heart to the glamour of such a temptation.

"The fact that Takebe didn't do anything wrong is a mere result of circumstance. For me it was otherwise. When I thought to go forward, I went forward. But when I did so, my feelings were not timid. I did not command them, nor did I compel them in any way. But I never let them out of my sight. That was all! I did not let myself get moralistic. I was truly pure. I might have wrestled with myself from thinking too much about it, but that's nothing to be ashamed of . . ." Looking back on himself, the guest gave himself good marks. Whether or not he was right to is not this writer's concern. But surely he *was* right to try to see himself clearly . . .

Just then a man in a livery coat, apparently a gardener, came running along the far side of the hedge. As soon as he caught sight of the wife's face, he bowed hurriedly and called out, "Madam. There's a fire. Over there. It was set off by that worst thunderbolt."

The man immediately dashed off again. From where he had pointed to, some white smoke, which one might have mistaken for a remnant of the low clouds, quietly climbed into the now windless sky. With a start, the wife exclaimed, "But that's close by the river . . . do you think it's all right?"

"Didn't that man say the lightning struck the water-wheel shed?"

"No, he never said that. What are you talking about?"

"Perhaps. But somehow I feel as if he did say that."

"Wake up, now. Do you think it's all right?"

"Yes, it's all right."

"Is it really all right?"

"It's all right, I tell you."

"It's bad when you don't mean what you say."

"If you like, we can send Takebe over for a look."

"You're as cool as a cucumber, aren't you?"

"It's not that . . . it's just that it's all right."

A few minutes later the houseboy, dutifully getting ready, dashed off in his stocking feet. His figure, half-visible above the rice ears, rapidly receded along the twists and turns of the paddy's ridge path and before long was lost to sight. Abruptly a shaft of sunshine broke through a rift in the clouds. Gliding across the green paddies, it fanned out in a broad sweep of light toward the west.

"Strange. Why did I think that man said the lightning hit the water-wheel shed? I felt sure he did."

"You were daydreaming. Besides, the shed *is* right around there."

"And that's where the lightning struck. Sometimes a thing comes clear to me all by itself. It's as if I was a god. Ask them when they get back. I know that's what happened."

"Oh, here they come!"

In the gently slanting sunlight, across the beautiful, wet, shining color of the rice paddies far in the distance, the tiny figures of the houseboy and her husband were spotted by the keen-eyed wife.

"Oh. Where?"

"Way over there, by that tree. The one with the dense foliage. Just to the left. See them?"

"Which tree?"

"What poor eyes you have. You still don't see? Well, so much for your theory about the water-wheel shed . . . no, no, much more toward us."

"This and the water-wheel shed are two different things."

Touching shoulders, they gave their warmth to each other. They were so close that they were almost cheek to cheek. But they were completely unaware of that . . . now and then a low peal of thunder echoed quietly in the distance. But already any danger was all gone.

In the distance the husband began to wave his hat.

庭

The Garden

芥 川　竜 之 介

AKUTAGAWA RYUNOSUKE

It was the garden of an old family named Nakamura. In the Edo period (1603–1868) their house had been an official inn for daimyo and the nobility.

For ten years or so after the Meiji Restoration, the garden somehow preserved its old appearance. There was a pond in the shape of a gourd, and the pines of an artificial knoll dipped their branches to its calm surface. There were also two summer houses, called Stork's Nest Inn and Pure Heart Pavilion. From a mountain ledge at one end of the pond a stream whitely cascaded. A stone lantern, which had been named by Princess Kazu no Miya as she journeyed from the capital, stood among yellow roses that grew and spread with the years. But flowers could not disguise the air of desolation that hung over the garden. Particularly in early spring, when the trees inside and outside the garden put out their buds at the same time, one sensed with unease an uncouth power that was all the more evident for the picturesque, contrived scenery. A gallant old Nakamura gentleman lived here in retirement with his aged wife, who suffered from boils around the head. Sitting by the *kotatsu* in the main house that gave onto the garden, they passed the day pleasantly enough at go or cards. Sometimes, however, when he had been beaten five or six times running, the old man would become very angry.

The eldest son and family head, with his young wife, who was also his cousin, lived in a separate building connected to the main house by a roofed corridor. This son, whom I will call Bunshitsu, "Detached Ward," had a violent temper. Naturally his sickly wife and younger brothers and even the old man were afraid of him. Only Seigetsu, a mendicant sage then resident in the town, came often to see him. The son took an uncharacteristic delight in serving him saké and challenging him to calligraphic contests. "'The mountain cuckoo, in the lingering fragrance of flowers—' Seigetsu." "'Now and again, the glimmering cascade—' Bunshitsu." Such linked verses as these have survived.

Besides Bunshitsu, there were two other sons. The second had been adopted by relatives in the grain business, and the youngest worked for a major wine merchant in a town about fifteen miles away. As if they'd agreed on it beforehand, they almost never came home. Besides living at a distance, the third son was temperamentally incompatible with the present head of the family. The second son, as a result of wild living, was scarcely to be seen even at his adoptive home.

In two or three years the garden's desolation gradually increased. The pond had begun to clog with duck-weed, and dead trees mingled with live in the planta-tions. Meanwhile, during a summer of severe drought, the old man had died suddenly of a cerebral hemor-rhage. Four or five days before this, as he had sat drinking some cheap saké, a court noble in white cer-emonial robes had repeatedly entered and emerged from the Pure Heart Pavilion across the pond. Such was the vision, at any rate, that appeared to him in the noonday light. Late the following spring, having ap-propriated the money of his adoptive family, the sec-ond son eloped with a waitress. That autumn, the eldest son's wife prematurely gave birth to a boy.

After his father's death, the eldest son lived in the main house with his mother. The detached quarters had been rented to the headmaster of the local grade school. The headmaster was an adherent of Fukuzawa Yukichi's utilitarian theories, and persuaded the eldest son to plant fruit trees in the garden. Now when spring came around, peaches, apricots, and plums mingled their blossoms among the familiar pines and willows. Occa-sionally the headmaster would stroll through the or-chard with the son, making such comments as "Splendid for flower viewing as well. Two birds with one stone." But the artificial knoll, the pond, and the summer houses looked all the more poorly for it. One might have said that a man-made desolation had been superimposed on that created by nature.

That fall the mountain behind the house was swept by the worst forest fire in years. Afterward the stream that cascaded to the pond abruptly gave out. Early that winter the eldest son became sick. According to the doctor it was consumption, or tuberculosis as it's now called. As he spent his days in and out of bed, the son's bad humor merely got worse. It even happened that in January of the next year, after a passionate argument, he flung a hand warmer at the youngest brother, who'd come on his New Year's calls. After that the youngest brother did not see him again, not even when he died. This event took place upwards of a year later. Tended by his unsleeping wife, the eldest son drew his last breath behind mosquito netting. "How the frogs are singing. Where's Seigetsu?" were his last words. But Seigetsu—perhaps he'd tired of the scenery here—had long ago stopped coming even to beg.

When the first anniversary of the eldest son's death had passed, the third son married his employer's youngest daughter. As the headmaster had been transferred, he and his bride moved into the now vacant detached quarters. They furnished them with a black lacquer chest of drawers and gay red and white cloths. Meanwhile, however, the widow had taken to her bed in the main house. She had her husband's disease. The fatherless only child, Ren'ichi, from the time his mother coughed up blood was put to bed every night with his grandmother. Before retiring, the old lady always tied a towel around her head. Nevertheless, the mice would creep out late at night, drawn by the stench of her boils. Of course, if she had ever forgotten the towel, the mice would have nibbled at them. At the close of the year the eldest son's wife died, like the extinguished wick of an oil lamp. The day after the funeral the Stork's Nest Inn on the north side of the artificial knoll collapsed under a heavy fall of snow.

When spring came around once more, only the thatched cottage of the Pure Heart Pavilion remained by the stagnant pond. The rest of the garden had reverted to a wild, mixed growth of trees.

On an evening when the clouds had a look of snow about them, the second son returned to his father's house. Ten years had passed since his elopement. Although I say "his father's house," it was, in fact, his younger brother's house. His brother did not seem particularly unhappy to see him, nor did he appear overly rejoiced. It was, so to speak, as an event of no interest that he accepted the return of his prodigal brother.

From the time of his arrival the second son shut himself up in the prayer room of the main house, keeping close to the fire. He was afflicted with a malignant disease. In the room was an altar on which memorial tablets for his father and brother had been placed. So as not to see them, he had drawn shut the doors of the shrine. Aside from the three meals a day that he took with them, he hardly ever met with his mother and his younger brother and wife. Only the orphaned Ren'ichi would occasionally visit him in his room. The second son would draw ships and mountains for him on his cardboard slate. Sometimes with a faltering hand he would write out old songs for the samisen, such as one about a teahouse girl and flower viewing at Mukojima.

Time passed, and it was spring again. In the garden, peach and apricot put out their meager blooms amid the luxuriant greenery, and the Pure Heart Pavilion was reflected in the pond's leaden mirror. But the elder brother, as usual secluding himself in the family chapel, seldom got up even in the daytime. One day the twanging of a samisen reached his ears, accompanied by a voice singing in bits and snatches. It sang how in the battle of Suwa a vassal of the Matsumotos, Yoshie by name, had led a cannon attack. The elder brother raised his head slightly where he lay. Surely it was his mother, in the tearoom? The song went on about Yoshie's gallant advance under fire. Was his mother singing to her grandchild? Still she sang, in the Otsu-e *kae-uta* style. But that was a song popular twenty or thirty years ago, which the old man was said to have learnt from a courtesan. The song ended in praise of the life that, gone with the dew, had left behind an immortal name. The elder brother's eyes, in a face grown bearded with neglect, had taken on a strange gleam.

Two or three days later the youngest son found his brother trenching the north side of the artificial knoll overgrown with butterburs. His breath coming short, he clumsily wielded his hoe. There was something of a serious enthusiasm in his farcical appearance.

"What are you doing, big brother?" the youngest son asked from behind, not taking the cigarette from his lips.

"Me?" The elder brother looked up at him as if dazzled. "I'm thinking of letting a stream through here."

"Letting a stream through?"

"I want to make the garden as it was."

The younger brother merely smiled slyly. After that he made no further inquiries.

Every day the second son, taking his hoe, earnestly continued his work. Weakened by illness as he was, however, he found it a harsh task. In addition to tiring easily he was prone to the various mishaps of one unused to labor, such as raising blisters on his palms and ripping off his nails. Sometimes throwing away his hoe, he would lie down on the ground like a dead man. Around him the flowers and young leaves smoldered in the shimmering garden heat. After a quiet interval, however, he would struggle to his feet and stubbornly set to again.

Nevertheless, even after many days the garden did not show much change for the better. Water plants flourished in the pond, and in the plantations the various trees grew unpruned. Especially after the fruit trees had shed their flowers, the garden seemed more of a wilderness than ever. Not only that, but no one in the family sympathized with his efforts. The enterprising younger brother was immersed in speculations in sericulture and the price of rice. His wife felt a womanly aversion for the elder brother's illness. Even his mother, on account of his condition, feared that he would go too far in his gardening. But the elder brother, setting his face against man and nature, went on restoring the garden piecemeal.

One morning after it had rained, he went into the garden and found Ren'ichi placing stones along the edge of the stream bed overhung by butterburs.

"Uncle." Ren'ichi looked up at him happily. "From now on, let me help you."

"Let you help me?" As it had not for a long, long time, a smile appeared on the elder brother's face. From that day Ren'ichi went nowhere but out into the garden to help his uncle. To entertain his nephew as they rested in the shade, the elder brother told him stories of the unfamiliar, the sea, Tokyo, the railroad. Exactly as if hypnotized, Ren'ichi bit into an unripe plum and listened agog.

The rainy season that year was a dry one. Braving the

beating sunlight and the sultry closeness of the tall grass, the aging invalid and the boy gradually went farther afield as they chopped down trees and dug around the pond. But although they managed to prevail over the external obstacles, there was nothing they could do about those within themselves. Almost as in a vision, the elder brother could see the garden as it once had been. When it came to exact memory of details, however, such as the grouping of shrubs and the layout of paths, his mind failed him. Sometimes he would abruptly pause in his labors, leaning on his hoe as if it were a staff, and stare vaguely around him.

"What's the matter?" Ren'ichi would invariably ask, lifting worried eyes to his uncle's face.

"I wonder how this part used to be," his uncle would merely mutter to himself, uneasy and sweating. "I don't believe this maple was here before."

Ren'ichi could only slap at an ant on his mud-daubed hand.

Nor were such internal obstacles the only ones. Gradually as the summer deepened, the elder brother, perhaps because of his ceaseless overworking of himself, became confused in his mind. Filling in the pond where he had excavated it, planting a pine where he'd removed one—such lapses were frequent. What particularly irritated Ren'ichi was the felling of a willow by the water's edge to make pilings. "You just got through planting this tree." Ren'ichi scowled at his uncle.

"Oh? Somehow it's not clear to me anymore." With melancholy eyes his uncle looked out over the noonday pond.

Nevertheless, as the fall came on, the garden emerged dimly from among the swarm of trees and grasses. Of course, unlike in the past, there was no longer a Stork's Nest Inn and the cascade was gone. In fact, the old elegant charm imparted to it by a famous landscape gardener was almost nowhere to be found. But there was a "garden." The pond once more reflected the round, artificial knoll in its clarified waters. Once more the pines, in front of the Pure Heart Pavilion, calmly extended their branches. But when the garden was completed, the elder brother took to his bed for good. Days went by, his fever did not go down, and his bones ached.

"It's because like a fool you drove yourself too hard," his mother complained almost constantly as she sat by his pillow.

But her son was happy. Of course, there were any number of things he would have liked to improve in the garden. But that could not be helped. The work had been its own reward. In that he was content. Ten years of hardship had taught him renunciation, and renunciation had saved him.

Late that fall, no one knew exactly when, the elder brother died. The one to find him was Ren'ichi. Shouting, he ran across to his relatives' quarters. The family immediately gathered around the dead man with alarmed faces. "Look. It's as if he was smiling." The youngest son turned to his mother.

"Oh, and today the shrine doors are open." His wife was looking at the altar rather than see the corpse.

After the funeral Ren'ichi took to sitting by himself in the Pure Heart Pavilion. As if bewildered, he would stare for hours at the late-autumn trees and waters.

Such was the garden of the old Nakamura family, which belonged to the daimyo's inn of this town located along one of the old highways. Less than ten years after its restoration the garden was destroyed, together with the house. A railroad station was built on the site, with a small restaurant in front.

Already by then, none of the main house of the Nakamuras remained. The mother, of course, had long since died. The third son, after his schemes had fallen through, was said to have gone to Osaka.

Every day the train pulled into the station, and then pulled out. The young stationmaster sat inside at a large desk. Occasionally he would look up from his work at the green mountains or chat with the hands about the neighborhood. In none of their anecdotes was the Nakamura family mentioned, nor did they imagine that where they were now there had been an artificial knoll and summer houses.

Meanwhile, Ren'ichi was in Tokyo, studying painting at a certain Western art school in Akasaka. There was nothing in the atmosphere of the studio—the light from the overhead windows, the smell of the paints, the model with her hair done in the "cleft peach" style—to remind him in any way of the old house and garden. But sometimes, as he handled his brush, there would arise in his mind the face of a lonely old man. The face smiled at him as he toiled away, and surely he heard a voice say, "When you were a boy, you helped me in my work. Now let me help you in yours . . . "

Even now, in poverty, Ren'ichi continues to paint every day. Of the third son, there is no word at all.

Grass

十一谷 義三郎

JUICHIYA GISABURO

The two Sugi brothers were brought up almost in the same cradle as the supervisor's daughter Utatsuko. When they saw the breasts of Utatsuko's mother, they felt a faint, sweet thrill as if she were their mother. Utatsuko, when she was crowned by their father's big hand with a crimson hat, went into a trance of pride and pleasure. The skeins of subtly colored thread that circled from hand to hand among the three children had many times woven beautiful dreams in time to their songs. The younger brother's hand, stealing around from behind, had covered Utatsuko's girlish eyebrows. The older brother, holding her about the waist, had spun Utatsuko round and round in the sunlight as if twirling a bright paper pinwheel.

But then, one day, in their sunny, lively world of fantasy, a decisive incident occurred. On that day the younger brother was "it" in their game of hide-and-seek. While his older brother and the girl ran off hand in hand, the younger brother withdrew behind a shed. Leaning against its wooden side, he began to count to fifty in a voice that flew up into the clear, pale-blue sky. Meanwhile, his brother and Utatsuko, quickly stepping through the weeds at the back of the garden, scrambled up the trunk of a fig tree that grew there.

When he'd counted to fifty, the younger brother came running out from behind the shed. Then passing his eyes over the tops of the weeds and tall grasses that swayed and shone in the breeze, he stood still awhile.

Suddenly a green fig came flying through the air and landed at his feet. When he looked up, a shout of joy broke out from high up in the tree across from him. His older brother and the girl, perched on the same branch, the pure white corners of their mouths stained with fig juice, were laughing. The younger brother ran up under the tree.

"Welcome. Have a fig on us," his brother said.

"Yes. Have one of our figs," the girl chimed in.

Putting his hand to the tree trunk, the younger brother raised his eyes to the pair and glared at them. It was then that he saw that there was something on his brother's cheek. The sunlight, filtered through the leaves, shed many different-shaped spots and patches across their fair skin so that it was difficult to be sure, but when he took a long, hard look, wasn't that a big spider, its legs stretched out, that clung to his brother's cheek like an exotic tattoo? Falling back two or three steps, the younger brother, paling and without a word, pointed up at his brother's cheek.

"Oh, oh, oh," the girl called out, the bole shuddering with her agitation. The weird, nervous spider must have sensed the atmosphere of fear. It began to move from the older brother's cheek to his slender neck. When the older brother casually put up his hand, the spider bunched itself on the back of the hand and wagged its abdomen. Hastily the older brother brushed it away with the other hand. In that instant he lost his balance and fell to the ground.

The younger brother and the girl tensed and their eyes grew wide. Lying face down, a hand cupped over one eye, the older brother wept and sobbed. From the clefts of his fingers, dark blood oozed out. In the air above him, the spider's ugly body, its legs drawn up, bobbed about and jerked on its thread as the upper branches trembled.

The girl, as if something inside her had burst, abruptly started to wail up in the tree. The younger brother also wept, with big teardrops. Then running toward the house as fast as he could, he cried along with the girl's voice in the distance. From that day on, his brother's left eye was always shaded by a black lens in his glasses.

The older brother could no longer be bothered to search for dragonflies in their dragonfly hunts or to find the place where a kite had landed. He did not even take part in the brilliant games of catch, of running wild in the trampled weeds and grasses. After he'd begun to wear the glasses with the black lens in them, he had grown pale and put on weight, becoming a child in whom a quiet purity was all the more felt. Words of pity for him were often spoken by adults in the presence of his younger brother and others. Utatsuko was always giving him finely knitted woolens and pinning glass-bead jewelry on him.

The younger brother was a high-spirited, healthy boy. But at some time or other he had begun to feel a melancholy.

One evening, with the older brother between them, Utatsuko and the younger brother went to the village shrine festival. Coming back, they excitedly talked about everything they'd seen—the colored, folding paper-work and the popguns, the magician who had calmly held his hands over the fire. When they came to a deserted part of the road, the older brother went on ahead whistling to himself. The younger brother sang a marching song at the top of his voice. Utatsuko walked along looking up at the sky or smilingly listening to their songs or fondling the Kyoto doll she'd bought at the fair. After they'd gone on a while, she suddenly ran forward and grabbed the older brother, pulling him back. Out of the dusky air a large horse's head appeared.

"I didn't see him at all," the older brother said. Clutching his hand, the girl was breathing fast.

When he saw this, the younger brother at once fell silent. Leaving them behind, he walked on quickly. Discontent and loneliness welled up in his heart.

That evening after they'd gone to bed, the younger brother lay wide awake until the small hours. Then making sure of his brother's quiet breathing in sleep beside him, he stealthily got up and, taking his brother's glasses from his bedside, went out onto the veranda. Opening the rain shutter of the privy, he threw them as hard as he could at the sky where stars glittered. Afterward, coming back to bed, he murmured over and over the name of God, which he had heard at church. Without his knowing it, his eyes filled with tears. When he closed his eyelids and slept, he dreamt that he was standing by Utatsuko's side, looking on as his brother was devoured by a horse.

The older brother, who by now was a middle school student, had become more taciturn than ever. The younger brother regarded even the shoes that his brother wore with a feeling akin to adoration. When, from a far room, he listened to his brother singing *lieder*, he felt the other had ascended to a place which no number of steppingstones would ever allow him to arrive at.

One day he heard the following story from one of his brother's friends.

That day his brother's class, in gym period, had been instructed to walk across the high beam. His brother, not heeding the teacher's warning to him not to, tried to cross the beam as his classmates had done. When he'd come halfway, he abruptly teetered and almost fell off. He clung to the beam like the stuffed monkey on a pole seen at festivals. It had been too much for him to try to walk a straight line in midair with only one good eye. The older brother made his way down a long pole that hung from that part of the beam. The teacher, smiling unpleasantly, said, "See what happened?"

When everyone had crossed over, the older brother once again began to climb the ladder at one end of the beam. Getting red in the face, the teacher scolded him. The older brother smiled and said it would be all right. Then he went up the ladder.

When he'd gotten a third of the way across, he again lost his footing. He clung precariously to the beam flat on his stomach. The teacher and the students, looking up from below, turned pale with alarm. "Come down.

Come down," the teacher called up in a shrill voice. Ignoring him, the older brother once more got to his feet and stood erect on the high beam. This time he made his way across it cautiously, with short, mincing steps of half a foot each. Below him everyone watched, laughing nervously with pale faces.

After the older brother had crossed the beam and come down, the teacher snapped, "You fool." For the rest of the period the brother had been made to stand underneath the beam as punishment, the friend said.

The older brother had not mentioned any of this to the family. The younger brother began to feel a kind of fear, even, of his brother.

The younger brother and Utatsuko went to grade school together. On rainy days they came home under the same umbrella. On fine days, drawn to moonflowers, darbies, and reeds, they would nibble together on the stems of roadside plants. Although the natural target of their ill-humored classmates' spiteful teasing and schoolyard graffiti, they were always happy together.

The girl now felt a certain distance between herself and the older brother. Even when, after school, she sat at the older brother's feet with the younger brother for help with their homework, she would now and then smile at the younger brother as if asking him to come to her rescue. With the older brother she did not talk as easily as she once had.

The family business of the Sugis was a saké brewery. The brewery was situated near the sea about a third of a mile from their house. Every day after school the younger brother went there in accordance with his father's wishes. Snuffing up the fresh scent of the wood used for saké kegs, clad only in a loincloth, he helped stoke the hot fires under the vats of brew. His body grew steadily stronger. His pure white skin became the talk of the other workers.

Utatsuko attended the local girls' school. Often, perhaps bringing some needlework she'd done there, she would come to the house with a songbook under her arm and enter the older brother's room. Now and then the younger brother eavesdropped on their conversation. Later he would look into her eyes as if trying to find something in them. Her mouth as she spoke, her hands that displayed a tender fullness of flesh, and all the slight, subtle expressions of herself came to make him afraid. He secretly went to church.

One summer evening the three of them took a rowboat out to sea. The younger brother was rowing. The older brother and the girl, sitting side by side, faced him. Their conversation, intercepted by the sound of the creaking oarlocks and the boat plunging through the waves, did not reach the younger brother's ear. But he felt keyed up by their two faces that floated in front of his eyes in the chill light of dusk.

There was no other boat in sight. The younger brother stripped down.

"How far are we going?" the girl asked.

Not answering, the younger brother rowed with all his strength. From his shoulders to his arms, the pure white bulges of his muscles rippled beneath the sweat that flowed all over them. The boat pitched violently forward under his laboring body. In the sky a star shone out. They went on advancing into the lonely, endless sea.

The girl, putting one hand on the older brother's

knee, held on tight to the gunnel with the other. Disheveled by the wind, her hair blew apart in strands across the older brother's expressionless face.

"I don't like it. I don't like it." The girl trembled as she spoke.

"Too lonely for you? Don't be a fool." The older brother grinned at her.

Stopping the oars, the younger brother let the boat drift. His big chest was slowly heaving toward the couple.

"You must be tired," his older brother said.

"No. It would be fun to go out as far as we can."

"It would at that."

By now it was completely dark. From the surface nearby, there was the sound of gray mullet leaping out of the water. Several jellyfish, like the shaven pates of priests, drifted by. The girl looked at the surrounding sea.

"Shouldn't we be going back?"

The younger brother answered her with a loud laugh.

"It would be nice to keep rowing until we lost our senses."

This time it was the older brother who laughed loudly.

"How would it end, though?" the younger brother went on.

"For who?"

"Who?"

"You'd die."

"Yes, I'd probably die."

"You'd die, and that's why it's not worth it."

As he spoke, the older brother looked up at the night sky. He turned to the girl. "Can you see them?"

"See what?"

"The stars."

"But they're shining so brightly."

"It's pitch-dark. Where's the Big Dipper?"

The girl raised her hand and pointed. The older brother brought his black-spectacled face exactly in line with it.

The younger brother stood up with the oars in his hands. The boat rocked sharply.

"I'm cold." The girl shifted in her seat. The younger brother threw his light summer kimono onto her lap. After that, he began to row toward the offing again. The girl vehemently shook her head.

"We're going back now." The older brother spoke as if giving an order.

Paying him no mind, the younger brother rowed onward. The boat reared and bucked through the waves like a crazed animal. Going dead white, the girl clung to the older brother. Biting his lip, the older brother stared at the younger brother.

The younger brother lifted his eyes to the sky spread out above him. He felt a joy that was as if the stars of heaven had melted into his sweat. He listened to the sound of the waves sweeping by under the boat. Their sound was like part of him, as if surging up from his heart. He looked at his arms and thighs, their muscularity strained to the utmost. He felt as if there was happiness in everything. Hot tears spurted from his eyes. Dropping the oars, he cried out in a loud voice.

The older brother and the girl gazed at him with wide, empty eyes. The boat glided onward toward the open sea.

"'I know thy works, that thou art neither cold nor hot: I would thou wert cold or hot.'" Repeating this verse from the Bible, which he'd read in bed the night before, the younger brother went out back, still in his pajamas. The heads of the plants and grasses were bowed down by the weight of the dew. Under the dim, pale light of the sun shrouded in mist, the sesame had opened its flowers. Looking up at the sky, he breathed in deeply the fresh smell of morning. In a corner of the garden his brother was squatting by the side of the well. When he heard the sound of the younger brother's approaching footsteps, he turned around and smiled. With his glasses off, his blind left eye was like a bit of white clam meat enclosed in its shell.

Two or three stalks of the tall, corollated plant called "frog catcher" lay on the ground beside him. A delicate scalpel glittered in the older brother's hand. He thrust it into the mouth of a large frog that he'd laid out on a tin shingle. Skillfully using both hands, he peeled back the frog's skin and cut away the translucent flesh. The clean vitals of the frog were exposed. Its heart was still beating convulsively.

"I suppose you enjoy this." The younger brother smiled uncertainly.

"It's not so different from a human being."

"Oh."

For a while the two gazed silently at the dissected frog body. Then the older brother tossed the frog, shingle and all, into the well. The stomach, liver, and rectum, detaching themselves from the shingle, floated up and down piecemeal. Washing off the blade, the older brother wiped it two or three times and stood up. The sunlight, dazzlingly bright now, poured down on them. Side by side the two made their way back toward the house.

"A lot more fun than reading the Bible, eh?" Smiling and squinting as he spoke, the one-eyed older brother peered into the younger brother's eyes.

When he had graduated from middle school, the older brother entered a science school in the northeast. The day he left, the younger brother and Utatsuko, piling the older brother's wicker trunk onto a small cart, saw him off tó the village station. Even when the train had pulled out, Utatsuko stood and gazed after it until it was long out of sight. Gripping the shafts of the cart, the younger brother waited quietly for her. Then thinking their own private thoughts, they went back along the dark road. On the way rain began to fall. Leaving the cart by the roadside, the younger brother turned back to where the girl was coming along about sixty feet behind.

"It's late. We should hurry."

Saying this, he took the girl's hand. Her eyes had filled with tears. Suddenly her lips trembling, she looked at him.

"Ride in the cart." His heart pounding, he put his hand on the girl's shoulder. Once more sharply scrutinizing him, she abruptly gave him a push in the chest and ran off. Going rigid, he stood and watched her figure into the distance. Returning to the cart, he lighted a paper lantern. The wheels of the cart made a lonely, creaking sound as he came home after her.

After their father's death the younger brother carried on the family business. The older brother, having come home after graduation, built a laboratory in the garden and spent nearly the whole day shut up in it. The older brother married Utatsuko. They were happy.

One day the older brother, rather excited, dragged the younger brother into the laboratory. Passing between cages filled with a rustling noise of water lizards that for several months had been raised on mouse and chicken livers in preparation for a serum, they came to a big worktable. On the table was a row of several jars of spiders pickled in alcohol. In a glass dish in front, a big spider crouched motionless on its stomach. A close look showed that seven of its four-paired simple eyes had been crushed. A blackish slime oozed out of them.

The younger brother covertly glanced up from the spider at the pallid face of the black-spectacled older brother.

"It's not blind." Saying this, the older brother put the tip of a glass rod that he'd elongated over the flame of a spirit lamp up close to the spider's eye. The spider, on legs that bristled with brown hairs a fifth of an inch long, sluggishly turned away. The older brother smiled coolly. Then he explained the history of the sacrificial victims lined up in front of him.

First, he had captured a male spider and a female spider. After piercing with a glass needle one eye of the handsome, glossy-haired male spider, he mated it with the female. A batch of baby spiders was born. When he examined these under a magnifying glass, each was found to possess the full number of perfectly normal eyes. The offspring had mated with each other, and afterward swarms of grandchildren had been born. Among them was one strange fellow. Raising him, the older brother had today experimented on him. With the glass needle he had put out each of the spider's good eyes. Leaving him his one doubtful eye, he had given him an eyesight test.

The spiders that had been pickled were the grand-parents and their married pairs of children.

"And, in short?" the younger brother asked, looking up at the older brother.

Blushing slightly, the other replied, "In short, it means that none of my children will be born one-eyed."

"Oh? Is your wife expecting? How long have you known?"

"What? Oh, later, later, I mean." The older brother tossed the spider from the glass dish out the window.

Feeling slightly melancholy, the younger brother went out of the laboratory into the garden. He thought that his brother's felicity was less important than the amount of taxes he would have to pay that year. With that thought he felt as if the spider that he had just seen was crawling about rustlingly inside his head. Suddenly angry, he spat out his saliva hard.

When he got back to the house, the older brother's wife came into the sitting room with a photograph. Accepting it from her with a smile, the younger brother tossed it into a small bookcase on a table. The bookcase was full of the photographs of girls being offered in marriage to him.

"That's the girl," his brother's wife said.

His smile stiffening on his lips, the younger brother stretched out on the tatami. The red waist-string of the woman was right before his eyes. He shut his eyes. Then he repeated the sentence from the Bible that he was always saying to himself: "'Doth the wild ass bray when he hath grass?'" His brother's wife looked at him severely. Afterward he abruptly got up and went out onto the veranda. Across the way at the open window of the laboratory, the upper half of his brother's body was visible. After stealing a glance at it, the younger brother shut his eyes again.

Mount Hiei

比
叡
山

横 光 利 一　Although it was eight years since
their marriage, every year Sadao
YOKOMITSU RIICHI　and his wife had dearly wanted
to go to Kyoto. Although they'd wanted to go so often,
their work conflicted and there were the children to
take care of. There were no opportunities for a trip to
the Kansai with the whole family. But now there was a
letter from Sadao's brother-in-law saying that he wanted
to observe the thirteenth anniversary of their father's
death and by all means to come; so pushing other
things into the background, they had finally gone down
to Kyoto in late March. Since this was his wife Chieko's
first trip west of Tokyo, Sadao thought it would be a
good idea to show her the place where he had spent his
boyhood. He also wanted to show his older boy, Kiyoshi,
who this year would be starting his first year in school,
the grade school that his father had first attended.
Although he often visited the Kyoto–Osaka region on

Osaka region on his own, this time Sadao would have to exert himself as a guide.

Sadao and his family put up at his elder sister's house. The day after their arrival, one of his sister's girls, Sadao's two boys, with Sadao and his wife and his sister, six people in all, went to the temple at Otani where their parents' bones reposed. Although his parents were dead, Sadao had gone to the temple to show them the children for the first time. Even the wind, blowing across the arched stone bridge against the napes of their necks, had a peaceful feeling about it. Carrying his second son who was not yet two years old, looking up at the red plum blossoms that were already past their prime, Sadao mounted the stone stairs. Kiyoshi and his cousin Toshiko, who was a year older than he was, had already raced up the steps and were out of sight. In the laboriousness of his ascent Sadao felt how much his body had weakened. Thinking on his way up of his many friends who that year had died one after the other, thinking that even if he died his children would come here like this, thinking about what feelings his spirit would peer out at them with from inside the temple, with these and other thoughts that were in no way different from those of ordinary pious men and women who made temple visits, for a while absorbed in reverie, Sadao made his way up after the children. But when he saw his sister and Chieko, how with no apparent emotion at coming before the bones of his parents they were praising the scenery and pleasantly chatting together, he thought that the most old-fashioned person among them was himself. Despite that, although coming to Kyoto many times by himself, he had not paid a single visit to the graves.

Before Sadao reached the top of the stairs, the children, who had gone on ahead, after playing tag in the upper compound had come back down from there and were playing tag again, with shrieks of merriment, around their mothers' kimono skirts.

"Quietly. Play more quietly. Your cough's come back again," his sister scolded Toshiko.

But the children, cousins who had met for the first time, not even listening to their parents' voices, straightaway scampered up the stairs again.

All together now the family went up the stairs and paid respects at the ossuary. After that there would be the reading of a sutra in the main hall. But until the preparations for the reading were complete, they were to wait in a room across the garden. It was a gloomy, cold room that felt as if the sun never shone into it. The tatami was as firm and hard as a board, the ceiling high. But the paper sliding doors along all four sides of the room, thick with gold flake and with gorgeous birds and flowers in the Eitoku style, took one's breath away. As the pictures on two old screens that stood folded up in a corner caught Sadao's eye, he stared at them, forgetting even his own children. Here and there in a lakeside forest whose leaves had all fallen, white flowers like magnolias floated up to the eye, as in a dream. From the water's edge beneath, a snowy heron looked as if it were just about to lift off and fly away. Compared to the dreamy flowers and forest, the heron had a strength and plenitude of life that astonished Sadao with a feeling of excellent wisdom. As, thinking that it must be the work of Sotatsu, Sadao fixed his eyes on it, tea was served. The children docilely ate their sugar-sprinkled Japanese crackers. Only Sadao's two-year-old, crawling around on his belly as if swimming in the scattered fragments of finely broken-up sweetmeats that clung to him from his face to both hands, started energetically kicking at the screens as Sadao studied them.

"Now, now."

Sadao, moving the screens out of range of the baby's feet, again gazed at them insatiably. But although there was a fire in the brazier, it was terribly cold in the room. Not only would everyone catch colds at this rate, but Sadao himself was already sneezing continuously. Meanwhile, the preparations for the sutra reading had finally been completed. When they were shown into the main hall, though, not only was it even colder but there was neither a brazier nor a single sitting cushion. Toshiko and Kiyoshi sat lined up beside Sadao, while Chieko sat by his sister, who held the two-year-old in her arms. When Sadao looked around, all was in order except that the baby, his legs sticking out from the sister's embrace, still had his shoes on. But since they were brand-new and had not touched any floor, they could, in a sense, be considered a sort of substitute for *tabi*. As Sadao, not paying them any mind, silently watched the priest make his entrance, his sister noticed the shoes.

"Ara. Kei-chan still has his shoes on. What bad manners. This won't do at all."

Smiling, she began to take off Keiji's shoes.

"It's all right, it's all right," Sadao said.

"That's right. He's darling, probably just like his grandfather."

At this from his sister, even Chieko, who'd started to remove the shoes herself, left them as they were. Kiyoshi and Toshiko, not once looking at the altar, were still at their games from when they'd been outside. Their shoulders hunched with the effort, they stifled their giggles.

From the time the reading began, the family waited in silence for the sutra to come to a close. In the shivery draft that blew at him from behind, Sadao kept wishing that the long sutra would end quickly. But when he thought that if this were not his father's but somebody else's death anniversary, he probably would not feel that way, he realized that it was because he'd always been indulged by his father. The figure of his father as he had been in life came back to him again. He had liked his father, and after their separation by death his desire to see him again had only grown with the years. As his father had died of a cerebral hemorrhage in Seoul when Sadao was twenty-five years old, he hadn't even been with him at his death. Ten years afterward Sadao had flown to Seoul with some friends and older colleagues. Even then, as the plane had neared the sky over Seoul, he'd felt as if his father's spirit were wandering there in the heavens. He remembered how the tears had welled up.

At last the lengthy sutra came to an end. When the family went out onto the wide veranda, the sunlit city lay beneath them in a single view.

"Well, we've done our duty now."

Behind his sister as she said this, Chieko also, spreading her shawl over her shoulders, said, "I really feel relieved after that." She started down the steps of the high veranda.

After this, it would be all right to take his family anywhere he felt like.

The next day, leaving the children with his sister, he and Chieko went off to Osaka and Nara. Afterward, he thought, they would make a tour of the famous sites of Kyoto that they hadn't seen yet and, lastly, go out to Otsu over Mount Hiei. Otsu was where he had first gone to school. He especially wanted to see how tall the little cherry tree that he had planted at the time of his graduation from sixth grade had grown in the thirty years since then.

The day of their ascent of Mount Hiei, Sadao and Chieko, both rather tired from walking around every day, left the baby at the sister's house and, taking Kiyoshi with them, went up the mountain in a cable car. Sadao had memories of having climbed Mount Hiei from Otsu twice in his grade school days, but this was his first ascent from the Kyoto side. When the cable car got under way, Chieko, saying that it made her nervous, refused to look up even once. But as they ascended, the roof tiles of the old capital, submerged in the mist, were beautiful, Sadao thought.

"Take a look. It's just like being in an airplane," Sadao said, taking hold of Kiyoshi's shoulder.

After they'd gotten off at the end of the line, the road going up to the top split into two. When Sadao, going on ahead, passed through the spacious temple square, the road, entering a forest, gradually began to go downhill.

"That's odd. I've made a mistake."

There were no passersby of whom he could ask the way, so he retraced his steps. At this blunder of Sadao's, who when it came to the Kyoto-Osaka area usually had an air of knowing everything, Chieko took him to task. "See? You have nothing to look so important about."

Finally making their way back along the road muddy with melted snow to their starting point, they met up with another group, and Sadao and his family tagged along behind them. Although the mountain road was quite muddy with thaw in places where the sunlight fell on it, in the mountain shadows, each time Sadao trod on the lingering snow, his straw sandals creaked. Chieko, now and then stopping and looking out over the peaks of the mountain range still covered with snow that stretched from Tanba to Settsu, kept exclaiming in admiration, "Oh, it's beautiful. It's beautiful." When they'd walked about half a mile, they had to cross a valley in a second vehicle dangling from a wire rope. This ride felt even more like flying than the first one.

"This is even more like being on an airplane."

"If it's this, I feel all right. Somehow I didn't like the cable car."

Kiyoshi, held by Chieko, suddenly pointed up ahead and yelled, "Look, look! There's another one coming."

From the other side a car making a return trip came floating toward them. For a moment everyone, mouths hanging open, gazed interestedly at the car. Just at that moment, by the relay pylon, the car abruptly slipped down. Holding their breath, the passengers looked at each other. But when the pylon appeared behind the car that had gone on by, they all, as if understanding for the first time, suddenly raised their voices in shouts of laughter. "That's what it was. That's what it was." Already, by then, another car was approaching from the far side. It went on by everyone's surprised face. The occupants of both cars, in their lighthearted feelings of relief, waved hand towels at each other, even merrier than before.

When, getting out of the car, Kiyoshi took his first

step on the firm ground, he said to Chieko in a loud voice, "That was scary before. When the car went clunk like that, I thought it was going to fall."

At this, even the people who after getting off had gone on a long way ahead turned around and let out another burst of laughter.

As it was still well over a mile to the main temple at the summit, Sadao suggested they take a sedan chair, but Chieko said she wanted to walk. The sedan-chair bearers, strenuously explaining the problem of the slushy road, kept following the three. But Sadao and Chieko walked on without listening to them, though indeed there was snow everywhere, so deep that their straw sandals went in over the tops.

"How about it? Shall we ride?" Sadao turned around again.

"No, let's walk. Unless we walk, even though it's like this, what have we come for?" Chieko answered.

Although Sadao knew that the road from here on out was level, Kiyoshi was tired, and the coldness of the wet sandals would be a problem later on. He tried again. "Why don't we ride? I don't feel right about this."

"I'm not riding. There's nothing left to climb anyway, is there?" Chieko, stubbornly going on by herself, tramped through the snow.

"I don't know. You're going to have trouble." Saying this, Sadao tucked up the edges of his kimono.

The road continued endlessly through a dark, dense cedar forest. Chieko and Sadao, keeping Kiyoshi between them, made their way over the snow that looked the hardest. As the bracing, chilly air tingled against their cheeks, nightingales sang amid a constant whir of wingbeats. Sadao, as he walked, suddenly thought that the great teacher Dengyo, by establishing his headquarters in this area close to the capital, had suffered a loss to Kobo of Mount Koya. It was too close to Kyoto hereabouts, and whether he wished it or not the influence of the capital would have been pervasive. It must have been a problem. On the other hand, Kobo had been the better strategist. Sadao was also acquainted with Mount Koya. It seemed to him that when Kobo chose that region his power of vision had enabled him to see a thousand years ahead. If Dengyo, instead of relying on his own talent, had possessed the excellent spirit of reliance on nature, he would at least, rather than here, have crossed over Hira and established his main temple at the border of Echizen. If he had done that, besides having both land and water communication with the capital, he would not have had to have the Miidera temple, the enemy at his back, in his sight.

Above Sadao's head, as he walked along absorbed in such musings, the singing voices of the nightingales were growing more lively. But Sadao did not pay much attention to them. He was thinking that the short-sighted actions of Dengyo, who relied on himself, were like those of his wife, who, rejecting a sedan chair, was trying to make her way on foot through this snow when there was no telling how far it went on. If that was so, was he himself like Kobo? With this thought, Sadao once again considered the great-mindedness of Kobo. Availing himself of the power of nature to the utmost, he waged a battle of endurance with the government in Kyoto. In brief, if one compared him to Sadao, Kobo was the type to make use of the sedan chair and negotiate the uncertain, snowy road to his destination. When difficulties arose between the government and Mount Koya, Kobo concealed his whereabouts and came out again when the problem was solved. In contrast to the recklessness of Dengyo, who incessantly bore down on the capital beneath Mount Hiei with the force of his personality and scholarship, Kobo, who spent his entire life in safety, understood the strategies of government that, even greater than the power of nature, wielded the formidable and foremost power of this world. Sadao did not consider that actions undertaken without regard to the supreme authority were those of a great spirit risking all. If one had asked his reason, he would have said that if the actions of a Dengyo who was always pushing himself forward were allowed to continue, the hardships of the devotees who came after him would necessarily destroy the reserves of strength of the whole Tendai sect.

Actually Sadao, as he observed the unsteady gait of Kiyoshi, who, sandwiched between his parents, was sulkily trudging on, felt a constant, unbearable unease that the child would not be able to keep up too much longer. Meanwhile, the sedan-chair bearers, who had been persistently trailing them, had at some point fallen back and were no longer to be seen. In their place, however, an old woman, keeping a sharp eye on how Kiyoshi was doing, was still following them. Now she came up, saying to let her carry the child as far as the cable for the Sakamoto descent.

"How about it? Shall we have just Kiyoshi carried?" Sadao suggested again.

"It's all right. He can walk," Chieko said, turning around and looking at Kiyoshi.

"Even so, it's still a long way. A child like this can't

walk that far. But I'll lower the price." Saying this, the old woman wedged herself between Kiyoshi and Sadao.

"But this child has strong legs. He's all right."

"Let her carry him. Let her carry him," Sadao repeated.

"There's still a long way to go. I'll make it cheaper. I'm on my way home anyway, so just let me carry him."

Chieko, seeming to give up in this contest with the old woman who was constantly sidling up to them, asked Kiyoshi, "Kiyoshi-chan, what shall we do? Do you want to be carried?"

"I'm walking," said Kiyoshi, disengaging himself from the old woman.

At times like this Kiyoshi, who for a long time had been an only child, invariably took his mother's side.

"Are you going back as far as Sakamoto?" Chieko asked the old woman.

"Yes, that's right. I go back and forth every day."

"Are there people with children to be carried, around here?"

"Lately there haven't been any. I've gone empty-handed every day." The old woman seemed to have resigned herself to not carrying Kiyoshi. With the expression of a fellow wayfarer, she began walking in a free and easy manner alongside them.

Sadao felt his mood, which had begun to lose its balance, at last regain its equilibrium. But Kiyoshi, aware that his parents had almost had a quarrel over him, stuck close to his mother when Sadao came up to his side. Sadao, when he thought that this old woman would be with them from now on as far as the next cable station, even though she had restored his mood, felt the unease of not knowing when his irritation of before would again coil around his mind . . . This time he walked on ahead of everybody. Even as he walked, he thought that he was not likely to feel any more satisfaction than right now . . . From his own, he tried to imagine the lonely thoughts of Dengyo as he walked along the snowy road. No doubt Dengyo had passed this way any number of times from Kyoto. What sort of satisfaction had he felt? Once he had established his temple here, even his prayers for the salvation of mankind, in the loneliness of such surroundings, must have been little different from the everyday thoughts that came and went in the minds of ordinary people. And yet, just then Sadao felt that he could understand Dengyo's satisfaction in having chosen this mountaintop that looked down on Kyoto on one side and the picturesque scenery of Lake Biwa on another. In contrast to that, his own present satisfaction, the simple satisfaction of having entered into a peaceful frame of mind in which he thought of nothing, was good, but as he thought of how even that was not easy for him, he wanted to immediately come to the end of this snowy road out into the clearing from which Lake Biwa was visible.

Soon the road, which had been shadowy and dark up to now, abruptly came out into a spacious area where the sun shone brightly. It was the central compound, the site of the main temple. From the eaves of the temple, which stood in a hollow somewhat away from the great plaza, the drops of melted snow were falling like rain.

"Well, here we are." Sadao turned around to Chieko and Kiyoshi.

It didn't seem possible to get as far as the front of the

temple in their straw sandals. So the three, quickly making their way to the edge of the square, stood looking down. The lake, enfolded by the fields of early spring, glittering in the sun, lay spread out beneath them.

"Oh, how big it is. I didn't think Lake Biwa was this big. My, my," Chieko said.

For Sadao too, it was the first time he had seen Lake Biwa in many years. But it seemed to him that compared to the Lake Biwa he had viewed from here as a boy, the colors of the scenery were shallow and faded. In particular the pines of Karasaki, once recognizable at a glance, had completely wasted away. One could no longer tell where Karasaki was. But for a main temple and its grounds as a suburb of Kyoto, this was certainly the ideal place, Sadao thought. The trouble was, it was too ideal. If one occupied a site like this, at no time would the jealousy and glares of envy gathering about it from all sides abate. Now, at last, Sadao felt the lofty authority and prestige of Dengyo, who had selected this place, but the psychology that lived by always looking down on Kyoto and Lake Biwa, which after Dengyo's death became arrogance, highhandedness, and the rambunctious behavior of the monks, could easily be imagined. It would be difficult to crush, unless one were like the warlord Nobunaga a believer in Christianity, which was the wellspring of European thought. It seemed to Sadao that the gods' enshrinement in this sort of prestigious location could only have the effect of roiling up the hearts of the monks who were their custodians and, on the contrary, making it harder for them to pray for the salvation of mankind. In contrast, the lowliness of a Shinran, putting roots down in the city, the realistic faith that flowed into the tradesmen's houses, it seemed to Sadao, was similar to the spirit of Laotzu, who taught that the center of gravity must always be lower, lower.

However, even if that were so, even if he was looking down at this Lake Biwa at his feet, Sadao could not easily regain his peace of mind. Dengyo, besides being determined to influence the government of his time, must, after all, have set his heart on this mountaintop in order to obtain spiritual peace. If so, it was a complete mistake. Also, the decision to build the main sanctuary in a hollow, lower than the plaza, a plan that rendered the view below worthless, it seemed to Sadao, sprang from a strategy of penance; but the romantic defect of the temple's being on a mountaintop would naturally have had a bad effect on the sect's welfare.

With Kiyoshi and Chieko in tow, Sadao walked along the road, now somewhat downhill. Probably because it was brighter and the snow had melted more here than on the road toward Kyoto, the voices of the nightingales were livelier than ever. Along the way a vendor was selling blue-lacquered bamboo flutes that imitated the nightingales' song. Sadao bought three, one for himself and two for Kiyoshi. The little flutes, by the way one pressed one's fingertip against the end-stop, emitted various notes of the nightingale. When Sadao showed Kiyoshi how to play one of the notes, Kiyoshi, who had grown sulky with fatigue, suddenly broke into a smile and played it himself. The voices of the nightingales—were they following after them?—continued overhead like the welling up of a spring.

For a while Sadao walked along in the pleasure and interest of getting a little better each time he played the flute, whereupon Kiyoshi too, playing first one flute, then the other, his face lit up by the speckles of sunshine that slid and flowed down through the treetops, walked along slowly behind Sadao.

"It's just as if I'd brought two children with me. Come along quickly," Chieko said, waiting for Kiyoshi to catch up. Each time he was called by his parents, Kiyoshi hurried toward them, but before long would stop again. As the road went along the edge of a cliff where there were no trees and the voices of the nightingales all died away, Sadao and Kiyoshi, before and behind, blowing their flutes in turn, made like nightingales. Before long, Kiyoshi, who by degrees had become a skillful flutist, even managed such trills as "kekkyo, kekkyo, ho-kekkyo."

"His nightingale is still a baby bird. Mine is the parent bird. Why don't you give it a try?" Sadao smilingly said to Chieko.

"Ho, ho-kekkyo, ho, kekkyo."

Although Chieko declined to accompany him, each time the road rounded the cliff and the lake appeared below, putting her hand to her forehead, she would stop and happily take in the view.

Soon the three of them arrived at the cable station. There was still a little time before the car left, so going to the edge of the observation platform that had been cut into the head of a peak that jutted out into the deep valley, they sat down on a bench. Through the pointy tops of a dense yew-tree forest, Sadao could see the lake. But drawing up his legs on the bench, he stretched out full length, face up. In his fatigue he felt as if his back were cleaving fast to the boards of the bench. And in the pleasure of feeling his fatigue being slowly absorbed by the wood, for the first time his heart became clear and empty. He was no longer thinking about the wife and child who sat by his side. As absentmindedly he let his eye roam free in the sky, where there was not a shred of cloud, he felt that if he were to die now it would be a peaceful death. He no longer had any desires, he thought. Well, he would like a pillow, but it was no great matter if there weren't any.

Chieko, whether because she was tired, was silent and did not move. Only Kiyoshi still played on his flute, repeating the phrase "ho, kekkyo, kekkyo."

For a while Sadao lay basking in the sun. Soon though, when it came time for the cable car to leave, even this moment of peace would instantly become a dream of the past, he thought. Just then, unexpectedly, there floated into his mind the faces of his friends who did not have children. Feeling as if this were a strange event that ought not to have occurred, he wondered how, despite their childlessness, they could endure life day by day. Becoming one with the faces of the monks of Enryaku Temple who had run amuck, his friends' faces would not leave his mind. But then, thinking that such things were as they were and that probably his friends regarded with amusement and distaste the carnal muck of desire, Sadao once again lifted his eyes to the clear, serene heart of the sky.

"Ye gods, look down upon me. I have children here below." Sadao stretched out leisurely, until he lay as if spread-eagled on a chopping board. The matter of Dengyo was all one to him now. But the time went by unexpectedly quickly. As he was slipping into a doze, Chieko said abruptly, "They're already clipping tickets. If we don't hurry, we'll be late."

Let it leave. I don't care. With this audacious thought, Sadao stood up. His eyes on Kiyoshi and Chieko, who were running up the road toward the station, he brought up the rear.

When Sadao boarded the car, the bell immediately rang. The car, as if to plunge into the heart of the lake, slid straight down toward it.

"Ho, kekkyo, kekkyo, ho, kekkyo, kekkyo." Kiyoshi, close up against the window, went on playing his flute.

Ivy Gates

蔦の門

岡本 かの子
OKAMOTO KANOKO

For some reason there is often ivy on the gates of the houses where I live. That is so at my present house, and it was so at my house in Shiba Shirogane before I moved here. Of course, there was none at the houses before that in Shiba Imazato and Aoyama Minamicho, but at the house before them in Aoyama Onden there likewise was ivy. Since there has been ivy at three of the houses I have lived in, as I've moved around the western and southern parts of Tokyo, in Shiba and Akasaka, clearly I have an affinity for ivy gates.

Once I've grown accustomed to seeing it, the luxuriant growth of the creepers that completely mantle the gate all the way down to the latch, parting evenly from the top of the gate and hanging down front and back like a young woman drying her hair, simply gives me a cool, flourishing feeling. But at other times, when I am going out with my family and somebody is slow getting dressed, and I've come out ahead and am tired of standing by myself on the stone pavement of the entryway, I jab my irritation at this growth of leaves. And then, perforce, I think about this happenstance of ivy gates.

After all, if we were a busy family that was always going in and out and jerking open and slamming the gate, even if there were ivy, it would certainly not luxuriate. Unless we were a family that particularly liked to let nature have its way, we wouldn't put up with such luxuriant ivy. Probably, in addition to happenstance, there were reasons somewhat closer to home in this matter of ivy gates. This answer to my own question was extremely prosaic, but the people of my house, binding shut the front gate as a sort of trellis for the ivy and inconveniencing themselves by entering and leaving through the little wicket gate alongside as if they were fugitives, whether they knew it or not, truly loved this modest ivy. Perhaps, every time it was necessary to move, we had tacitly agreed among ourselves, in the way we went about it, to look for a house that had ivy on the gate. When I thought about it, I remembered that when we lived in a house with an ivyless gate, there was a lonely, alienated feeling about entering and leaving, as if a reflection of electric light on an office-worker's visor had slanted glancingly right into one's eyes. Our experience was that we had never lived long in such houses.

In its midsummer profusion of foliage, the ivy might even be compared to a dense green wall, as its thick leaves, overlapping like fish scales, buried the gate. From autumn into early winter the ivy was as beautiful as if it had put on any number of goldish-vermilion raincoats of brocaded straw. Each morning of frost there were more yellowing and decayed leaves, and even when there was no wind, they fell and scattered. In winter, only the stems and tendrils, delicately and tenaciously woven together, twisting back to their original arabesque when you unwound them, remained. Like the bones or network of nerves of some prehistoric reptile that had dried out and hardened into a woody fossil, at their joints they put out thorny feelers like suction-cupped tentacles. They gave me goose flesh. But looked at another way, they were like the elaborate designs of steel curlicues on Renaissance gates.

It was at the time of new greenery that looking at the ivy gave one a pleasurable, braced-up feeling. The young, green, translucent leaves cascaded from the top of the gate like a newly formed waterfall after rain. The stems and shoots at the tips of the creepers, the color of stone bamboo, that emerged from their pale green crept out each one by itself to occupy the empty spaces on the boards of the gate. There was a lovable freedom and youthfulness in the disorderly energy with which they grew and lengthened. The nature of the soil at our house in Shiba Shirogane was evidently the best for this kind of creeping plant. Along their creepers the soft, plump young leaves, countlessly coiling around each other, bunching up into handfuls that vied with each other in length, swarmed all over the gate.

"They're just like the tasseled woolen shawls that we wore in the old days."

Even our old maidservant, Maki, who was rather indifferent to plants and trees and nature, was impressed by the beautiful ivy. It was a clear day in early summer when the fresh maturity of late spring still lingered. Shading her eyes from the sun with her hand, Maki looked up at the ivied gate. "Some days the tips shoot out two or three inches. They're lovable when they're like this."

It was as if the quick-tempered Maki, by being able to calculate with her eye the spread of the growth of the tips, had for the first time discovered in herself a love for nature. Although an honest person, Maki was set in her ways to the point of inflexibility. Because of this, her two marriages had ended in divorce. Obliged to work as a maidservant in the house of strangers many years, this aging woman, who somewhere in herself possessed a hard shell of ego, had at least had the gentle side of her drawn out by these ivy tips. It pleased me. Past fifty and on the outs with all her relatives, childless, Maki herself had come to feel subconsciously the hardness of her lot. Hadn't the natural development of her emotions and the necessity to find something to love in her later years appeared to some extent even in this matter of the ivy? Feeling the sadness of her situation, I looked closely at Maki.

Her body was pretty much that of an old woman. Around her jaw, in profile, two or three brown vertical wrinkles had become conspicuous.

"Take care of them, even though they're just ivy. It'll soothe your feelings."

"Yes," Maki answered absently. She already seemed to be thinking of other things in regard to this ivy.

One afternoon four or five days later I heard the scolding voice of the old maidservant outside the gate. The voice was near the window of my study and was distracting me from my work. Thinking I would have

her stop, I shoved my toes into a pair of house sandals
and went out front. The clusters of young ivy leaves,
crawling sideways across the inside of the gate, were
like an ocean current that, checked by promontories, is
rapidly withdrawing its ebb tide out to sea. Displaying
great undulations, they were like a tide on the move.
The new shoots, overly numerous, forlornly groping in
the open spaces for something to fasten upon, swayed
precariously by a slight breeze, were like the tide's
creepers of foam. Somewhat dizzy from having stood
up so abruptly from my desk and dazzled by the unac-
customed sunlight, I fell into a sort of melting, swaying
trance that was pleasurable rather than otherwise. Simply standing there, breathing in the mild, resinous smell
of the fresh needle clusters of the pine tree, I heard,
listening and yet not listening to it, the quarrel outside
the gate.

"Ye-e-e-s. Honest. It wasn't me. It was another girl.
And I know who that other girl is."

The pert, precocious voice belonged to Hiroko, whose
family ran a tea shop in the neighborhood. The giggling
voices of four or five of her playmates could be heard a
little in back of her.

"That's a lie! Show me both your hands." It was the
voice of Maki. Having been answered back a lot already, Maki had lost some of her self-confidence and
sounded confused.

"All right," the girl replied, in the put-on voice of a
good child obediently doing what is asked of it. I could
just see her, right through the ivied gate, holding out
her hands in a big, magnanimous gesture. And I could
imagine the instant look of perplexity on Maki's face.

"H'm," the old maidservant muttered.

Again there were the giggling voices of the children. I too smiled for some reason. After a moment Maki returned to the attack.

"Then who tore off these ivy shoots? Tell me. Who was it? You can't tell me."

"Yes, I can. But I won't tell you. If I told you, I know that girl would be scolded by Auntie. To tell you when I knew she would be scolded, that's lacking in human feeling."

"'Lacking in human feeling.' Ha-ha-ha-ha." Perhaps amused by the adult-sounding phrase that Hiroko had used, the girls raised a peal of boyish laughter.

"These children are too talkative by far." Maki was getting excited. Even I could imagine her indignation. This old woman, who had been thrown into loneliness by everything in life, had evidently received a blow to the heart from this phrase. "Go away. A girl like you should become a woman orator," she scolded harshly.

By now the children, with Hiroko in the lead, had started to run away. They were rather far in the distance. The old maidservant, evidently thinking that appeasement was the best means of prevention, called after them in an unnaturally sweet voice.

"Oh, you all . . . you're all good children, so you won't tear off these ivy shoots. Please, I beg of you."

Even the children, appealed to this way, gave their lukewarm assent. "Aa." "U'm." There was the sound of their scampering off. At last I opened the wicket gate and stepped outside.

"Maki. What happened?"

"Oh, madam, just look. What a hateful thing to do. Hiroko was the leader of the gang and did this to the ivy shoots. I'm thinking of complaining to her parents."

When I looked at where she was pointing, I saw that the ivy on the gate had been torn off in a straight line just at the height of a child's reach. The tear was as regular as the short bangs of a modern girl's "water imp" haircut. There was something flippant and funny about it, as if a barber had gone too far in following the fashion. "What a terrible thing. Even for children to do," I said, sounding displeased. But in the way the ivy had been torn off in a straight line at just the height that showed how high up a child could reach, there was a mischievousness, a childlike naturalness. I could not but think better of it.

"They can't tear it off any higher than this. And they're children. They'll soon get tired of doing it."

"But . . ."

"It's all right."

As I've said, Hiroko's people managed a small tea shop two or three blocks away. In front and along the left side of the shop there were modest display cases with glass doors containing a common assortment of round gift teapots, large and small, and paper-wrapped boxes of tea.

In a complete green-tea set of handmolded pottery, a lacquer, jujube-shaped canister for use in the tea ceremony and a bamboo tea whisk were gathering dust. Along the right-hand side of the shop there was a three-shelved case. Ranged on the top shelf were little pots of refined green tea with purple cords. The pots of superior-grade green tea on the middle shelf were opened only rarely for a customer. What sold was mainly the coarse green tea in big pots on the bottom shelf. The economical "beach tea" and "dust tea" also sold comparatively well.

The pots of refined green tea were for show only; there was nothing inside them. Even the best of the superior tea, to save the trouble of transferring it to the pots, was stacked up in little tinfoil-wrapped boxes from the supplier in Shizuoka. Rummaging among the boxes, the shop people would finally find what you wanted and measure the tea for you out of those boxes. "That was why there was nothing to do but wait," Maki said.

"You mean you still go to that shop to buy tea?" I asked. "Isn't that the shop where that child who was tormenting you lives?"

As if bashful, Maki lowered her eyes. "Yes. But they give you a full measure there."

All of Maki's cunning went into this explanation. But it wasn't that I didn't have some idea of what was going on.

From the day of the incident of the torn-off ivy, Maki had suddenly become nervously vigilant about the front gate. If there was the slightest sound of a child's voice, Maki, saying, "It's that brat Hiroko," would rush outside.

Actually, two or three times since then, the children had done the same kind of thing. But in less than a month, with Maki's watchfulness and the children's getting tired of it as I'd predicted they would, it had stopped. Fresh-colored shoots grew downward in profusion from the line where the children had torn off the ivy. Early-summer cicadas sang, and goldfish vendors came by. Even so, at the sound of children's voices, Maki, muttering, "It's that brat Hiroko again," would rush outside.

Apparently the children played elsewhere these days.

There was no longer the sound of their voices outside the gate. Maki, for whom rushing outside had become a purpose in life, seemed disconsolate. Even when, with nothing to do, she'd flopped herself down on the cool board floor of the kitchen, she would suddenly wrinkle up her face and say, as if talking to herself, "That brat Hiroko. That brat Hiroko."

Starting from that time when the old maidservant had scolded her so, the little girl had coiled herself around Maki's heart, I surmised. She must feel lonely unless she could at least say the girl's name to herself.

Therefore, it was not that I wasn't able to grasp the feelings with which Maki, deliberately crossing several streets and enduring the inconvenience, went to buy tea in the girl's shop. Not pursuing Maki's unskillful explanation, I said, "So. That's good. Hiroko has stopped tearing off the ivy. You can be her patron now."

Perhaps because she'd taken heart at these diplomatic words of mine, Maki began to openly frequent Hiroko's shop. She brought back various stories about the people in the shop.

My house is a house that drinks a considerable amount of tea. Most members of my family, who do not drink saké, often put on fresh tea as a stimulus or for a change of mood. Maki was able to visit Hiroko's shop more than twice a month.

According to Maki, Hiroko's shop was indeed the shop of Hiroko's parents. But her father and mother had died early on in her life. For the sake of the orphaned Hiroko, her aunt and uncle had moved in to take care of her and look after the shop. The uncle was an office worker. He would leave the house around noon and come back toward evening. He was a good-natured, rather feckless-seeming man, whose one pleasure in life was going to the neighborhood chess parlor for an evening game. The aunt, a strong-minded woman, managed the household well but was of frail health. Often she had to take to her bed. Both were approaching middle age, and if they didn't have a child in two or three years, were thinking of taking the necessary steps to either adopt Hiroko or become her official guardians. Also, the income from the tea shop was an important part of their livelihood.

"It's pathetic. When she's in that shop, she's a completely different child. She just sits there all cowering and timid. It's because she has no real parents," Maki said.

Loneliness attracts loneliness after all, I thought. I wanted once to hear our old maidservant and the younger girl having a conversation in the shop.

Although it was not for that purpose, I happened to go to the framer's next door to the girl's shop to have a hanging scroll of a memorial sutra mounted. As I was sitting outside the framer's shop, Maki, whom I'd sent on an errand to the flower shop before leaving the house myself, came around from the far side of the street and entered the girl's shop. Since there was a big shop sign that said "Master Framer" between us, Maki did not see that I was there. The proprietor of the frame shop had gone into the back to look for samples of mounting paper and was taking a long time. I could hear quite clearly the voices talking in the tea shop next door.

"Why aren't you serving me any tea today?" Maki's voice, as usual, seemed to thrust at her interlocutor.

"In our shop, unless you've bought more than twenty

sen worth, we don't serve complimentary tea." Hiroko's voice too was its usual pert, precocious self.

"Don't I always buy a lot of tea? I'm a regular customer. Even if just this once I make a small purchase, you should still serve me some tea."

"You don't understand, Auntie. Usually you buy more than twenty sen worth. That's why I serve you tea. But today you've only bought a cap for a tea strainer for seven sen. That's why I can't serve you any tea."

"You know I came here to buy tea four or five days ago. There's still a lot of it left at home. That's why I'm not buying any today. Next time when we're all out, I'll come and buy a lot. Please give me some tea."

"But no matter what Auntie says, it's a rule of the house. I can't serve any tea to a seven-sen customer."

"My, what a heartless girl you are."

The old maidservant, a bitter smile in her voice, stood up to leave. And here a scene took place that pulls at my heart a little.

As Maki was leaving the shop, Hiroko called after her. "Auntie. The back seam of your *yukata* is out of line. I'll straighten it for you."

"It doesn't matter," Maki answered curtly. But then she seemed to come back into the shop a few steps. While she was straightening the seam, Hiroko whispered something to her that I couldn't hear. A moment later Maki, her face full of deep emotion, passed by in front of me. She was thinking about something so hard that she didn't notice.

After I'd returned home, I asked her what Hiroko had whispered and what she'd been thinking about. Maki told me that as Hiroko had pretended to straighten the back seam of the *yukata*, she had whispered to her, "Auntie. Please forgive me. My people are in the back watching me today, so I can't break the shop rules. If I do, there'll be a lot of trouble. Please understand." After telling me this, Maki added, "That child is such a tomboy when she's outside, but she serves me tea just like a young lady. She's so charming that I always ask for some. But when she has to behave for her aunt and uncle, like today, she'd go crazy if she couldn't go outside and play."

It was Maki who, when Hiroko was a little older and came to her for advice, stopped her from leaving home and becoming a waitress. And it was Maki who, when Hiroko had been adopted by her aunt and uncle, prevented them from doing whatever they wished with her. While my ivy gate was displaying the changing aspects of how many rounds of seasons, the two had become deeply involved in each other's lives and come to rely on each other. As loneliness had attracted loneliness, already loneliness and loneliness were no longer loneliness and loneliness. Maki developed a calm, motherly discernment, which even imparted a gentle orderliness to her personal appearance. In Hiroko too a modest, diligent disposition showed itself. At my place, when you went around to the kitchen, you entered the wicket by the ivy gate and passed through the grounds alongside the house. Any number of times I saw the old woman and the girl, like a mother and child of slightly disparate ages, in affectionate farewell or welcome scenes at the ivy gate, and was even moved to a tear or two.

The old woman remembered a story from her childhood (recently it was the subject of a radio program, in which survivors from that time related their experiences) about the origin of nursing. At the Battle of Ueno, it seems, the nurses of the wounded and sick were male. After a change to female nurses, the results were immeasurably better. From her own experience too Maki had learned that a poor woman, whether married or single, would have a miserable life unless she possessed some specialized skill. Earnestly adjuring Hiroko, she recommended that she become a nurse. Giving something out of her own earnings toward Hiroko's expenses, she entered her in a Red Cross nursing school and made her study hard.

Taking along Maki, my family moved from Shiba Shirogane to our present house in Akasaka. This time there was only a meager growth of ivy on the wall alongside the gate. But I pulled the creepers over onto the gate and now it is flourishing there.

Maki is a very old woman now. Leaving the housework and the kitchen chores to the young maids, she lives in her room. It's enough for her if she occasionally joins in the maids' gossip.

Nevertheless, from late spring to early summer, when the ivy is putting out shoots, she personally attends to the morning and evening sweeping up at the front gate. Is it because even now, in the lively sprouting of the ivy, she looks back with nostalgic pleasure to the beginning of her relationship with Hiroko, their going back and forth like mother and child? Against the backdrop of dense ivy like a green Gobelin tapestry, carefully stretching her long body, bent in two separate places, from the hips and in the back, the old woman leans on her broom and looks around at the ivy. In the mist of the summer morning she stands out clearly, white and fresh, like an

ivory carving. When a little child, up early, comes tod-
dling toward her, with all the strength in her crippled
body she takes it up in her arms and lets it pull off as
many ivy shoots as it wants. That ivy, which she used to
get so angry about when it was picked, she now smilingly lets the child have its way with. Has Maki realized, in her old age, that the love of the shoots and buds
of plants and trees cannot, after all, equal the love of a
human child?

When I think of that, for some reason I can't help it,
this verse by Saigyo floats up in my heart: "This is my
life, my mountain in the night."

Autumn Wind

中 山 義 秀

NAKAYAMA GISHU

I spent this summer at a hot-spring place in the northeast. I'd had a mild breakdown and had purposely chosen this out-of-the-way mountain resort to avoid people. I was disappointed to find it crowded with guests from the city.

There was an old clerk, Kyuhachi, who now and then drank with me and told me unusual stories of the past.

"It was before the inn had changed so," he began, but the local clientele who did their own cooking had always stayed away during the summer, a prosperous season of city people attracted by the cheap rates.

Early one August two women had arrived at the inn shortly after noon in a strange kind of sedan chair. In those days there weren't any cars, so guests rode the five miles from the station in an open bus. It was a newly opened mountain road full of bumps and jolts, and for invalids and those otherwise not up to it litters had been provided at the teahouse in front of the station.

At this remote inn on an upland plain there were not the facilities for entertainment there are now, and the guests found it dull. Their curiosity aroused by these two ladies in palanquins, they lined up along the veranda for a look.

From the first palanquin a fat old lady got out. In the other was a young woman, who surprisingly was lame. The clerk who'd been sent to meet them carried her on his shoulders to their room.

This news soon got around the inn. It was surmised by those soaking in the bath that like most new arrivals the women would come immediately to wash off their sweat.

True to form, the old lady, but herself alone, soon appeared carrying her toilet articles. Unashamed of her age and nothing dismayed by the mixed bathing that was old practice in these parts, she entered the bath-house with aplomb.

It was not a small tub, but there was a steady cascade of hot water from a faucet, and as the old lady submerged her corpulent body in it, the tub abruptly overflowed. Completely at ease despite the covert stares of her fellow bathers, she slapped water on her face and then breathed a deep sigh. Opening her eyes wide, as if noticing the others for the first time, she stared at each of them. In a loud voice that competed with the noise of the water—perhaps it was her way of saying hello—she gave out a long stream of complaints. The bath was a little too hot. Traveling in the middle of the day was an ordeal. It was the first time she'd ridden in one of those things. The inn was not as nice as she and her friend had hoped. The problem at a hot spring in the mountains was the food. She could not enjoy herself unless she had fresh sashimi every day.

The people around her said nothing. But their faces expressed openly their opinion of this vulgar old woman. Quick to notice such rudeness, the old lady looked puzzled awhile and then, suddenly sulky, went to wash herself off. With her broad back to the others she gave herself a thorough scrub and, propping up her mirror, applied some light makeup. Throwing on a *yukata*, she flounced out of the bathhouse.

Bad would be a mild word for the comments after her departure.

"Who was *that?*" someone began.

"Some vulgar old woman."

"Probably a sex maniac."

"The young lady's strange too."

"No lady, if you ask me."

"Can't make them out at all."

The guests were more curious than ever about the young woman, but the two did not leave their room after that. One of the more inquisitive guests was told by the maid that the young woman had had her bed made immediately and had lain down, while the old lady, back from the bath, sat by her pillow drinking beer.

Late that night Kyuhachi and some woodcutters whom he drank with were soaking in the bath when a sound of unsteady footsteps came along the quiet, hushed corridor. It was the old lady, with the young woman on her back.

In a good mood Kyuhachi and his friends silently luxuriated in the hot water, their heads resting on the sides of the tub. From the ceiling, a steam-clouded bulb cast a dim light over them.

Approaching the bath, the two women seemed to notice the men for the first time. But the prospect of bathing late at night with these uncouth locals did not appear to bother them. On the contrary, their presence seemed to interest the old lady somewhat. Even after the pair had entered the bath, the woodcutters continued to relax indifferently. With a special, grim expression, the old lady kept a close watch on them.

Behind her, the young woman crouched in the water and quietly bathed herself. Studying her out of the corner of his eye, Kyuhachi observed that she was not lame in the legs and that her external appearance in no way differed from an ordinary woman's. She was short, with a charming figure and shoulders inclined to roundness. Similarly full, her face had none of the invalid's pallor but rather a rich attractiveness. A peculiarity was her thick eyelashes and large eyes. Hers was a gentle face, completely unlike the old lady's, which as she frowned looked bad-tempered and hateful.

Soon the old lady gave a strange, premonitory cough and began to question the woodcutters.

"Do you gentlemen work here?"

Raising his head, one of the men answered her.

"We're mountain sawyers, ma'am."

"Is that so? Well, if you're from the mountains, you're all good fellows."

Her stern face filling with wrinkles, the old lady suddenly became friendly.

"I was wondering at first. You looked too unselfish to be working here."

But the man seemed unmoved by the compliment. Leaning his head back again, he closed his eyes.

"Have you been here long?" the old lady persisted.

"About two weeks."

"Then you won't be staying much longer."

"No, we're here until the start of fall. Even if we went back now, there wouldn't be any work."

"That's true. Summer's the time for resting. Please don't hurry."

Again and thoroughly, the old lady looked each man in the face. Dripping water, they were sitting along the edge of the bath. Suddenly she lowered her voice.

"By the way, this is something I thought of just now, but . . . if you're going to be here . . . that girl . . ." she gestured with her head at the young woman behind her. "Do you think you could take care of her? She's not quite right around the hips. As you can see, she can't even get out of the water without help. When I say 'take care of her' I mean if you could help her in and out and even when she goes to the bathroom. I'm an old woman, and I can't afford to be on vacation. I have to go back tomorrow, and just didn't know what to do. I've asked the people here, but without this"—with her fingers she made a circle, the sign for money—"they do nothing, so I'm worried. It's embarrassing for a girl, and doesn't help her get well. On the other hand, the guests think only of themselves. They're different from an old woman like myself."

The old lady waved with her hand at one of the woodcutters.

"You won't mind if it's for a girl, will you? You look as rugged and honest as a bear—I know you won't just stand by. You'll show her a little chivalry. Please. I beg of you."

At this all the woodcutters in a row and even Kyuhachi, who'd been put down by the old lady as an avaricious underling, burst out laughing.

The next day the old lady distributed a case of beer among the maids, and after going to the woodcutters' room to repeat her request, left the inn at once, this time in the usual open bus.

Kyuhachi, if the truth be known, was astounded less by the old lady's selfishness than by her temerity in leaving a young woman alone with the rough-and-ready woodcutters. The other guests had their doubts. Although she had referred to the girl as her daughter, it hardly seemed likely that she was her true child.

At that time woodcutters were generally thought to spend their days drinking and gambling beyond the reach of the law. Prone to bloody scuffles, they were considered desperadoes to whom a murder or two meant nothing.

Trooping in with their supplies on their backs— bedding, rice, miso, soy sauce, and a keg of saké—the six men were a painful embarrassment to the inn, which had begun to prosper at last thanks to the city guests.

An outright refusal, however, might anger the men into taking matters into their own hands. Led by their reluctant hosts to a room ordinarily used as a store-room, where they would not attract too much attention, they were tacitly sequestered there. The explanation given the guests was that they were charcoal makers employed by the inn.

As a matter of fact, they did make charcoal during

the winter. Originally mountain settlers, they left the cultivation of the stony fields to their wives and old men. Unless they themselves, men in their prime, cut trees and burnt charcoal, they could not make a living.

Thus, a visit to a hot-spring inn, even if they did their own cooking, was an infrequent event in their lives. And they never went to one patronized by city people. Unaware of how the inn had changed, they had come on the hearsay of someone who had been here many years ago. That is how out of touch they were, living in the mountains.

Abashed by the inn's splendor and the fine city people, unlike what they had heard, the men behaved extraordinarily well. Even when they drank there were no unruly outbreaks. Secluded in their dusky storeroom, they played at flower cards or chess.

Choosing, whenever possible, times when people were not around, they exercised discretion in taking baths. By just so much, however, did their boredom increase. Kyuhachi, who as an old-timer had more or less the run of the place and was more at ease with the old local guests than the city people, naturally became their friend and joined in their drinking parties.

Far from being put out by the old lady's request, therefore, the men welcomed it. The girl's room was in a detached building, distant if one went around by the corridor, near if one cut through the garden. The old lady's instructions were scrupulously observed by the men, who sent one of their number in turns to visit the girl. Not only did they take her to the toilet and bath, but they changed her position for her (she was in bed all day) and even did maid's work around the room.

Certainly the men were extremely tender toward the

girl. But they all of them had wives and children themselves. Ranging in age from thirty-four or -five to forty or so, they appeared much older than their years. Rather than performing services for a young woman, it was as if they were taking care of a daughter whose disability was in no way repulsive to them.

They took her especially often to the bath. Her affliction had been described by the old lady as "contusions," and the men thought the more baths she had the better. But they disliked for others to see her this way, and chose times early in the morning or late at night. Also they believed that bathing at such hours did her the most good.

The girl had an open nature unusual in one so young. She accepted their help cheerfully, without reserve or strain. She was not talkative, but on account of her natural virtue this created not the slightest impression of unsociability.

Tired of lying alone in bed, she borrowed storybooks and novels from the inn and read them avidly. But when the men came to see her, she would immediately raise her eyes from the book and smile at them. Her face at such moments, offering a flashing glimpse of gold teeth, was incomparably charming.

She was fond of fruit and always kept a pile of those in season by her pillow for the woodsmen. She also liked flowers, and at her request the men brought down various flowering plants from the mountain. These she would arrange by her bedside and look at.

As the days passed, the men gradually became less reserved with her. Even when there was no particular reason to, they all came over to see her. The girl welcomed their visits, generously treating them to beer.

Not to be outdone by such hospitality, they brought over their own back-country saké. After all, the men were not savages, and rather than drink in their gloomy, sweltering room with the same old unshaven faces for company, they much preferred to drink in her room, where they were cheered up and even the saké tasted better.

From her bed, the girl smilingly watched them as they drank. Occasionally she would tease them. "You're very quiet drinkers. Please sing something."

"You don't mind if we do?" the men asked good-humoredly.

With unexpected boldness the girl answered, "Of course not. I'm not an ordinary invalid, and you're here to help me get better."

This made the men bashful. Evidently they had no great confidence in their singing ability.

"Oh, you wouldn't like our kind of songs. We've never had a geisha in even once," they deprecated themselves.

"The clerk, then. Clerks always have some talent or other."

Kyuhachi's forte was pack-horse-drivers' songs. By profession a boatman, he had ruined himself gambling and been unable to return to his hometown. Since then he'd left off gambling, but even now sang the songs of that time. He had a reputation among the guests, and it was said that they would pour out saké for him and ask to hear his songs.

Pack-horse-drivers' songs seemed to be a special favorite of the woodcutters. Closing their eyes, they listened attentively. At the end, they all praised his voice. The girl chimed in, "Such a mellow, evocative song. It's the first time I've heard it. A trifle drawn out, though."

Kyuhachi was irked by this apparent criticism of his specialty. "It was originally a boatman's song, in time with the oar. No matter how it sounds to you, it has to be that way."

The girl quickly nodded submission to this tart reply. "That's true. Please forgive my impertinence."

From that moment, however, Kyuhachi began to view the girl in a different light. For a long time he'd had an easy life at this mountain hot spring. Unlike the new clerks, he did not worry too much about the guests' opinions and evaluations. Generally whatever happened was all right with him.

Therefore, he had discounted as gossip what he'd heard about the girl. Having been given bad marks for his singing, however, he began to wonder if she was quite so uninitiated as he'd assumed. Of course, there were any number of things that, once one doubted, took on an ambiguous aspect.

First of all, from her way of speaking and moving her body, it was impossible to think that she was a virgin. Furthermore, even if she'd been brought up in a red-light district, an inexperienced girl all by herself could not have smilingly invited the bearlike woodcutters to drink and make merry. Her behavior at those gatherings suggested a practiced skill. Her being alone now naturally enlivened the parties. Lying on her back in bed or sometimes on her stomach, she helped the time pass delightfully. There was an overflowing, sensual charm about her movements unlike those of a crippled person.

On the other hand, there was something extremely

childish about her. When she clapped her hands in glee at the woodcutters' funny stories, her laughter gurgling up in irrepressible giggles, she was completely the innocent young girl. When one stole a look at her as she napped, the charming line of her long eyelashes along the lower lid, the glimpsed row of little teeth, the air of quiet breathing about the fullness of throat and cheek all made her seem no older than seventeen or eighteen.

"How old are you, Matsu-chan?"

Matsu-chan's big eyes would sparkle with mischief like a child's.

"Fourteen."

"Don't tease your elders, now. Was that old lady really your mother?"

Even to this kind of direct question, she would nod smilingly.

"Yes. She's big and fat, but she's a good mother."

Her questioner did not believe her at all, but when the girl spoke to him so sweetly, for that moment he suddenly felt that he did. It was Matsuko's gentle disposition and fun-loving heart that moved her hearers. No one, when they had come to know this girl, could dislike or scold her.

It was unjust, a crime to harbor various suspicions about her. Perhaps after all it was the manly way to do as the woodcutters, oblivious to rumor, did, and treat her kindly without exercising one's evil thoughts. Having thus reconsidered, Kyuhachi tried to correct his thoughts. But doubt, once it had been sown, was not easily uprooted. Kyuhachi continued with the woodcutters to do her favors and, when he had time, would go to her room to listen to the stories she read from her books or play flower cards at a penny a draw. Before he was aware of it, however, he had formed the bad habit of covertly observing her.

Kyuhachi was not the only one who had his eye on Matsuko.

Nearly all the guests—then some sixty or seventy persons, in what is now the old building—watched Matsuko being cosseted by the woodcutters with the eyes of hawks and cormorants.

Perhaps from the conceit peculiar to city people, the guests—this was so even with the woodcutters—did not take kindly the intrusion of their social inferiors. When or how was unclear, but they had sniffed out the facts about Matsuko. At an inn frequented by people of various districts and conditions, it was bound to come out. According to the story, Matsuko, as Kyuhachi had suspected, was not after all an average young girl. Far from it. She was a waitress at a seaside brothel, a woman at the absolute bottom even of her profession. In other words, she was what northeasterners call a "wildflower rice dumpling."

Even the normally unfazeable Kyuhachi was shocked by this. It was not unusual for those who had been in that trade as geisha-courtesans, say, or teahouse women to come and take the waters as the wives of guests. But this woman from the abyss who had taken on fishermen and young sprouts of farmers, factory hands and mechanics, coolies and pack-horse drivers was truly beyond the pale.

People of her class were simply not treated as human beings. Geisha prostitution was a socially acceptable profession, and as such received the protection of the police. But girls like Matsuko, ostensibly waitresses but really and secretly whores, were thrown in jail the moment they were caught. Their contracts with their employers were rather vague affairs that covered bodily services only. The contract could, however, if the person was weak, end by sucking the marrow from her bones. It was a calling that naturally attracted cool, crafty women. Matsuko enjoyed a rather high standing among such types and, having a pleasant disposition and appearance, got her pick of the customers. She was the most popular girl in that town by the sea. Thus she was made much of by her madam, who had accompanied her even to this hot spring. Actually Matsuko, when she was not doing business, was not markedly different from your average hot-spring guest. No doubt it was because she was still young and not that far gone in her vices. There was even considerable reserve and refinement about her that set her apart from the low-class lady guests.

The ones to be pitied in all this were the woodcutters, who, unaware of her profession, had nursed Matsuko like a daughter. Thanks to her, the days had lost their weight of tedium and sped by unnoticed.

As worried about her sickness as if it were theirs, they anxiously observed her daily progress. If she could walk just a little by herself, they wanted to take her as far as their room, and looked forward to the day she could go out or anywhere she liked. Setting aside everything for her, they waited eagerly for her to get well. Sometimes, on the way to the bath, they would detach her clinging hands from their shoulders and say, "Try walking a little. If you lean on us all the time, you'll never be able to walk."

Matsuko would docilely spread her hands like a bird

flapping its wings and teeter forward a few steps, but then had to grab their shoulders again or a nearby post.

While Kyuhachi was thinking of privately warning the woodcutters before they were too deeply taken in by her, the other guests were becoming increasingly outspoken. Although this was a hot-spring inn, it had none of the usual erotic connotations common to that kind of place. Run by the same people for many years, it was a respectable place to which one took one's family. The presence of such a woman was felt to endanger the moral welfare of the children. Moreover, her pelvic problem was no doubt due to some bad disease, and if a family should catch it there would be all sorts of trouble. Already there were guests who showed signs of being about to leave. Of course, even among these morally alert patrons there must have been some at least who had come here on the sly for treatment of similar ailments. But the inn was dependent on public opinion. More exactly, it had begun to prosper because of the city guests and their expensive tastes, and was not about to forfeit their goodwill and its own reputation for the sake of a girl prostitute.

As an old-timer and particularly as one who was friendly with Matsuko, Kyuhachi was assigned by the proprietor to get her out of the inn on some suitable pretext. It was a harsh task, but as one of the help he had no choice. Naturally enough, he did not have the courage to tell Matsuko himself. After painful indecision, Kyuhachi went to the woodcutters and laid the facts before them.

Sooner or later they would have to know, he reasoned, and rather than unwisely dupe them it seemed better to tell them now. Also, the wrath of the simple woodcutters when they learned they'd been fooled might be worse than anything. Kyuhachi figured that a frank revelation of the truth would forestall their anger.

Going to their room, Kyuhachi told the woodcutters of the guests' complaints. Sitting cross-legged, chins cupped in their hands, the men listened silently. Even when they heard who Matsuko was, they did not seem very surprised. No doubt they were privately astounded, but outwardly there was not so much as a twitched eyebrow.

But when Kyuhachi came to the part about Matsuko's having to leave because of what the guests thought, the woodcutters' expressions began to change. It was not overly pleasant for Kyuhachi as the blood drained from their sun-darkened faces, which took on a curious bluish-leaden color. Just when he thought they would start raving like animals, there was a strange silence in which he could not even hear them breathe. Hearing him out, they did not answer when he'd finished.

"That's the nasty part of this business. We have to please the public. Even if what the guests say is wrong, we can't go against it. I know you must be offended, but please consider our position."

After this lame apology, one of the men finally spoke.

"She can't walk yet. Are you going to turn her out that way?"

"It's extremely regrettable, but that's how the guests feel. We have to ask her to leave."

"But no matter what the guests say, it's unfair to drive out a sick person who's come for the hot baths."

As if taking this for a signal, the six woodcutters looked at him with sharp, suspicious eyes.

Thinking now it's coming, Kyuhachi said hurriedly,

"No, if I meant that, you'd be right to be angry. We just want her to go elsewhere."

"You mean there's another place around here?"

"Yes. If you bear left across the plain down there, around seven miles on, behind Burntover Mountain, there's a little hot-spring shack where workers from the forest district stay. Now that it's summer I expect the local farmpeople are using it. Usually there's a care-taker there. It can accommodate ten people or so."

The woodcutters exchanged looks as they heard this, and appeared to be thinking something over. Kyuhachi saw his chance.

"If it's all right with Matsuko, I can go to the station tomorrow morning and have the litter sent up."

At this, in a completely altered, cheerful tone of voice, the woodcutters answered, "Oh, you don't have to do that. Up to now we've done nothing but eat and fool around. If it's Matsuko, we'll carry her there on our backs. We'll all go."

They all broke into good-natured laughter. Then one of them said, "This may just turn out to be better for Matsuko. She's not going to get well where she isn't wanted. What she needs is a nice, quiet place where she's at home. We should recommend it to her."

Relieved, Kyuhachi said, "That would be wonderful, if you could tell her that. It would be different coming from you, and easier for her too. I'd be much obliged."

Kyuhachi left quickly, before the woodcutters could change their minds.

The next morning, when he thought they would have finished breakfast, Kyuhachi went to the wood-cutters' room to see how things were going. The men were busy packing.

"What, you really *are* going together?"

At his surprised exclamation, the men laughed sheepishly.

"Kyu-san, we're ashamed to admit it, but we've fallen in love with that girl. We don't want to leave her. You must think we're a bunch of softheads. Just pretend you don't see us."

As they spoke, the men completed their preparations. After that, they took care of Matsuko's things and paid the bill. When it was time for them to leave, all the guests came out into the corridors. Certainly their departure was worth seeing. Five of the men divided the baggage among themselves, while the sixth shouldered a kind of scaffolding in which a cushion had been placed. This was for Matsuko.

When Kyuhachi had carried her from her room and seated her in it, Matsuko opened a bright red parasol that hid her from view. Whatever the woodcutters had told her, she seemed in no way offended with Kyuhachi. Taking something in a twist of paper from her obi and softly pressing it into his hand, she said with her usual charming laugh, "Thank you so much for all you've done. Please be well."

As the procession of six men and a girl started off, the children of the guests who closely lined the corridors of the first and second floors clapped their hands and sang out in time with their clapping. When they heard that, the men turned their heads and clownishly banged their hands on the crowns of their round, wicker sunhats. Doing so, they jogged down the road to the plain.

Once the August midday was past, there were many signs of fall on this upland plain. There was a peculiar emptiness about the sky, and in the colors of the brimful light one sensed a certain perfume. The inn looked out over a vast field of pampas grass. The tall plumes, although one could not hear the wind, swayed back and forth at the edge of the field.

The solitary red parasol, with the men before and behind it, bobbed away over the green swell of the prairie. Slowly borne forward, it was like a beautiful petal shouldered by a wave.

"Good-bye, good-bye," Kyuhachi heard himself calling after it and waving. But his voice, drowned in the autumn wind, no longer reached it.

The Titmouse 日雀

川　端　康　成
KAWABATA YASUNARI

When he saw the item in the newspaper about a big fire in Agematsu of Kiso, Matsuo called to his wife.

"What happened to that titmouse, I wonder . . . " Matsuo spoke as if it had been his wife who had gone with him to Kiso.

"Aren't you talking to the wrong person about that titmouse?" Haruko felt like saying. But she held her peace and read the item. The Tokyo newspaper did not report in any great detail this fire in a distant country town, and she could take it in at a glance.

"It doesn't say that anyone died or was injured. Somebody in the house must have taken the titmouse with him when he fled the fire." Haruko spoke as casually as she could.

"Is that so? You think it was saved, then?" Matsuo's tone of voice seemed to say that Haruko would know more about the titmouse than he would. But then a moment later he murmured as if to himself, "It was a fine titmouse . . . "

Tilting his head slightly, he dreamily narrowed his eyes as if he were listening to a titmouse. Haruko too, as if right over there the little bird were singing out in its clear, high voice, listened for it, unconsciously alert.

It really did seem to Haruko that Matsuo was remembering the song of the titmouse. It did not seem to her that he was remembering the woman he had taken with him to Kiso. Although that was not likely, and no doubt he was remembering the woman as well as the titmouse, it did seem that way to Haruko, perhaps because she was misled by the somewhat childish look on Matsuo's face. Therefore, there was no question of her saying it was good. For Haruko it was better if he remembered the woman rather than something like a titmouse.

"They had the cage in an outer box papered on four sides, hanging from the house pillar at the desk. It was up high. They might have forgotten to take it with them when they ran out of the house."

Haruko looked as if pitying Matsuo as he went on like this. And then she felt a faint chill along her spine.

"That's probably because they had more important things to worry about than a titmouse."

When one thought about it, there was something eerie in the fact that although many houses had burned down and many people were likely in distress, apparently only the fate of a single little bird weighed on Matsuo. But then, if he had no relatives or acquaintances in Agematsu, it was perhaps not strange that all he was anxious about was one solitary titmouse. People did have that side to them. Furthermore, if the titmouse were the fine bird that Matsuo said it was, weighed in the exact and exacting scales of Heaven, one small bird might well outweigh an entire town. The past held countless instances of people who'd lived and died with that kind of faith. There had even been people who had plunged into the flames and death for the sake of such treasures.

In the loneliness imparted to her by her husband, Haruko had even lain awake staring at such thoughts. In the several years of their marriage, had she even once gone to sleep before her husband? At first, as the nights of falling asleep after her husband continued without letup, Haruko had mistakenly supposed that to lie awake so late was a woman's fate. Even so, she was well aware, now, that something of the sort was the case.

"I should have bought that titmouse and brought it back after all," Matsuo said.

"Yes." Bowing her head in assent, Haruko went on, "Being the person you are, you would soon have confessed anyway."

It had been no good to come home without buying the titmouse, so as to conceal from Haruko his affair with the woman. Matsuo could not help telling her almost immediately.

After being away for two or three days that time, Matsuo had gone around everywhere to bird shops in search of a titmouse. Just as Haruko was thinking it odd, he let slip the remark that there were no birds in the Tokyo shops with a good singing voice like the one he'd heard in Agematsu of Kiso. Inadvertently he ended up talking about the woman he'd taken there as well.

On the way to Nezame-no-toko, he said, he had quar-
reled with the woman about the titmouse. When they
had gotten off the train in Agematsu, it was, of course,
with the idea of seeing the scenic mountain river of
Nezame-no-toko. Before they had come through the
ticket gate, however, Matsuo heard the prolonged trill
of a titmouse. The woman did not hear it. Hurrying
after the voice as if in a dream, Matsuo located the bird.
It was in a cage hanging behind the front desk of a
lumber dealer's shop. After standing outside the gate,
listening raptly, Matsuo entered the shop.

"A truly beautiful song. A fine bird."

The lumber dealer, merely staring round-eyed at
Matsuo as he came behind the desk, unsociably resumed doing his accounts. But he was unable to conceal
his complacent pride in the bird. Plumping himself
down all uninvited, Matsuo was treated to a discourse
on titmice. Before now, Matsuo had not been particularly fond of titmice and, furthermore, knew nothing
about them.

His having praised it as a fine bird had been an act of
intuition. And judging from the lumber dealer's boast-
ful talk, he knew his intuition had been accurate. Indeed, Matsuo was a man whose wayward, willful
method of work was valued for its strangely acute
intuition. The company he worked for was a large
organization with interests in almost every field, from
various kinds of machine industries to mining, real
estate, banking, insurance, transportation, and textiles.
But Matsuo held no precisely defined position. Nor did
he have any specialty. All he did was sniff out the
prospects of various enterprises and submit them for
research. Although seemingly a useless person, he drew

a rather high salary. He was, so to speak, a curious kind of successful person. While saying it did no good to be greedy, Matsuo, simply going by his own taste, had also bought pottery, antiques, and occasionally land and houses on his own account. Most of them had proved to be lucky discoveries, and he'd made a good deal of money. But he was a man who was as disinterested as flowing water.

"Is there someone like you at every company, a man like a diviner?" Somewhat uneasy about her husband's status in the business world, Haruko had asked this.

But Matsuo had calmly replied, "There may be. I don't really know. But the company is not about to let me go. They're afraid I would go elsewhere. And I don't like being lumped with diviners. What I do is a kind of art."

If he followed too conventional a method, he said, the needful intuition was lost. But despite his confidence in his work, what a lonely figure he was in everyday life. Perhaps that was the shadow cast by the loneliness of a wife who had such a man for a husband.

His trip to Shinshu also had been for the purpose of sniffing out land that was likely to become a resort area. Sometimes, he had casually remarked, it was necessary to take along a womanfriend.

Evidently thinking that Matsuo was a fellow titmouse fancier, the Agematsu lumber dealer had elaborated complacently about such things as the singing contest at Matsumoto. The woman had waited outside, bored. Matsuo earnestly asked the lumber dealer to let him have the titmouse. But the latter had stubbornly refused, saying that no amount of money would persuade him to sell the bird.

Unable to resign himself, even after he'd left the shop, Matsuo had stopped, turned around, and listened to the titmouse's song. Then when they'd walked out of the town and gone on a while, the shopboy from the lumber dealer's had come after them on a bicycle. They would sell the titmouse. The price was thirty yen.

Although wanting to go right back and buy the bird, Matsuo had a feeling that if he took it home Haruko would know that he'd had a woman with him. Even though both places were in Shinshu, his business had been in North Shinano, not Agematsu. It would seem well to say that he'd taken a side trip to Agematsu to see the river at Nezame-no-toko, but even Matsuo was aware that such a coverup would be totally inept and soon be seen through. He asked the woman to take care of the titmouse for him a while. But the woman had something of an antipathy to the titmouse by then and would not agree. Forgetful of the shopboy looking on, Matsuo had importuned her like a child. But the woman had shown equal obstinacy. Talking endlessly of nothing but the titmouse, Matsuo hadn't even looked at the fantastic river crags of Nezame-no-toko.

Evidently he had soon afterward parted from the woman. It was surely not on account of the titmouse. He never stayed long with any of his women.

Thinking that at any rate it wouldn't last long, Haruko had until now been inclined to forgive Matsuo any number of times and, furthermore, had made that the excuse for her resignation. But this also, when one thought it over coolly, was a strange thing. At first Haruko had been unable to believe that so many women could get involved with a man who had a wife. Even after her childish incredulity had faded away, however,

Haruko found it a not easily decipherable riddle why those women parted from Matsuo so quickly. Was there some great defect in Matsuo? Was it only she, ignorant that Matsuo was not a man whom one should be with for long, who went on living with him? There did not even seem to be, here, the difference between a wife and an adulteress.

And yet none of those women whom Matsuo had parted from ever came around afterward to cause unpleasantness at the house. According to Matsuo, even after they'd separated, none of the women felt any dislike for him. Matsuo himself, of course, had nothing particularly bad to say of them.

Once Haruko knew about the affair, Matsuo would come to her after he'd seen the woman and confess everything in a rather innocent manner. It was already a custom for Haruko to listen with a meek, acquiescent demeanor. But at such times, in her heart, she would open wide her sad eyes and stare at Matsuo.

Matsuo was evidently able to forget without any trouble the woman he had separated from. But Haruko could not forget. And so it had come about that Haruko remembered well the women that Matsuo had forgotten. It was as if it were Haruko's duty to remember instead of Matsuo's. Perhaps this kind of thing, not merely in connection with love affairs, tends to be the case among married couples. But in Matsuo's case it seemed to go a little too far.

With the woman also, once her life had changed, it did not happen that she kept deep in her heart the memory of her affair with Matsuo. And Matsuo himself forgot. Why was it that only the looker-on, Haruko, had the memory powerfully incised in her heart?

Matsuo was a passionately fond parent. He would not go to bed unless he had their three-year-old girl in his arms.

"How terrible if she should turn out to be like you," Haruko said one night.

"What? She's a girl. She'll be all right."

"Before you go to sleep, I have a request to make."

"H'm." Deftly picking the child up, Matsuo went off to the toilet. Watching him from behind, Haruko felt like bursting into loud laughter. What must he look like at some other woman's place, she thought.

"If I had been with you, I could have bought that titmouse in Agematsu and brought it home. Next time we'll go together."

Although saying this, when Matsuo went to Nikko he took somebody else with him.

It was just at the start of the rainy season, and the little mountain birds were singing at their best. Even while viewing Kegon Falls, Matsuo listened only for the songs of the robins and titmice. Even while fishing for salmon trout at Lake Yunoko, each time a titmouse sang, he would count the notes in its trill. The high, clear song echoed out over the lake beautifully. But there was no bird that sustained its song through seven notes. None of them could have perched at the feet of the titmouse of Agematsu in Kiso. Matsuo told Haruko about it as soon as he got home.

After arriving at the station in Nikko, Matsuo had taken it into his head to walk around looking at the little birds in the shops. It was already dusk, and the woman complained. In this town white-eyes were very popular. In one shop that Matsuo finally found, the owner was a cabinetmaker by profession, but having a liking for birds, he raised them from chicks and even shipped them off to Tokyo, it seemed. In the shanty-like shop at the end of an alley, there was hardly room to sit down. There were only three white-eyes. Saying that they were a more interesting bird than titmice, the owner commenced a discourse on white-eyes. Matsuo stepped up to one of the three cages. The bird inside was the owner's prize possession. But Matsuo was not as impressed by it as he had been by the titmouse of Agematsu.

"It's not such a fine bird" was his comment.

The owner, perhaps mistaking Matsuo for a bird connoisseur, immediately lowered the price. Thinking he might as well buy the bird, Matsuo asked the woman to take care of it for him. The woman, saying it would be a nuisance, refused. Having been made to walk through the misty rain, her striped, crepe kimono shrinking on her, by now she was in a thoroughly bad humor.

Even when he talked to Haruko of these things, the Nikko white-eye and the Kiso titmouse did not seem to linger in Matsuo's heart.

The incident of the Kiso titmouse had occurred in early autumn of the year before last, that of the Nikko white-eye in early summer last year. Matsuo had shortly afterward parted from the woman he'd gone with to Nikko.

From about the beginning of this year, Matsuo, for some reason, had begun to put on weight. He himself was very displeased by it. He had a naturally round face, and nowadays when he looked down a little, it gave him a woman's double chin. His earlobes were plump and fleshy. His eyelids were full and gentle-looking. When his face was turned to the side, seen from behind there was a somewhat lonely feeling about it. It was strange.

"It's unnatural, me getting fat like this. I think there must be something wrong with me." Stroking his now protuberant belly, Matsuo seemed stupefied with disgust.

"You're drinking too much saké. If you would abstain a little . . ."

Lately, Haruko thought, there did not seem to be any women.

"What? If I make my mind up to it, I can lose weight." Matsuo smiled. "Come to that, you've gotten fat yourself, haven't you, Haruko?"

"Perhaps I have . . . " Haruko looked at her wrists and lap.

"The child is healthy too." Matsuo spoke as if to himself.

What self-conceit! A feeling of indignation abruptly welled up from the pit of Haruko's stomach. Closing her eyes, she endured it. If she told her husband that there had hardly been a day she hadn't thought of leaving him, how surprised he would be, Haruko thought.

Suddenly, with the face of a happy child, Matsuo said, "I'm told by everyone that I'm a happy man, that I have a special disposition, but I've never thought anything in particular of my good points. It's as if that were why I have them."

"Can that be? Don't you have very strong confidence in yourself?"

"Not all that much. Even women don't have any respect for me."

Haruko had the feeling that she was hearing something extraordinary.

One day in the rainy season, as Haruko was tidying up the clothes closet, she found several mildewed articles. Intensely disliking that kind of thing, she was hastily clearing out the contents of the closet when a visitor called. Even before the voice of the visitor she heard the singing voice of a little bird. It was the lumber dealer from Agematsu of Kiso. He had come to Tokyo on business, he said, and had brought the titmouse along with him.

Haruko, for some reason, was more flustered than she should have been. No doubt the lumber dealer understood that the woman whom Matsuo had had with him the year before last was not his wife. But what must he be thinking as he looked at Haruko? Even when Haruko said that her husband was out, the dealer, saying that he had come all this way with it, insisted on leaving the bird.

"If you should have no use for it, I'll be in Tokyo another two or three days. Give me a call at my inn, and I'll come and take it away."

"Yes. But my husband is whimsical. He's never actually kept a bird."

The dealer had a puzzled expression, as if he thought Haruko were not telling the truth. Finally Haruko paid him. The price was twenty yen, ten yen lower than in her husband's story.

Matsuo, who came home in the evening, was as delighted as a child with the titmouse. He would not come away from the side of the cage.

"Is it really the bird from that time? Afterward I

thought he might have brought a different bird. I was a little worried."

"No, it's the same bird. No question about it—it's that bird."

Four or five days later, however, there was another visitor, this time the cabinetmaker from Nikko. He'd brought two titmice with him. Haruko, already smiling, docilely accepted delivery. The price, once again, was low.

Matsuo, when he returned from work, thinking that he heard a bird sing, casually opened the door of the cage, and the two birds flew out.

"Oh dear. What have you done?"

Haruko immediately stepped down into the garden in pursuit of the birds.

"That kind of bird is no good. Don't chase them." Matsuo's tone was nonchalant.

Haruko silently gazed for a moment at the sky into which the birds had escaped. Since Matsuo had spoken firmly, with no sign of regret, she could not complain. A feeling of respect even stirred faintly in her.

It was strange to Haruko that, at a time when her husband seemed to have forgotten about such things as titmice, both the lumber dealer of Kiso and the cabinetmaker of Nikko had remembered their promises and purposely brought the birds with them to Tokyo.

And it was strange to Haruko that it was she, the wife, who took daily care of this little bird that, with the other two, was a memento of Matsuo's love affairs.

Once when Matsuo was out of the house, Haruko sat by the side of the cage and gazed in earnestly at the diminutive titmouse, small even for a small bird. The song of this prized bird, clear and high, continuing so long it was painful, passed purely into Haruko's heart. Closing her eyes, she gave herself up to it. It was as if something that had passed from the world of the gods into the life of her husband had come echoing to her straight as an arrow. Nodding to herself, Haruko felt the tears rise to her eyes.

One Woman
and the War

坂 口 安 吾

SAKAGUCHI ANGO

The old man, the one I called the Mantis, called me Madam or Sister. The fat old man just called me Madam. That's why I liked him better. Each time the Mantis called me Sister, I would look unconcerned, as if I hadn't noticed, but I made up my mind to give him a hard time for it soon after.

Both the Mantis and Fatty were around sixty years old. The Mantis owned a factory in the neighborhood, and Fatty had a well-cleaning business. Getting together in the intervals between sirens, we shot craps. Usually Nomura and Fatty won, and the Mantis and I usually lost. The Mantis would get all excited, call me Sister, and make awful faces. Sometimes he would make a lewd, slobbering face at me. The Mantis was a terrific miser. When he paid the money he'd lost, he would take out the bills and one by one smooth out the wrinkles in them. He couldn't let go of them. When the other players said, "It's dirty to put spit on them, come on, hand them over," he would scrunch up his face as if he were about to cry.

Sometimes I would get on my bike and go over to invite the Mantis and Fatty out. We all believed that Japan was going to lose, but the Mantis believed it with a vengeance. He seemed to be happy about Japan's impending defeat. Half the Japanese, eight-tenths of the men and two-tenths of the women, were going to die. He counted himself among the babies and tottering old geezers of the surviving two-tenths of the men. In his scheme he promised to remember me and treat me nice among the hundreds or thousands of his concubines.

The terror of these old guys under an air raid was something to see. It overflowed with the lewd tenacity of life. And yet their interest in the destruction of others was more active than any young person's. When Chiba or Hachioji or Hiratsuka had been bombed, they would go to see the sights. If the damage had been light, they would come back looking disappointed. They would lean over the half-burned corpse of a woman and examine it so closely that they couldn't help but touch it, even though others were watching.

Each time there was an air raid, the Mantis came to invite me to see the sights of the area that had been bombed, but after the second time I no longer went. Both Fatty and the Mantis hated the war because there were no sweet things to eat and no good times, but in this poverty of life they felt sorry only for themselves. They felt nothing for anyone they knew or any of their countrymen. Their thought was "let everyone be killed except me." As the raids grew more and more intense, their true natures were stripped bare layer by layer. Toward the end they shamelessly came out and said it. Their eyes, strangely glittering, became demoniacal. Sniffing out human misfortune, scrounging around for it, they prayed for it to happen.

One day it was hot, so in a short skirt and no stockings I got on my bike and went to ask the Mantis out. The Mantis had been burned out of his house and was living in his shelter. Hereabouts also, now that the neighborhood had become a burned-over plain, no one got angry even if you didn't wear *monpe*, the loose, baggy trousers that women were expected to wear as a mark of solidarity with the war effort. The Mantis stared at my bare legs as if he was out of breath. Putting something in his kimono, he came out of his shelter. On the way to my place he said, "I'll only show this to you," then sat down by a bush that had survived the flames and took out a book of pornographic woodcuts. It had a beautiful binding, like an album, and an old Japanese jacket.

"Aren't you giving it to me?"

"Of course not!"

The Mantis was consternated. When he had turned around and was fiddling with something, I grabbed the book and jumped on to my bike. It was as much as the Mantis could do to get unsteadily to his feet and, mouth hanging open, watch me as I nonchalantly straddled the bike.

"The hell with you!"

"You bitch!" The Mantis bared his white teeth.

The Mantis hated me. I'm aware that men in general, from the age of forty or so, change completely in their attitude toward women. When they get to be that age, they lose their spiritual longings, dreams, and hopes of consolation. I get enough sentimentality at home, they think. They can't help but think that tender feeling doesn't exist outside the smell of salty rice-bran paste and diapers. So they become infatuated with the woman's body. It's from this time on that men really go overboard on women. From the start, without a thought of the soul, they're besotted with a dream of the flesh from which they never awaken. Men of this age think they see through women, know all their tricks, and, if anything, generally feel dislike for the feminine. But since their desire is already nothing more than carnal lust, it doesn't change because of their dislike. More often it's stirred up by it.

They don't have any such mushy thoughts as love. They think only of their own interests and the transactions of the flesh. But while the glamour of a woman's body is a spring that does not dry up in ten or fifteen years, men's money is not a spring. It's easy, before too much time goes by, for a man to make a broken-down old beggar of himself.

At times I thought I would like to make a beggar of the Mantis. I thought about it almost every day. After making him crawl around me like a puppy dog, I would rip his fur off him, gouge out his eyes, and kick him out, I thought. But I didn't have enough interest to actually do it. The Mantis was a decrepit, dirty old man. Since he already had one foot in the grave, why not give him the final shove, I thought, but when it came down to it, I didn't even feel like doing that.

Probably, I thought, it is because I love Nomura, and Nomura doesn't like that kind of thing. But Nomura didn't believe that I loved him. He seemed to think that people were being somewhat nicer to each other because of the war.

In the old days I was a streetwalker. I was a woman who hung around in front of the latticework of shops, calling out, "Hey there, big boy, hey." There was one man I fell for. I became his mistress and the madam of a bar he owned. But my heart was in the gutter, and I slept with just about all the customers. Nomura was one of them. On account of the war, the bar had to close down. Bedeviled by such things as compulsory work-service, I had to get at least nominally married. I decided to move in with the carefree bachelor Nomura, who didn't let himself be bothered by anything. Greeting me with a sour smile, he remarked that as Japan was sure to lose the war, the country would be a chaos afterward. "We'll put off everything till then," he said. Neither he nor I had any thoughts of a conventional marriage.

But I had always liked Nomura, and I gradually fell in love with him. I came to think that if only Nomura wanted it, I'd like to be his lifelong mate. A whore by nature, I was a woman who had to have fun on the side. A woman like me does not believe in such things as chastity. My body was my plaything, and I was going to play with my toy all my life.

Nomura thought I was a woman who could not be satisfied by one man, a woman who would go from man to man. But love and sex are two different things. I had to have my fun. My body was parched for sex; naturally perverse, I was a truly bad woman, I thought. But was I the only one who wanted some fun? I loved Nomura, though it was different from having fun. For his part Nomura intended to leave me and find himself a regular wife. First of all, he thought that before he left me he would be killed in the war. Even if he was lucky enough to survive, he thought he would be taken off somewhere to do slave labor. That was pretty much what I thought too, and I wanted to make him a good wife at least for as long as the war lasted.

The night our neighborhood was bombed was the fifteenth of April.

I liked the night bombing runs of the squadrons of B-29s. For daytime bombing, they flew very high up and you couldn't see them well. There was no light and color, and so I disliked it. When Haneda Airport was bombed, five or six small black fighter-planes, each leisurely twirling its wings, came down in a nose dive as straight as a plumb line. The war really was beautiful. It was a beauty you could not anticipate; you could only glimpse it in the midst of your terror. As soon as you were aware of it, it was gone. War was without fakery, without regrets, and it was extravagant. I didn't begrudge losing my house, my neighborhood, my life to it. Because there was nothing that I was sufficiently attached to that I would begrudge losing. But when, holding my breath, I watched a divebomb attack in which the sudden suction of a maelstrom of air pressure roared in my ears, the planes had already passed low overhead and the machine guns had stitched the air with their staccato outbursts. I didn't even have enough sense to hit the ground. When I came to my senses, there was somebody lying on the road not thirty feet away, and in the wall of his house there were about thirty holes two inches across. From then on I disliked the daytime raids. I felt an empty displeasure, like a schoolgirl of not even average looks who has been molested by some conceited, barbarous, middle school delinquent. Even just a few days before the end of the war, I got a shower of sand in a noonday attack by small fighter-planes. When I was repairing the air-raid shelter with Nomura, a black plane came flying in at an altitude of only about seventeen hundred feet. It released something that looked like an oil drum. I screamed and Nomura shouted, "Hit the ground!" Although we were right outside the shelter, there was no time to run inside. In no hurry, I lay down on the ground and looked at Nomura. Under my chin and belly the ground trembled, and I felt as if the wind of the blast would flip me over on my back. It was after that that I got showered with sand. Nomura was a man who really took care of me at times like that. I thought if Nomura was alive he would come and lift me up in his arms, so I played dead. Sure enough, he lifted me up, kissed me, and started tickling me. Laughing in each other's arms, we rolled around. The bomb this time had gone too deep into the earth, so that only the house next to next door was blown away. The roofs and windows of the neighborhood were undamaged.

The night air raids were magnificent. The war had robbed me of various pleasures, so I hated it, but after the night bombings began, I no longer hated the war. Although I'd disliked the blackout darkness of the nights, after the night raids started, I felt a deep harmony, as if that darkness had soaked into me and were a precious part of myself.

But, if I were asked what about the night bombings was the most magnificent, truth to tell, my real feeling, more than anything else, was one of pleasure at the vastness of the destruction. The dull silver B-29s too, as they suddenly hove into view amid the arrows of the searchlights, were beautiful. And the antiaircraft guns spitting fire, the droning B-29s that swam through the noise of the guns, and the incendiary bombs that burst in the sky like fireworks. But only the vast, world-destroying conflagration on the ground gave me complete satisfaction.

It made me feel nostalgic. The town in the northeast where I was taken by a procurer after my parents abandoned me was surrounded by little mountains. I had the feeling that that hometown scenery of mountains whose lingering patches of snow made them look like scurfy, balding heads was always burning in hellfire. Everything burn, I always cried in my heart. The town, the fields, the trees, the sky, even the birds, burn and set fire to the sky, water burn, the sea burn! My chest would tighten, and I would cover my face with my hands despite myself to keep the tears from gushing out.

I thought it would be good too if my hatred burned away. When I was staring at the flames, it was painful to realize that I hated people. I began to seek unreasonably for proofs that I was loved by Nomura. Nomura only loved my body. That was all right with me. I was loved. Under Nomura's heavy caresses, I thought about all sorts of sad things. When he let up on the caresses, I would scream, "More, more, more." And I would get the strangest feeling of wanting to cry and embrace myself.

I secretly waited for the day when our neighborhood would be engulfed in a sea of hellfire. From the Mantis I got some industrial potassium cyanide, and during the air raids I kept it with me next to my skin. I intended to do away with myself before I died in agony in billows of smoke. I didn't think I particularly wanted to die, but I harbored a vague fear of suffocating to death in the smoke.

The dull silver bombers usually flew over a sea of flames in some other neighborhood but that night, floating up in the arrowy shafts of light, they tilted overhead, swayed, and passed on by. It was gradually becoming a sea of fire all around us. By and by the sky was shrouded in red smoke. Noise, noise, noise, the screams of the falling bombs, the explosions, the anti-aircraft guns, and then the crackling sound of flames coming nearer. A roaring arose.

"Let's get out of here," Nomura said.

On the road a confused mass of people was fleeing for refuge. I kept feeling that those people were different from myself. I suddenly thought that just today, even if it meant dying, I would not join that chaotic, shameless, headlong stampede of strangers. I was alone. But I wanted just Nomura to be with me. The vague meaning of why I had the potassium cyanide next to my skin began to be clear. From a while before I had been listening for something. But I could not grasp what it was.

"Let's wait a little longer. Are you afraid of dying?"

"I don't want to die. Each time a bomb comes down, my heart seems to stop."

"Me too. It's worse for me. But I don't want to run for it with all those others."

Then an unexpected determination welled up in me. I felt a deep-rooted yearning. I felt sorry for myself. I was a child. I wanted to cry. Even if others died, even if the houses of others burned, I wanted just us to live. Our house mustn't burn either, I thought. I couldn't think about anything else except saving our house until the last moment of the last day.

"Please put out the flames!" I screamed at Nomura, as if throwing myself on him. "Please don't let your house burn. Your house, my house. I don't want this house to burn."

An incredulous look of surprise came over Nomura's face, full of real feeling and pity. I was willing to entrust myself to Nomura. It would be good to give my heart, my body, my everything joyfully to Nomura. I was stifled with sobs. Nomura, to find my lips, held my jaw in his big hand. The sky above us was as black as sin. I had never once wanted to go to heaven. But I had never even dreamed that in hell I could feel this kind of rapture. The sea of fire, which entirely surrounded us, seethed with more pain and violence than any other fire I had ever seen. My tears flowed endlessly. Losing my breath because of my tears, I felt suffocated. My broken cries were cries of happiness.

My body, in the hues of the fire, took on a faint, glimmering whiteness. Nomura, unable to let go of me, deluged me with caresses. But then decisively I pulled my clothes back on, as if putting a lid on a box. Nomura stood up and ran off with a bucket in his hand. I picked up a bucket too. After that, we fought the fire in a delirium. The house was enclosed by the trees and shrubs of the garden. We were lucky that there was a road upwind and that the house next door was a bungalow. Even though the sea of fire was all around us, the flames were burning toward us on one side only, and we were able to put them out one by one. And the height of the fire, the flames surging up madly in a blazing hurricane, lasted only about fifteen minutes.

During that time you could not even go near the flames, but afterward it was like an ordinary bonfire that had spread out in all directions. Before the house next door went up in a fury of flame, we threw buckets of water all over our house. When the fire next door died down, we ran to the back of the house where it had spread to the kitchen eaves and put it out with three or four buckets. With that, the danger passed. Until the fire moved on to another house had been our hour of crisis. Almost in a trance we fetched water and flung it over the house.

Flat on my back in the garden, I fought for breath. Even when Nomura said something, I didn't feel like answering. When he took me in his arms, I realized that my left hand was still unconsciously gripping the bucket. I was content. I felt as if I had never wept myself as satisfyingly empty as this. It was an emptiness that made me feel like a baby who has just been born. My heart was emptier and more desolate than the vast conflagration, but it was an emptiness that was full of my life. "Tighter, tighter, tighter, hold me tighter," I screamed. Nomura made love to my body—my nose, my mouth, my eyes, my ears, my cheeks, my throat. He made too much love. In strange ways he made me laugh, made me angry, he tormented me, but I was satisfied. Knowing that he was happy in his frenzy for my body, I was happy. I wasn't thinking about anything. There was nothing in particular to think about. I just thought about when I was a child. Scattered memories. I wasn't comparing them to now. I just remembered them. And in the pain of those memories I was even cruel to Nomura. While being made love to by

Nomura, I thought about the face of a man, the body of a man who was not Nomura. I even tried thinking about the Mantis. Anything, if I thought about it, was tiresome. Nevertheless, I was glad that Nomura was drunk, was drowning in love for my body.

I had always disliked holier-than-thou, fancy things like heaven and the Lord, but I'd never thought until now that I was a woman from hell. Except for our block, our neighborhood had become a burned-out plain for miles around. And yet I felt somehow discouraged when I realized that the neighborhood wasn't going to burn any more. I disliked the burned-out plain all around us. Because it was not going to burn again. So that even when the B-29s came back, I was unable to feel the same excitement as before.

But the time was coming when the enemy would invade, when all through Japan the arrows of bullets would crisscross in the wind, when bombs would be falling like crazy, the time of the end when people would keel over right and left like so many baby spiders. That day was what I was living for. The day after our neighborhood was bombed, I went around looking at the vast, burned-out area. "It's just not enough," I muttered to myself. Why does everything that human beings do and make have to end so unsatisfyingly? I saw only shadows, I held nothing in my arms. I yearned, the marrow in my bones was dried out like a drought-stricken field, cracks opened up in my back. Each time I heard the radio warn that a large formation of three hundred or five hundred B-29s was on the way, what, only five hundred, I would think. Why isn't it three thousand or five thousand yet? That's nothing, I would think, restless and unsatisfied. I took pleasure in imagining a raid by a formation so large that the whole sky would be overspread by a cloud of bombers.

The Mantis was burned out. Fatty was burned out.

The Mantis came to ask me to let him stay with us, but I cruelly refused. Before, around here, he had built an expensive air-raid shelter, almost one of a kind. He was able to store most of his household goods in it, and was safe as long as he didn't get a direct hit. Mocking us for our meager shelter, he'd say things like "Have you sent your possessions out to the country?" and "Do you have a lid for this shelter?" and "I envy you people who have nothing to worry about even if you're burned out." Actually he was jeering at our unpreparedness and looking forward to our stupid distress when we did get burned out. The Mantis was a devil praying for defeat. It irritated him that the numbers of the B-29 squadrons were not ten thousand or twenty thousand. He believed that all Tokyo would become a burned-out plain, and that even that burned-out plain would be thoroughly cratered by heavy artillery blasts. Even then, he believed his shelter would hold up as long as it didn't take a direct hit. With a complacent air, he told us how he would crawl out of it with his hands up, crying "I'm an old man. Don't shoot." He'd thought ahead that far. "People who hold on to their money and don't build shelters are fools," he'd say. "Money's going to become scraps of paper. Hanging on to scraps of paper, what fools you are."

That's why I said to the Mantis, "You built your shelter for a time like this, didn't you? Go live in your shelter you're so proud of."

"It's full up with my things," the Mantis replied.

"That's not my problem. If we'd been burned out, would you have let us stay with you?"

"Well, no, I wouldn't have." With a dour smile and this unpleasantry, the Mantis went away.

The Mantis was about as tactful as the real insect. Paying us a visit in the midst of the smoldering fires and ruins, "You weren't burned out," he would greet us, clearly unable to hide his disappointment, his face a mask of chagrin. "You weren't burned out," he'd say, but nothing else, not even "You were lucky" or "Congratulations." What soothed his feelings somewhat was the prospect that in the end every house was sure to burn down, collapse, be blown away, that any house left standing would be a target and be riddled with machine-gun fire, that a single burst from a small fighter-plane might blow away life and all. "My shelter is very small," the Mantis would say with undisguised lewdness. "When the time comes, I can take only one person. That's so. At the very most I can put you up, but only you."

To be truthful, if the bombs came calling and blew up Nomura and the house, leaving only me alive, I didn't think I would mind that much. Then I would go to the Mantis's shelter. I would wreck his family, make his old wife die in convulsions. Then I would give the Mantis a fit and finish him off the same way, I thought. Even in regard to my road in life afterward, I felt no unease about living. But I thought about the pleasure of fleeing the battleground with Nomura, making our way here and there, crawling into barley fields, swimming across rivers in Nomura's arms, taking refuge in the farthest interior of the mountains, putting up a shack unbeknown to anyone, and for the next several years living in secret away from the enemy's searching eyes.

Now that the war is over, it seems natural that the old life has resumed, but during the war it never even occurred to me that life would go on as in the past. I thought that most Japanese would be killed, that those in hiding would be dragged out and shot. I imagined the pleasures of playing around with Nomura and fleeing and hiding from the eyes of the enemy troops. How many years would that continue? Even if it went on many years, in the end we would come down from the mountains to my hometown, the day of peace would arrive, and the boring days of peacetime, as in the past, would open out before us also. Then, I thought, we would probably separate. Ultimately my fantasy came to an end with me losing Nomura. I didn't even try to think of such things as the two of us growing old together. I was able to think of anything else. Even if I went to work in a whorehouse, deceiving old men and having young lovers, that was fine.

I liked Nomura. I loved him. But to ask what I loved about him, why I loved him, I think, is stupid for a woman like me. I had no larger reason for love than that I could live together with him without displeasure. I never forgot that there were lots of other men, lots of men more handsome than Nomura. While being held and caressed by Nomura, I often thought about those men. But it's stupid to have qualms about such things. Even then, I had my sweet fantasies.

It's said that people can think of all sorts of things, but I think they can only have very limited thoughts. That's because during the war I never even dreamed that this kind of life of the past could come back so quickly. I felt a yearning, a turbulence, a pathos, as if Nomura and I, one flesh as we faced this fate called the war, were desperately standing up against our death. Impatient with the sterility of sex, disliking the tiresome things around me, hating Nomura and the Mantis, everybody, cursing them, not letting Nomura touch me, not wanting to answer when I was spoken to, at such times I would get on my bike and ride out through the fire ruins. When young factory workers or air-defense guards teased or reproved me for my bare legs, I would get angry with myself and think maybe I should wear a pair of *monpe*.

But in my heart I felt sorry for Nomura. He was sure to be killed in the war. I believed that eighty, ninety, even a hundred percent. Because I was a woman I would survive, and afterward I could do anything, I thought.

I wanted to keep as one scrap of my memories the fact that I had been the loving wife of one man. I thought of that man, tenderly loving me, being killed in the war, and me living on into postwar Japan, an interesting world of craters, rubble, and chunks of concrete, and when I'd done whatever I pleased, murmuring, "My dear husband died in the war." It gave me such a quiet pleasure.

But I thought it was very sad about Nomura. I really felt sorry for him. The foremost reason for that, the matchless, absolute reason, was that Nomura himself, squarely contemplating the day of the end, the most miserable day of the end of the war, had no illusions whatsoever. Nomura believed that all Japanese men, even if they didn't die in the war, would survive only as slaves. He believed there would no longer be a Japan.

Only the women would survive, and give birth to mixed-race children. Another country would be born, he thought. Nomura's beliefs were not idle ones, and there was no way to console him. Nomura would caress me. He believed that there was only a short time left for caresses. As he caressed me, Nomura would grow enraged with hate. There is the fate of Japan, I thought. This was how Japan was dying, the Japan that had given birth to me. I didn't hate Japan. But seeing the last gasps of the old Japan in Nomura's enraged caresses, I hated women who, with Japan coming to this, made love, their foreheads streaming with sweat, in an ecstasy. That is how I felt. I gave my body to Nomura to do with as he pleased.

"You women will survive. You'll make out all right."

Sometimes with a giggle Nomura would tease me. I didn't give in to him.

"I'm sick of people who slobber and paw me like a puppy dog. I want an honest love."

"'Honest'? What's that mean?"

"It means decent."

"'Decent'? You mean a spiritual love?"

Blinking at me, Nomura made a face as if he'd been tickled.

"I'll be sent somewhere to the South Pacific for slave labor. Even if I've done nothing but seduce one of the native women, I'll have the breath flogged out of me."

"That's why even you will have to make spiritual love to the native girls."

"That's right. I sure can't fuck any mermaids."

Our conversations were always about this kind of dirty, foolish thing.

One night our bedroom was flooded with moonlight. Nomura carried me over to the window where the moon was shining full in. Throwing me down, he tussled with me. We could see each other's face clearly, and even the blue veins under our skin stood out distinctly.

Nomura told me a story of the olden times, from the Heian period . . .

> A man hears the sound of koto music deep in a forest. Approaching it through the wind in the pines, he comes to a towered gate where a lady is playing the koto. Overcome by her glamour, the man exchanges pledges of love with the lady. But she is wearing a veil, and even in the moonlight he cannot see her face clearly. Afterward the man yearns for this woman of a single night, but with the koto playing as a clue, he learns that the lady is the empress of that time . . .

It was that kind of story.

"When we've lost the war, perhaps we'll become that kind of elegant country. The country perishes, the mountains and rivers remain, they say. And the women. The wind in the pines, the moonlight, and women. The women of Japan will have nothing to wear but housedresses, but the love stories of dreams will begin."

Looking pityingly at my face in the moonlight, Nomura would not let me go. I could see his deep unwillingness to give me up. Thanks to this duration of the war that was completely beyond our control, we could make love and cherish each other in this simple, innocent, nostalgic way. It came home to me very deeply.

"I'll be the kind of loving wife you want. In whatever way you want, I'll be more loving."

"Is that so? But it's fine as it's been up to now."

"But tell me. What is your ideal woman?"

"It's you," Nomura said after a while, with a smile. "You are my last woman. That's a fact. That much at least, ideal or not, is right in front of me."

I couldn't keep myself from biting Nomura on the neck. He had truly accepted his fate. That a man's acceptance of his fate could be so childish and lovable! If he could always accept things this way, I wanted always to be his loving wife. I closed my eyes, and thought the young kamikaze pilots must be this childish and lovable. They must be even more so. Any woman, in any way, would love them and be loved by them, I thought.

When the war ended, I hadn't thought of that kind of ending, and so I felt bewildered, as if a promise had been broken. Things were out of kilter, and I didn't know what to do. Of course, everything was out of kilter—the Japanese government, the military men, the priests, the scholars, the spies, the barbers, the black marketeers, the geishas. The Mantis was furious. He was boiling with anger. "What is this? Why stop now?" he sputtered. "Why do they stop before Tokyo is burned out? Why stop before all of Japan is destroyed?" The Mantis wanted all Japanese to have a worse time of it than he had had. Although I despised the Mantis for his obscene, sordid, misanthropic prayer, when I thought about it, I realized that I had secretly had the same wish, and loathed myself. I tried to think I'd been a little different, but it wasn't so. I despised the Mantis even more.

The American planes began flying through the skies of Japan at low altitudes. Squadrons of B-29s would pass back and forth right overhead. I quickly got tired of seeing them. They were merely unfamiliar, four-engined, beautiful, streamlined airplanes. They were not the dull silver bombers that, scissored by arrowy shafts of light, had burst into view in the dark skies of wartime. On the fuselages of those silver bombers the fiery colors of hell had been reflected. I had loved those bombers, and it was bitter to have to realize that those lovers of mine had already been lost. The war was over! Already it had been pushed back into the distant, irrecoverable past. No matter how I tried, I could not bring it back.

"Even the war was like a dream," I could not help muttering. Perhaps everything was a dream, but the war was an especially unsatisfying, irretrievable dream that I had not seen enough of.

"Your lover boys are gone." Nomura saw into my heart.

When I thought that from now on the mediocre, tedious days of peacetime would come, each one inevitably divided up into night and day, sleeping time and eating time, I could not but curse my lot. Why hadn't I died in the war?

I was a woman who could not endure boredom. I gambled, I danced, I slept around, but I was always bored. I made a plaything of my body and by doing so had both the self-confidence and the means to live my life without worrying about money. I knew nothing of ordinary remorse and sentimentality. I had no desire for the good opinion of others. Nor did I want to be loved by a man. Or I wanted to be loved by a man so I could deceive him. But I didn't want to be loved by him so I could love him. I absolutely disbelieved in things like eternal love. Why were people supposed to hate war and love peace, I wondered.

I wanted to live like a tiger, a bear, a fox, a badger in the deep forest, I thought, to love, to play, to fear, to flee, to hide, to hold my breath, to kill my breath, to risk my life.

Inviting Nomura, I went out for a walk. Nomura had been injured in the leg and was only just now able to walk again, but not for long distances. To rest his injured leg, he had to clutch my shoulder now and then, dangling the leg in the air. He was heavy, and it hurt me, but it was a thrill to feel him leaning on me. All over the burned-out ruins, wild grasses had sprung up.

"During the war I was very good to you. Now I'm going to give you a hard time."

"You mean you'll start sleeping around again?"

"Now that the war's over, I have to turn myself into a bombshell."

"An atom bomb?"

"No, a small one. A five-hundred pounder."

"You know who you are, don't you?"

Nomura smiled ruefully. As we stood there, glued together in the hot, grassy air of the burned-over plain, I felt as if it was an event in history. This too will become a memory. Everything passes. Like a dream. We are able to grasp nothing. And I too, I thought, was only the shadow of myself. Sooner or later Nomura and I would part company. I didn't even think it was sad. When we moved, our shadows moved. Why was everything so banal, like this shadow! I felt a strange, awful hatred for my shadow. My brain nearly exploded with it.

Borneo Diamond

ボルネオ・ダイヤ

林　芙美子

HAYASHI FUMIKO

Along the dark banks the lights of candles glimmered. Just a short while before, the last gleams of sunset had been effaced in the distant sky. The *iron-iron* weeds, which all day long had been drifting on the waters, no doubt had quietly moored themselves ashore somewhere for the night . . . The quiet was so intense that the sound of the sculling oars of the *tanbagans,* the native boats, as they came out from the shore, was unpleasantly clear. The sounds of the water, swirling around and dripping from the oars—*picha, picha*—were drunken in by the very heart of the listener, inviting an unbearable loneliness, a yearning for others. From time to time the "moaning trees" that surrounded the house swayed and soughed in the evening breeze.

Tamae, stark-naked, lay sprawled on her stomach inside the white mosquito netting. Her legs up on one of the long, bolster-like pillows called a "Dutch wife," exactly like a spread-eagled frog, Tamae was having herself massaged by a Javan masseuse. The masseuse, rubbing in coconut oil all over Tamae's body, with her hard palms was slowly kneading her back, slippery with oil, in circular motions that resembled one of the Japanese syllables. Pressing her face into a big towel, Tamae thought about the child she had left behind in Japan. I've come to a terribly faraway place, she thought to herself. A feeling even came over her that she would never be able to get back to Japan.

Perhaps because of the sullen, oppressive heat and the clamorous croaking of the frogs outside, she could not put her thoughts in order. No clear images rose up behind her eyes. When they had left Hiroshima, had it been raining . . . ? Her gallant traveler's figure of four months before now seemed merely that of a stranger. Was it evening when the boat had entered the wide mouth of the Barito River . . . ? Along embankments where mangroves flourished, the boat had slowly glided over the reddish, muddy water.

As if from dream to dream, one strange, unchanging season flowed into the next in Tamae's memory, spinning in place day after day like a top. A full four months had passed since her departure from the homeland. Since she had come to this place called Banjarmasin in South Borneo, every evening, without letup, it had rained. It was a heavy downpour, like cord ropes being let down. This being the tropics, the rain in its torrential violence raised a steamy mist that imbued the scenery with a milky-white color.

Among the women who had come to work in this kind of place were many who seemed to have reached the end of a long trail of hardship in Japan. But Tamae had come here on the spur of the moment, at someone's suggestion. That was the sort of young woman she was. Tamae was the daughter of a hairdresser. Her older brother, drafted into the army when the war with China had started up, had been killed in the landing at Woosung. Her next oldest brother, terrified of battle, had voluntarily taken a job with a munitions firm and gone to work at a plant in Mito. At the time Tamae had been a student in a girls' school. But when classes were canceled and the whole student body was marched every day from the school to the factory, Tamae grew sick and tired of it. A year before graduation, without telling her mother, she had left school and gotten a job as a waitress at a restaurant in Ueno Station. There she took up with the cook, a man named Matsuya. During the course of occasional rendezvous at an inn near the station, Tamae finally ended up pregnant. Tamae herself didn't know she was pregnant until almost the sixth month. Told by Matsuya that she looked funny, Tamae had only then thought that her physical condition was odd. Still only seventeen, Tamae didn't worry too much about her body's irregularities. Leaving home, she'd gone to live with Matsuya in his boardinghouse. Realizing for the first time and by slow degrees that the lot dealt to her by life was not a normal one, Tamae had grown somehow melancholy. In the spring of her eighteenth year, in a small clinic in Matsubacho, Tamae gave birth to a baby girl. When the child was born, Matsuya, without talking it over with Tamae, who was still in the hospital, had given the child to people in the Oji district of Tokyo. Still almost a child herself, Tamae hadn't felt too much regret for the child, but somehow it seemed unbearably sad to hand it over to strangers.

Since she had run away from home, Tamae could receive no rations. She lived on food that Matsuya contrived to get for her. It was boring to sit around cooped up in the room all day while Matsuya was at work. One day, going to an employment agency in the neighborhood, Tamae met the proprietress of an inn in Atami. Skillfully persuaded by the woman that instead of fussing around in a tedious life in Japan, how would it be if she tried going to the South Pacific to work, Tamae suddenly became of a mind to do so. She was given twenty-five hundred yen for departure expenses. Sending a thousand yen to her mother and leaving another thousand at Matsuya's boardinghouse, without telling anyone, Tamae had left for Hiroshima with five other women who had signed on with her.

Each of the five women had a different life story to tell. During the nearly three weeks' voyage from Hiroshima Tamae had had to listen to the same stories told over and over, day after day. Tamae was the youngest among the women. There was even a woman who was slightly over thirty. The party of eight consisted of the inn proprietress, a woman named Fukui, the five women along with Tamae, and a man in black sunglasses by the name of Sakata, who had come up from Borneo to escort them.

Day by day it grew warmer at sea. The women were bored beyond endurance by their monotonous existence in the hold of the ship. By degrees they were lured into something like a feeling of homesickness. The ship ostensibly being a hospital ship, not only the many soldiers who were aboard but even Tamae and her companions had to stay under hatches during the day. When they had to go to the bathroom up on the deck, they would throw a dirty old nurse's smock over their shoulders. At night the red cross painted on the sides of the ship was illuminated. Women and soldiers alike lolled about in the hold all day. Sprawled out on a dirty blanket, Tamae read old magazines she had borrowed from the soldiers. When she'd grown tired of that also, she would take something out of her rucksack and gobble it down. When she'd gotten tired even of doing that, Tamae would close her eyes and think about such things as the child who'd been given away for adoption and about Matsuya. When the image of Matsuya, searching for her, floated into Tamae's mind, the tears suddenly rose to her eyes. She even thought she would like to go back to Tokyo again. Her contract called for two years in Borneo. But if she went back after two years and sought out Matsuya, what sort of welcome would he give her . . . ? Always afraid that he would be drafted soon, Matsuya had sworn that if he were he would desert. But when it came to the matter of rations, Matsuya had grinned ruefully and said that for people like them there was after all no place to go.

The events of the past four months seemed vague and hazy. Tamae could think of Japan only as a dream of the distant past. Arriving in Borneo, for the first two or three days Tamae had felt an unbearable self-reproach. Everything was different from what had been promised in Tokyo. What she had been brought here for was her body.

In every room there were primitive tatami mats and a crudely lacquered table. For senior officials from Tokyo there was a room with an ornamental alcove. In the alcove hung a scroll picture of Mount Fuji, with a strange objet d'art that resembled a Korean lion shrine guardian. Out of place in this lush tropical clime the anomalous Japanese-style room seemed bare and poverty-stricken.

When the Javan masseuse had gone, Tamae got up and went to the bathing room. There she sluiced several cups of water over herself. In this house where there seemed to be neither morning nor night, a stream of officers, soldiers, and civilians in military employ was constantly passing through. A servant came to call Tamae any number of times. Even while feeling a hot indignation in her stomach—how was she going to stick to this kind of job for two years?—Tamae sat down at the mirror and began her makeup.

Sumiko, the woman who shared the room with her, was taking a week off from work. Saying she didn't feel well, she lay in bed all day and never helped entertain any of the guests. Languidly driving away the mosquitoes with a native fan made out of coconut fronds, sitting out on the shady veranda, Sumiko seemed to be thinking about something. But when Tamae sat down at her dressing stand, she at last came back into the room. "Tamae, won't you come for a boat ride with me, to cool off?" she invited. The tributaries at the mouth of the Barito River made a delta of the town Banjarmasin. The Martapura flowed right through the heart of the town. If one went out to the embankment, there were always some native boats moored alongside, for all the world like the One Yen taxis of faraway Tokyo. At any hour of the day or night they would gladly cruise the waters for you. "It might be refreshing out in the river breeze."

"But we'll be scolded again. Since we've come to a war area, we're not supposed to do selfish things."

"I don't care. Aren't the people who tell us that sort of thing all doing exactly as they please . . . ?"

Sumiko wound her sarong around her and put on a white voile blouse. Her lips were unpleasantly tumid, her color was bad, and—perhaps because of the dim lantern—her face seemed dark and gloomy. Her eyebrows and eyes, as if wet, stood out distinctly.

Tamae, sitting down hard on the rush mat in nothing but a chemise, lit up a cigarette. Her made-up face revealed the lively resilience of her feelings. It was also because Tamae had recently found a man whom she liked, but both her way of making up and her general demeanor were fully adult. Perhaps too she had accumulated the experience that such women do and the ability to discriminate exactly among men, but she looked a year or two older than her age. Decorating her hair with the fragrant white flower called *bunga sunpin*, which she had had the native maid buy for her in the market, Tamae put on a black voile garment. Feeling pretentious, as if she'd become a respectable woman, she peered into the mirror.

"Won't you come out on the river with me a little while? There's time. It's dark. They won't know."

"Well, I wonder now. Ma-chan is coming, but . . ."

"He'll wait for you. It's lonely by myself. Just keep me company. Aren't we all in the same boat, by coming out here . . . ?

"All right, all right, I'll come out with you."

Shoving on their leather sandals, the pair stepped down from the veranda onto the lawn. Fan-shaped "traveler's palms" towered up blackly against the dark sky, giving one the feeling of having come to a faraway place. When they came to the riverbank, the tide was already in. Muddy water had overflowed onto the road. The two walked along between the shoulder-high bushes and grasses.

"Tanbagan . . ." Sumiko called out to a boat.

From the black shadows of a tree that grew out over the water a boatman replied in a muffled voice, "Ya-a." There was the sound of an oar working, as the boat glided near to where they were standing. When they'd jumped down into the long, narrow, roofed boat, for a while it rocked right and left like a hammock.

Out on the water the intensely quiet night air pressed in around them. The dark shores of the river kept getting farther and farther away, vague in the evening mists. Abruptly Sumiko said, "Aaah, I want to go back to Japan. I've gotten homesick." Since it was so sudden, Tamae was unable to answer. But somehow that feeling of Sumiko's came pressing in on her.

When the boat reached the middle of the river, the boatman, alert to their wishes, left off working the oar and let the boat drift with the current. In the houses on the water along both banks, the lights of coconut-oil lamps flickered among the fireflies. Tamae sprawled out on the straw mats of the boat. The fragrance of her white *sunpin* flower, floating on the gentle breeze, diffused its sweet perfume over the surface of the river. "Sing us a song," Tamae called out banteringly in Indonesian to the boatman. The boatman gave a bashful-sounding laugh. But then in an unexpectedly youthful voice he began to sing one of the native four-line ditties. It was a beautifully mellow voice that echoed out over the water.

"Even if I didn't have anything, I'd like to be back in Japan. I know that once we were back, we'd probably want to be in Borneo again, but I'd like to go back to Tokyo just once." Even as she said this, Tamae did not really want all that much to go back.

"I'm different from you. I want to go back so bad I'd swim there if I could. I'm sorry I ever came to this kind of place. The madam says it's just nerves, but that's not so. Even when I was in bed with dengue fever, I was thinking I didn't want to die in this kind of place. If only it weren't for the war, I could go back right away, most likely."

"It's because that person died, isn't it? That's when you got discouraged all of a sudden."

Among their customers there had been a soldier whom Sumiko had been fond of. But about a month before, news had come of his death at an oil field in Moronpudakku, deep in the interior.

At some time or other the singing voice of the boatman had faded away. There was the sound of his oar again. Tamae thought she would like to spend the night in the cool boat. She wanted to stretch out at ease and sleep undisturbed by anyone.

It might have been around nine o'clock when Tamae and Sumiko got back to their room. When Tamae went to the front of the house, as usual several groups of drink-deranged guests were singing military songs and having arguments. Sumiko did not show herself out there.

When she'd had two or three powerful brandies forced on her, Tamae recovered her usual good spirits. She wasn't thinking about anything. Something like a brilliant, golden radiance, like ether, seemed to transpire from the pores of her body. Whatever the place, Tamae was not afraid. With a passion that was full of strength, she settled herself in. The history of her four months in Borneo faded away like a passing moment. When she felt the ease of knowing that the person called herself had been naturally and totally destroyed, she could settle down calmly wherever she was. The feeling called shame also vanished. She felt a confidence in herself that any man who came before her would go down on his knees. It was not the case that her present life was of no interest to Tamae.

Late that night Manabe came in an automobile from the diamond-mining district of Martapura to see her. When the two of them were alone in the small room, Tamae, in nothing but her chemise, stood in front of the electric fan. Spreading out her arms like a child, she drunkenly prattled away. Manabe, taking off his tropical suit and leaving it on the table, crawled inside the mosquito netting. In the corridor, as usual, the voices of foul-mouthed customers scrambling for a woman for the night flew back and forth. Tamae went on standing in front of the weakly functioning electric fan. With childish gestures, as if to deliberately show off her plump, white body, Tamae crooned in a low voice a song of which the words were unintelligible.

"Why don't you come over here?"

"Because I'm hot."

"You'll feel even hotter after you've been in front of the fan. Come over here . . ."

Docilely turning the fan toward the mosquito netting, Tamae went to Manabe. And then as she always did, she laid her head on Manabe's chest and began to nibble at the fingers of his right hand. Any number of times the two had lain together in bed like this, but not once had they had sex. Although engaged in a fierce war, Manabe simply held Tamae in his arms. In the morning they were able to look at each other with an indescribably refreshed feeling.

"You don't love me. That's what I think. You don't have the heart of a human being."

"It's not that kind of thing. I come here because I like you. You probably think it's unnatural, but I think my being able to meet you in this kind of place was fate. If the eyes of a hundred million Japanese weren't fastened on us, if it weren't for the war, I'm thinking I'd like to marry you. But it just wouldn't work out, would it? If something should happen, we'd be separated far and wide from this place."

"Wouldn't it be all right if we got married, fair and square?"

"Yes, but this is a war zone. The army's here. It would be simple if only I weren't working for them, but as it is, there's nothing we can do . . ."

"Yes, yes, that's how it is. And you have a wife and children, Ma-chan . . . you mustn't be unfaithful to them."

Manabe was silent. After a while, taking from his pocket what looked like a wrapped dose of medicine, he placed a raw diamond gleaming yellowly on Tamae's sweaty palm. "It's a diamond I dug up myself. If you ever get back to Japan, you can have a ring made for it."

The diamond gleamed as if it were wet. Perhaps because they were in bed, from the brightening window the traveler's palms on the lawn seemed to Manabe to fan out like a bright fresco. In the morning atmosphere of this swampy region, everything seemed drenched with the dews of night. Holding the diamond in her fingers, for a while Tamae gazed entranced at its liquid light. The diamond itself seemed a surprisingly trivial object.

"Borneo diamonds aren't of good quality, but this one would be just right for a ring for you."

"How much could I sell this for?"

If you stood at the entrance of a factory in your neighborhood back in Japan, you would see many girls with ordinary faces like Tamae's. It was a dull-looking, flat-planed face with nothing particular about it, unless it were the delicate flower bud of the lips and the gentle eyes under the single-fold eyelids. It was a familiar-looking face, such that most people would have said to themselves, "I've seen that face before." When Tamae, practical as always, asked how much the diamond could be sold for, Manabe, feeling a slight letdown, replied, "Well now, I guess you could get five or six thousand yen for it." He meant to startle her.

"Oh, really? Is this kind of stone worth that much? I'm astonished. That's a fortune for me. I really could sell it for that much?" Tamae stared at the diamond with even more avidity. Manabe gazed absent-mindedly out the window. Putting her arm around his neck, Tamae planted several kisses on his sweaty cheek.

A graduate of the Department of Mining Metallurgy at Tokyo Imperial University, Manabe, at the time of the seizure of South Borneo, had been sent here by an industrial mining company as a civilian employee of the military. For the last two years or so he'd been living at the small official residence at the mine in Martapura. He had first met Tamae at a banquet given by the Japanese civil administrator. Tamae had immediately liked Manabe. One day, disguising herself as an Indonesian woman, she had walked the two and a half miles to Martapura to visit him. Manabe, for his part, although thinking at first that Tamae was a whimsical person, gradually got drawn in by her passion for him. He found it a nuisance that his fastidiousness would not let him descend to the final stage of their relationship. To use Tamae's body as a night's consolation was, in Zen terms, to experience the ultimate chagrin of sensual desire. Once the momentary flame of lust had passed, the peaceful world of the morning after brought a leisurely calm to Manabe. If his determination should start to waver, he would of his own accord become an ordinary man. The three poisons and five lusts would arise in him. Thoughts of murder, of felony, of fornication, of avarice, slander, prevarication, fine-sounding lies, falsehood, wrath, complaining, pride, covetous longing, envy . . . Engraved on Manabe's heart were the dying injunctions of a third-class disciple of the great Zen priest Muso, which he'd read as a student. To violently break off all connections with the world and single-heartedly seek out the secrets of one's soul, that was the highest stage of spiritual endeavor. To mingle in all knowledge confusedly, with an impure love of wisdom, that was the middle stage. To willfully darken the light of the soul in oneself, to ignorantly worship the spittle of the Buddha, that was the lowest stage. If, with the excuse that this was a war zone where life was uncertain, he were to buy Tamae's body for a night . . . but Manabe's scruples would not let him think that far. And yet when he thought about it carefully, this present dalliance with Tamae was after all not upright behavior. It was none other than darkening the light of the soul in himself. Somehow, precisely because this was a war zone, one had inhibitions. The idea of the eyes of numberless Japanese fastened on him also was frightening. And for the government student Manabe there dangled before his eyes the "honor" of the future. And yet how pleasing to his heart, in the lonely night of a foreign land, were these sweet, gentle words of the opposite sex, murmured for him alone. At the same official residence where Manabe lived was a man who instead of keeping a diary wrote to his wife every day. Manabe thought the pure feeling for home of that kind of young man was enviable.

While the army had been gallantly advancing to seize territory, there had been no time to think of anything else. But once the territory was occupied and things had settled down, the honorable regulations of the military grew timid and fearful in peaceful conditions. The change undermined stability. The more peaceful and placid things became, the more did military discipline slacken. That had been so in Manabe's case. When he'd been rushing around setting up mining operations in the occupied territory, he had felt that he was risking his life for Japan. But as little by little the results of his efforts began to appear, Manabe was tormented by thoughts of unendurable boredom. Vaguely infatuated by the sinuous walking figure of the maidservant of the Daya tribe that bore a close physical resemblance to the Japanese, half unconsciously seeking out those with beautiful bodies among the Malay and Javan women who sifted the diamond-bearing sands, he had blushed at his base desires.

The mining operations, under orders from the military, were desperately busy. But the liquid luster of the diamonds themselves always reminded Manabe of a woman's smooth and supple skin. Rather than the utilitarian aspects of the diamonds, which were used in various machines, Manabe took much more pleasure in imagining them as the adornments of beautiful women. Yellow, violet, purple, cobalt, pink, the many different diamonds, by the labor of how many tens of thousands of native coolies, emerged one by one from the sands like the stars of heaven. Those diamonds, which appeared so gradually and in such small numbers, were sadly enough ground into dust by the war plants of the homeland. Their romantic, lustrous beauty, when they left the mining district, like shooting stars turned to stone, dispersed like fleeting vapors, was like the ephemeral dew of the battlefield.

Manabe had sent a large, resplendent cobalt diamond to his wife. His wife had donated it a few days afterward to the government for the war effort. A letter arrived from her, completely missing the point, asking him to praise her for her patriotic sentiments and for having guessed his inmost wishes. It was a superb stone, such that he'd thought it unlikely that a diamond as beautiful as this would be found again in his mining district. Manabe was chagrined and angry at his wife's obtuseness. Her lack of feeling for jewels, her thinking of the diamonds as so many little letters to be typeset in a printing machine even seemed pathetic. Japanese women did not understand the true beauty of jewels, nor their worldly value. On the work-roughened finger of a Japanese woman, driven in a daily treadmill of toil, the excessively beautiful brilliance of a diamond might seem frightening. In these days of stagnant military rule Manabe felt something in common between the stupidity that oppressed a territory won at the cost of bloodshed for the benefit of the ignorant conquerors, who despised the native population as an inferior race but failed to notice their own gross misgovernment, and the heart of a Japanese woman that did not know the worth of a diamond. To be asked frankly by Tamae how much she could get for the diamond was, on the contrary, now a good feeling for Manabe.

Tamae sent the maidservant to the market for about twenty pieces of saté, chicken broiled with spicy sauce, and ate it with Manabe inside the mosquito netting. That day also would be hot. The vast, empty, cobalt-colored sky, peculiar to these southern regions, was as dazzling as if a myriad of tiny needles of light were being jabbed in one's eyes. The dusty streets of Banjarmasin, devoid of transportation facilities for the people aside from infrequent automobiles and bicycles, were hushed and deserted from morning to night. But the surface of the muddy river from bank to bank was crowded with a lively confusion of little boats, as if the contents of a toy box had been emptied out. Their bowl-shaped sunshades, so large that one could barely glimpse the hands working the oars beneath them, glided along like so many flowers adrift on the stream. Among the bustle of boats prodigious masses of the water weeds called *iron-iron*, jostling against each other, were pushed upstream by the tide. The flow of the water plants, so dense that one could not even see the water, if one watched it for a while, induced the illusion that the boat was sliding along on rails. One had the sensation of the earth itself turning. The houses on both sides of the river had their fronts open as shops. One could even stop the boat in front of a dry-goods store and make one's purchases. One could bargain at the water's edge for rice and sundries at their respective shops. The boats themselves sold articles like coffee and neatly ranged packs of cigarettes as they slowly circulated amongst the river traffic. Naked children, dividing the masses of weed at their roots, swam about. On this river, at least, man and nature, heedless of the war, disported themselves with each other as frolicsome as puppies, creating together a lovable world.

For the people of Borneo nothing must be as troublesome as this war. The only notable water hereabouts was rainwater, which made people lazy about brushing their teeth. Manabe himself had teeth stained brownish-yellow by nicotine. "You know what? Sumiko-san said she would be willing to swim all the way back to Tokyo . . . How about you?"

"How about you? You must want to see your mother . . . ?"

"Well, yes, I sometimes dream about her. But I've come all this way. There's nothing I can do about it . . . I think Sumiko's gotten slightly crazy. It's strange somehow. Since that soldier friend of hers was killed, she's been good for nothing. Maybe she's been brooding over him so much that . . . I think it's the weather myself. It's so hot here in Banjaru that you can't keep a cool head . . ." Tamae, very rudely, had both her legs up on Manabe's torso, and like an acrobat with her head half out of the bed was smoking a cigarette. The electric fan, left on all night, perhaps because its current was low, revolved its blades sluggishly, with a sound as if it were dragging a tin can.

"Your friend has lost a little weight. Somehow she seems lonely."

"You're right. Yet somehow she's gotten shrewd, and more beautiful lately. She says she's twenty-seven . . ."

"Oh, is she already that old?"

"Yes. She was born in Kobe. She tried being a waitress, a geisha, and things like that before coming out here."

"Oh? She doesn't seem the type."

"Last night the two of us went out together in a *tanbagan*. Sumiko-san was crying. She said she wanted to go back to Japan . . ."

When he heard that Sumiko had wept, Manabe felt sorry for her. This kind of insanely hot place was too much for anyone to cope with. Whatever else one said about it, it was hot. Abruptly pushing Tamae's body aside, Manabe got up and stepped outside the mosquito netting. When he looked into the mirror, his beard had sprouted anew in a single evening. His oily face was a muddy, impure, tea-brown color. Putting on his sweat-sticky tropical suit, he said, "I'll come see you again, then. Take care." He kissed Tamae's forehead through the white gauze of the mosquito netting. There was a sour odor of perfume. From where she lay in bed Tamae followed Manabe with her eyes. After a while, in the distance, there was the sound of an ancient engine starting up, then of Manabe's car blowing its horn as he drove away. Taking out from under her pillow the little packet, Tamae gazed intently at the diamond once more in the light. Suddenly, for no reason, the face of the child she had been separated from floated up behind her eyes. The yellow-tinged color of the diamond shone coldly. This was the first time in her life that Tamae had held a diamond in her hand. It was a delicate, subtle feeling. When she tried placing it on her ring finger, the diamond looked just a little lonely on the stubby, dimpled finger. In her heart Tamae thought that the red of a ruby would have become her better. Was this kind of stone really worth that much? Despite its high monetary value it had little glamour. The madam was always calling in a jeweler and having diamonds appraised. Should she perhaps palm off this diamond on the madam?

"Tamae-san. Something terrible has happened." Masaki had excitedly stuck her face in at the window. "Sumiko-san finally did it."

"Oh? What did she do?" Clutching the diamond packet, Tamae quickly slipped out of the bed.

"This." Sticking her tongue out, Masaki let her hands dangle.

"Oh, no! When? When did she do it?" Just as she was, in her underwear, Tamae shoved on her sandals and ran with Masaki to her and Sumiko's room. An army doctor and two or three soldiers from the landing forces had come. Entering the room, Tamae gazed for a while at the miserable sight. Looking at the dead person, she felt the desire to live boil up within her. Like an electric current, it flowed into her naked shoulders, her arms, and her calves, hotly numbing her.

"She must have done it this morning."

"She did it in the bathing room." The other women, gathered around the madam, were chattering away hysterically. When the army doctor and the soldiers had gone away, Sakata, giving instructions to a native servant, had Sumiko's body, which sadly brought to mind a shriveled flower, wrapped in a sheet and placed in a corner of the room. The bare feet of the corpse looked terribly flat and big. Sakata tried to clasp the hands together on the chest, but rigor mortis had already set in. Sumiko's summer kimono hung by her pillow. "She's just as she was yesterday evening." Tamae could not bear to squarely contemplate Sumiko as she lay there, her eyes slightly open, her tongue protruding, in her white voile blouse and calico sarong.

Suddenly Tamae and her co-workers had the day off. Having a lunch packed for them, they went for a drive out to the beach at Takison. The car, on loan from the civil administration, came complete with a Malay driver. If only he hadn't been smoking coconut-fiber cigarettes that gave off smelly clouds of smoke, it would have been a truly enjoyable drive. But Tamae had a heavy feeling. Her shallowness of heart, which right up until what proved to be their final parting last night had failed to perceive Sumiko's distress, how close she was to killing herself, tormented Tamae. Even though Sumiko was dead, nobody was particularly upset or cried for her. Strangely enough, only the madam, saying "She's better off now," had dabbed a handkerchief to her eyes and wept a little.

"The madam cried for her . . ." Masaki, in the car, said this as if she only now remembered it.

"It was just to distract herself . . ." This heartless comment came from the big, dark-complected Shizuko, whom they'd nicknamed Blackie.

When they arrived at the government-operated inn on a slight eminence above the beach, it was about midday. Even though it was muddy and tea-colored, when they had the limitless expanse of the sea before them, the women were already in great good spirits. Everyone started chattering away. But the reddish-brown color of this sea at Takison, in the eyes of these women who had thought the ocean was always blue, came to deepen their feelings of hardship. Peeling a hard-boiled egg, Tamae ate it. Sumiko's tragic countenance in death rose up behind her eyes. Perhaps I'm a bad woman . . . Dismayed, Tamae gazed at her recent, half-forgotten feelings in the distance of the empty sky. In the wooden-floored main room of the inn, a dilapidated, bungalow-type structure that seemed about to fall apart any minute, the women opened their lunches. The caretaker, a man of the Zuson tribe, brought them some lukewarm coffee. "It's so peaceful. It makes you wonder where the war is." Masaki, a woman of mature years whose kimono-clad figure brought to mind the "older sister" type of waitress you might see in a small restaurant in Asakusa or thereabouts, between drags on her cigarette, was gazing out to sea.

"Sumiko-san wanted so much to go back to Japan. Last night we went out together in a *tanbagan*. That was the last time . . . oh, how I wish she hadn't died. She didn't have to die."

"H'm. You're still a child, Tamae-san. Don't you know why her soldier friend was done in at Moronpudakku? He got something called solitary detention all because of Sumi-san. They were so in love that they were thinking of making a getaway and going native. When they bungled it, her friend got the death penalty. And when the man she loved died, Sumi-san herself didn't want to go on living under these faraway skies. She said she had felt more at peace when she could still walk out to where he was and see him . . . besides, she had very bad lungs. That was the kind of fate Sumi-san was up against." Shizuko explained things to Tamae.

A heavy wind, laden with moisture, thrashing the

foliage, had begun to blow. Far below, under the shade of the tropical trees, the car was parked out of the wind. The children of the village, scampering across the sand, were coming to look at the car. Small with distance, they were hunched over against the wind like shrimps as they ran.

Along the Mountain Ridge

岩尾根にて

北　杜夫

KITA MORIO

From far away that place of rock caught my eye. The skin of the gray rock here and there was tinged with green, and a narrow chimney, as if cut into it from the side, ran up the rock face.

To leave the path and go far afield, particularly to investigate the type of rock, was something close to second nature, bred in me when I was a boy. But these last few years I hadn't gone up against a cliff worthy of the name. Since losing two companions in two successive climbs, fastened to the same rope as myself, I'd reluctantly stayed away from the mountains.

Reacquainting my eye, after so long, with the protuberances, clefts, and canopies of the cliff spread out against the side of the mountain, I made my way to the base of the chimney, where rock fragments lay scattered about. By then, I think, the uncanny glamour of that enormous rock mass had already possessed me. The stone walls of the inside of the chimney were damp to the touch. But unlike my first idea of it, there seemed to be no lack of handholds or footholds. When I looked up, the gigantic niche carved into the sheer rock face gradually narrowed to where midway it curved and petered out. From a distance I'd figured that to get out of the chimney I would have to make a traverse. Above the chimney there was a patch of rocks and grasses, overhung by another vertical rock face. Assuming I could use pitons, was it, in fact, a feasible ascent? Of course, I would have to have had a partner, one who knew how to handle the rope. I was alone now, and had come unprepared for such a climb.

Just before the snows come, the mountains take on a strange brightness. Under the crystal-clear autumn sky, the dry, overlapped rock, brimful of gloomy shadow, seems very much heavier and denser. But today there was a low overcast. The craggy peaks, when I looked up, had their heads half in the gray clouds. The mountain seemed to have contracted in the damp atmosphere. As I stood there, I felt the chill from the desolate rock and the gray, monotone sky against my skin, silently stealing away my body heat.

Coming away from the base of the precipice, I made my way back across the fallen and slidden-down rock fragments. In the valley that I overlooked, the color of the rock was cold and there was no life in the green of the dwarf pines. Not even a bird call rose up. Nothing moved. Just as I thought this, a tiny black something slowly crossed my field of vision, right in front of my eyes, and landed on a stone at my feet. It was a black fly.

Even on mountains of the ten-thousand-foot class in the inland regions, flies are common. Although not a markedly different species from the lowland black fly, they seem bigger and dirtier. They are always to be found in beds of alpine flowers, and even when you're resting on a craggy summit, they soon come by. Perhaps they're messengers of the underworld, which follow us wherever we go.

The fly, sluggishly walking a couple of inches across the rock, rubbed its legs together briefly and then languidly took off. There was an unpleasant buzzing sound, and then the world was silent again. All around me, there were only subdued-colored clumps of boulders and lines of invisibly advancing pines, their green blackening, soon to be buried under snow.

I started walking again. Under my heavy mountain boots, as I trod hard, a number of brittle rock fragments fell away. Two or three flies danced up. Floating lightly upward, they drifted in midair a moment and flew away. There was something tired about their way of flying, as if they'd been numbed by the cold. I didn't pay them any mind. Skirting the sea of pines, I went around a huge rock that towered up on my right. I wanted to get back to the mountain-climbing trail I'd left a while ago. No matter how shrublike they may be, one must never set foot among dwarf pines on a mountainside unless there is a path.

Again there were flies. Any number of them clung to the pine needles and the rocks at my feet. At my approach they flew up slowly only to settle back down again. Their number increased with each step I took. I became aware of a certain odor, mingling with the cold, bracing air. It was like the smell of fermenting fruit. Then, from a thicket of pines about fifteen feet ahead, a swarm of flies numberless beyond imagination seethed out. A black, malodorous cloud, it seemed to have suddenly risen out of the earth. With a full-bottomed hum, it wavered up and down, spread out right and left. Soon I could make out individual flies. Most of them sank back down to where they'd come from. Some, however, alighted on my clothes. I could not shake them off. The previous smell, suddenly much stronger, assaulted my nostrils. It was a nauseating stench now. As I thought this, it went away and there was no smell at all. I moved to the side. The mass of flies seethed out again, swayed this way and that way, then coming together again disappeared. But a heavy buzzing hung in the air even after they were gone.

Squatting, I caught sight of a strange-colored object in among the bunched-up trunks of pines where the flies had subsided. Whitish cloth, on which flies clustered like sesame seeds, boots with their soles facing this way—it was undoubtedly the legs of a man. I could not make out the rest of the body. Recoiling two or three steps, I dislodged a stone and once more roused the swarm of flies. Stepping back farther, I waited for the black cloud of smelly, little flying things to vanish out of the air.

By and by, a lonely silence dominated the world of dwarf pines and drab-colored boulders that stretched to the horizon. Only my heartbeat, pulsing down to my feet shod in stout boots, pounded against the rock.

Walking slowly, I resumed my way back to the trail. In the valley far below, a shadow like a bird's skimmed the tops of the scrub pine forest and was gone. That was all. There was no sound. Picking up a stone, I threw it at the pine thicket I'd come away from. The black cloud of flies seethed out unmistakably. At this distance I could not hear any buzzing. But the unpleasant sense of it beat on my eardrums in waves. Picking up two or three stones, I threw them at random. This time there was no response. One stone, striking a rock with a clear echo, floated up into the air and was soundlessly swallowed by the ocean of pines below.

Hitching up my knapsack, I balanced its weight on my back. Turning around, making sure of my footing, I began walking again.

Even after I'd made it back to the trail, however, I merely felt environed by a kind of vague awareness. Perhaps the gigantic solidity of the mountain had swallowed up the movements of my little emotions. Keeping my eyes on the ground at my feet, I walked along briskly. After fifteen minutes or so I lowered my knapsack to the side of the path and sat down next to it. Feeling sharp hunger pangs, I took out a lump of bacon, cut off a thin slice of the fatty meat, and tossed it into my mouth. The last remaining fibers of fat made me feel nauseated. Pinching them out and throwing them away, I gulped down the whiskey that I'd poured into an aluminum cup. When I'm on a two- or three-day hike in the mountains, I live on bacon and whiskey. Mechanically I cut off another strip of bacon but could not make myself eat it. Just to look at the fat-striped meat was enough to turn my stomach. Wrapping it up again, I put it back in the knapsack. Instead, I tossed off several shots of whiskey one after the other. Because of my fatigue and the rarefied atmosphere, the alcohol quickly spread all through my body.

Already I was out of sight of the place among the dwarf pines where the dead body had come crashing down. Tapering off at an angle in its upper part, the chimney was not so clearly visible from here. More distinct than ever, though, the high, rocky brow of the cliff above it towered directly across from me. Most likely, though I couldn't see it, the top of the mountain was in back of that cliff. The path, making a wide detour around its base, meandered on ahead through the dwarf pines.

Aware of a pleasant tang on the tip of my tongue, I stupidly licked at the whiskey taste. Now and then, holding my wristwatch to my ear, I listened to its faint, steady tick marking off time in seconds and minutes.

Since my consciousness was very much diminished at this point, one could say that it was purely by chance that I caught sight of the human form clinging to the sheer rock face. At first I felt as if I were looking at an insect stuck to the surface of a stone wall. But as I realized that the stone wall was actually a rough, weathered cliff and the insect, in fact, a man, I might well have shouted in astonishment. But the whiskey had left my heart strangely cold and quiet.

Taking from the knapsack a pair of field glasses that I ordinarily used for bird-watching, I adjusted the focus. In the circular field of vision the pale, rugged skin of the rock appeared and, stuck fast to it, his legs slightly spread, was the man. He did not seem to be secured by a rope, and had a rather large knapsack on his back. It was the act of a mad fool, I thought. The only part of him in motion was his tousled head, turning slowly left and right. Minutes passed. Changing my grip on the glasses, I concentrated my gaze on the tiny, always turning, head. Just like a house lizard on the wall, the man did not make the slightest move. Then, inch by slow inch, the left leg was lifted. The bare toes groped for a foothold. When the left leg stopped moving, the right hand was shifted to where the left hand had been. With seemingly endless *lenteur*, the left hand moved to the left about a shoulder's breadth. As if in a slow-motion, acrobatic feat, the man's body moved upward about a foot and a half. Afterward there was a long pause.

It was painful to watch. I felt as if I could even hear the man's heart beating. I could see that there was a terrace about twelve feet above him, but the whole cliff seemed to be an overhang. "Stop, stop," I muttered. But the man began again to move. With a creepy slowness, he made his way up. I turned my eyes away. A few minutes went by. When I looked again, he was about three feet below the terrace. It baffled me how there alone he'd managed to get up so quickly. He was not moving now. His legs, torso, head, and arms stretched out right and left were absolutely still. But no. His right hand was groping upward. Crawling across the rock, feeling for handholds, not finding any, the hand was slowly drawn back to its starting point. After a long pause the same attempt was made and abandoned again. Then the man tried something different. Bending his knees, he contracted his body and then stretched straight up. Rising airily to its full height, his body seemed to come clear away from the rock. I averted my eyes. I had known what it was to hear a companion's body go hurtling down with rocks to be crushed far, far below. A second passed. Two seconds passed. I waited for tens of seconds, for minutes. When I raised my eyes to the cliff again, the man's shadow was still clinging to it. When I peered through the field glasses, he was just hauling himself up onto the terrace. The upper part of his body was not visible. As if in a silent movie, his bare feet waggled free from the bottoms of his trousers.

Safely on the terrace, the man got to his feet. But his movements were peculiar. He must be drunk with fatigue, I thought. Taking a few unsteady steps to the left and right, he did not rest or examine the cliff but stood in an undecided manner. Then abruptly he took hold of the rock. From there to the top, the slope was gradual, albeit with many bumps and prominences.

Yet the man's way of climbing it was unusual. In working one's way up a cliff, one follows a certain fixed rhythm, but his rhythm, rather than that of a human being, seemed more like an animal's. There was something about it that brought to mind some lower animal, for whom life and death are much simplified. By now I was unable to believe what I was seeing. Lowering the field glasses, I watched with my naked eye. It was easier that way, like watching an insect crawl up a stone wall. There was no great difference. When the small, solitary figure had disappeared over the top of the cliff, I picked up the aluminum cup that lay at my feet, carefully wiped off the grains of dirt that stuck to it with my handkerchief, and poured myself a drink. It's easy to get drunk on a high mountain. If I'd been my normal self, most likely I would never have done such a thing.

About two hours later I was at the top of the mountain. Here there was nothing but folds of overlapped rock. A cold wind, blowing up from a far-distant valley, swiftly stole the sweat and heat from my skin. Even after I'd taken out a sweater and put it on, I felt chilled. Sitting in the shadow of the rock, I drank the last of the whiskey.

Although the clouds were low, there was a clear view

of everything. Undulantly, in jagged notches and in-
dentations like the teeth of a saw, the mountain ridge
descended and rose up again into the ridge of the next
mountain. Each peak was like a giant who stood bar-
ring the way with bared chest, and the rocky detritus
was the flakes of his clear skin, worn off by endless
weathering. With a weird, scary uproar, the wind howled
past with enormous force, as if to shake the immovable
crag where I sat.

Shouldering my knapsack again, I placed a flat, ap-
propriately sized stone on the cairn alongside the path
and went on my way. The ridge split off into several
others, and I frequently stopped to look for a cairn.
Each time I did so, the strangled, moaning sound of the
wind grazed my ears. In the valley on one side a sea of
dwarf pine and scrub undulated stilly. The valley on
my other side, as when I had come up it, was deathly
silent. As if this mountain ridge were its farthest boundary, the wind seemed to be swept up from here into the
monotonous, gray sky. Buffeted underneath, I made
my way along unsteadily. It was a queer feeling. Perhaps you've experienced something like this yourself,
in a dream from which you haven't completely awaked,
or coming out from under anesthesia. I was three persons. I was making my way along this ridge like the
edge of a sword, from which I could take in at a glance
the valleys on either side; and at the same time I was
sprawled out dead in the pine scrub under a dense
swarm of flies; and also I was clinging limpet-like to the
rock face and groping for a handhold. These states of
mind were unlike each other, in fact, were absolutely
different existences, but their disparity wavered and
dissolved as if in a mist. They merged into a single

triple self. Now I was on the windy peaks, among the dwarf pines, in the gray clouds; now I was a dead body swarmed over by flies; now I was dangling in space, unable for dear life to get up over the edge of the overhang. Then the wind howled in my ears again, and coming back to myself I made my way along uncertainly.

Just then, unexpectedly, I saw a man in the distance. From here the sandy path descended and wound around a round-topped monticule to a small, flat area suitable for a campsite. The man was sitting there on a rock. By the way he hung his head, I could tell even from here that he was exhausted. It was as though this person "I" had divided, and half of myself were sitting over there. Approaching, I saw he was a man of about thirty, my own age. He was wearing a parka. At his feet there was a knapsack with a climber's pick stuck into it, and a portable cooking kit with the burner on. Sluggishly the man lifted his head and looked at me. He had the languor of some creature of the depths, slowly reacting to an intruder from beyond the world of the sea floor.

"Hello," the man said. I could not really tell whether his lips moved. But I heard a word like that.

When I'm in the mountains, I do not care to be hailed and even less to have conversations. Now, though, like a doll worked by strings, I stood there and watched the liquid come to a boil on the burner.

"How about a cup?" the man asked, in a fagged voice. His face was thin and bloodless, and I could not tell what, if anything, his dull eyes were looking at.

Nodding, I sat down on a rock beside him. He poured some of the coffee into an aluminum cup. Using a crumpled-up, old army glove as a potholder, he was about to pour himself some, then stopped. Staring off to the side for about ten seconds, he was lost in thought. Coming back to himself, he filled the cup to the brim. As I watched his strangely awkward, halting movements, I was assailed by a doubt that this was taking place in reality. It was as if I were seeing it in a dream. But the deliciously aromatic steam rose in wisps from the black coffee. The aluminum-alloy cup was so hot that even when I wrapped my handkerchief around it I had to shift it from hand to hand.

"Thanks," I said.

I couldn't tell whether the man had heard me. Sipping a mouthful of coffee, he brooded with an expressionless face.

"This really tastes good," he said abruptly.

"Yes," I answered vaguely. The illusion suddenly welled up in me that I myself had made this coffee.

Loosening the strings at the neck of his parka, the man silently stared off to the side. He was wearing thick, baggy trousers, their knees worn and frayed. His feet were shod in old but sturdy mountain boots. I caught a glimpse of triangular cleats. I also took a good look at his Kissling knapsack. What was it about this man? I could not get a feeling that he was a real other person.

"Just now," the man said, in a tone of voice that seemed almost unaware of my presence, "I watched you coming down. For a long time. Your method of descent is exactly like K's."

I followed his line of sight back up the steep avalanche slope that I had just come down. I felt as if it were I who had sat here for a long time, watching him come down from up there.

Quickly getting hold of myself, I grinned ruefully. "You're joking, of course!" K was a famous solitary climber, who'd fallen to his death in my most ardent mountaineering period. "I was slightly drunk," I added, half to myself.

"Drunk?" my companion muttered, also half to himself. "I feel funny too. Empty in the head, somehow. How did I get here?"

The words were uttered in a perfect monotone. I observed once more the absence of expression, the dull, glazed eyes, and the oddly uncoordinated way he held himself. But I wasn't myself either. Shaking myself, I tried to clear my mind.

For a while, sipping the rest of the coffee, neither of us said anything.

Somewhere far above us, the wind was singing wildly. But not a breath of air reached us here. The dead calm seemed to be inside us as well. I even felt a little sleepy.

"Do you mountain climb?"

After a long silence, one of us said this. I have only a fragmentary memory of the conversation that ensued. Actually I couldn't tell which of us was saying what. But between us, the following things were said:

"Do I mountain climb? I don't want to anymore. It scares me."

"Are you afraid you'll fall?"

"Yes. At least when I first take hold of the rock. But as I go up . . ."

"You mean you start to find your rhythm?"

"Yes. But there's another kind of uneasiness. It's completely different from the fear of falling."

"I know what you mean. It's as if something buried in us had suddenly surfaced."

"What is it?"

"Yes. What is it?"

"It's a kind of vague uneasiness."

"That's all you can say about it."

"I don't know what it is, and so I'm afraid of it. But when I feel it, it's as if I were more alive than at any other time."

"I've felt that way. It sits and waits in the deepest part of you."

"When I climb, it's as if I'd gotten it out of me."

"Probably you and I have to get it out of us."

"Have you ever had this experience?" one of us said. "In the night, when you're sitting on a high mountain ridge, you hear a kind of voice. It's like your own voice. It's as if you had split into two persons and were throwing your voice at yourself."

"It's the wind. That, and something like auto-suggestion."

"Whatever it is, it's no fun."

"I read about some mountain in Switzerland where you could always hear a voice. When they investigated, it was a trick of the wind."

"Even if you know it's the wind, it's no fun."

We listened intently for the sound of the wind, passing by far in the distance. Behind us, intercepting the wind, the unshaken bastion of stone towered up. In its shadow, as if hypnotized, we continued our conversation.

"But, you know," one of us said again, "for me, human beings are even more frightening. Whatever type of rock it is—inverted strata of quartz porphyry, say—you always know where you are. If it's the rock you're meant to fall from, you'll fall, and if it's not, you won't. Or even the most crumbly rock, with a bit of technique, it's as stable as any other."

"You mean human beings aren't stable?"

"This happened to me once," the other said. "It was during the off-season. I was sleeping in an empty hut with a man I'd met on my way up the mountain. In the middle of the night I was awakened by a noise. A shadow was moving about in the darkness of the hut by the flickering light of a candle. It was the man. 'What's the matter?' I called out. 'There's a spider around here,' he answered."

"'A spider'?"

"Yes. He said he'd seen a spider nearly a foot across, but it had suddenly vanished and he was looking for it."

"My god, how unpleasant."

"And he wasn't half-asleep, either. His voice was quite clear and calm."

"Was it a hallucination?"

"Who knows what it was? Talking about it now, it's rather funny. But then, it was like ice water down my spine. If a person's crazy, I don't know anything about the subject, but it seems to me that insanity must obey the laws of its condition. But this man was sane. That's why it was so terrifying. In other words, even in what we call sanity . . ."

"Well. Even so, you and I, we have the unstable element thoroughly under control."

The clouds had drifted lower. The atmosphere that absorbed them was chilly and damp. The world of rocks and dwarf pines was silent to its very depths. Shivering involuntarily, I shook myself.

By degrees the coldness of the air seemed to be waking me up.

"What are you thinking about?" This time, I remember clearly, it was the other man, with his catatonic impassivity, who spoke.

"There was a dead body," I said, conscious of my own voice. "It was somebody who'd been killed in a fall."

"'A dead body'?"

"The flies . . ." I started to say, then looked at my companion. I looked at the sweater that showed from the neck of his parka, at the color of his trousers torn at the knees. "The flies . . ."

"The flies were swarming on it? I know. The flies were really all over it, weren't they?"

"Oh, you saw it too?" Once again I looked hard at my companion.

"His skull was split open. The brains were out," the man said, with the same lack of expression and dead voice. "Yes. I thought I'd try to find out who he was. But the flies were everywhere on him. Some even got on me. I couldn't bring myself to touch him."

"Was it you?" I asked. I didn't feel particularly astonished. On the contrary, the mists in my head had cleared away and I felt rested and alert.

"What did you say?"

"I watched you climb that cliff."

"'Cliff'?"

"Right above where I saw the dead man."

The condition of my companion, whatever it was, underwent a change. Slowly his dull, glazed eyes acquired a light of vitality. It was like watching a man who has fainted regain consciousness. Seeing it happen was none too pleasant.

I was no longer the least bit drunk. This man and I were two different people. I wondered despite myself at the eerie conversation I'd been having with this stranger until a moment ago. Above all, it was clear to me that this man was no amateur mountain climber like myself. A while ago I'd been spellbound by his super-human technique.

"I understand now," he said in a low voice. His tone had changed, and he no longer stared emptily at nothing. "You saw me."

"It was frightening just to watch," I answered. "You still had your knapsack on. I thought you must be crazy. Do you always take risks like that?"

He gave me a sort of smile. It was a nervous smile, which stiffened and froze on his lips. His whole face went hard and distorted.

"You may not believe this, but I don't know myself. It was not really I who was climbing. It was my illness."

"Your 'illness'?"

"It's something like amnesia. I black out and can't remember anything afterward. I'm told that the first time it happened, I did something insane. I was expelled from the university mountaineering club."

"Is it something like sleepwalking?"

"I don't know. Even the doctor couldn't tell me what it was. I hadn't had an attack for a long time, but the shock of seeing that dead body may have set it off."

"But you had taken your boots off. You were climbing barefoot."

"Oh, really? Apparently that's the kind of thing I do.

The last time it happened, I came down a cliff with nothing but a bit of scrap rope."

"You mean if you knew what you were doing, you wouldn't have tried it?"

"Of course not. Even if I had, I would almost surely have fallen."

I observed him closely. His eyelids were twitching, and his fingers were trembling finely.

The clouds, from below, crawling up the skin of the rock like something alive, enveloped us. I looked at my wristwatch. It was time to be getting back down. I asked him about one other thing that was bothering me.

"Do you remember what we were talking about before?"

He shook his head.

"I know we were talking about something. But to be truthful, I don't know where we met or why we're together. In fact, I don't even know your name."

"It's nothing strange." I spoke with deliberate good humor. "Down there in the world it happens all the time when we're drunk."

After that, neither of us felt like saying anything more. Silently we tightened the cords of our knapsacks. The man stripped down to the sweater in which he had climbed the cliff.

When we came out onto the mountain ridge, the wind, raising a sharp howl, tousled our hair every which way. Hunched over, we made our way along the narrow ridge path.

"This wind is really something," the man said, turning around. I nodded.

"After this, there'll be several more days of good weather, and then snow for sure."

"If we hadn't found it, that body would have been buried under the snow until spring. Of course, it might have been better that way."

The wind drowned his low voice. I had to step up close to him, put my face right next to his.

"I'm frightened," he said in a whispery voice. "Sooner or later I'm going to fall. It's going to happen the next time I come to the mountains. I know it is."

"Let's slow down a little," I said, taking no notice of his words.

"I hate it," he muttered fiercely, staring deep into my eyes. "I'll be a dead body like that. I'll be swarmed over by a pitch-black mass of flies."

I averted my eyes from the man. The wind, raising its strangled, moaning voice in my ears, howled on. The craggy ridges, lead-colored and undulant, continued out of sight.

"Let's slow down a little." I repeated the meaningless words.

But the wind, instantly tearing the words from my parched lips, carried them away into the remotest reaches of this gigantic, towering world in which we faced each other.

Ugly Demons

醜魔たち

倉橋　由美子
KURAHASHI YUMIKO

That year I spent the summer in a cottage on the headland. The light breezes off the sea were as caressing as a woman's tongue. The sea and sky were sewn together at the horizon. Aside from that time each morning when, like an eyelid being opened, it was rent apart by and disgorged the great, blood-red eyeball of the sun, that seam was tightly closed. I was just like a demon shut up inside a shell. My ugliness was probably due to my fondness for despair. It goes without saying that this was something born of my hatred for the solid world outside that shell and for the going on of everyday life. But there was a young woman who, by angling for me with the hook called love, succeeded in firmly binding me to that actual world. It was from that time that my true despair began. This is why, in that decisive summer and in that word "love," I cannot but discover a unique, brilliant past. A brilliant past, like a whole armful of roundworms. That summer I was seventeen years old.

In the nights I spent at that cottage, any number of times in dreams I fondled that headland, which was like a stegosaurus clambering up onto the land dragging its tail behind it. Especially at the place where the jagged tail sank into the sea. Often my fingers, groping for the tip of that stegosaurus's tail, put all their strength into an attempt to pull the monster back under the sea. At such times, my desire became a devil that stood blackly athwart my way. Raising a hideously obscene scream, the monster was torn away from the land and, the thick hide of the whole world being rolled up along with it, was slimily hauled back into the depths. It was then, as the beast resisted me, that I would awake scattering the fruit juice of ecstasy. But outside the window was the dreamlike calm of the morning light. The headland lay stretched out like the smooth, beeswax-colored limbs of a woman. My dream had not changed the world in a single detail.

On such mornings M often came by. At first she brought with her the collie that had been raised in my house. How well they resembled each other, M and the collie, as they stuck out their faces side by side from the window of the car. With the sulkiness of the morning's awakening, with the familiar arrogance of an older brother toward his younger sister, with the petulance of a youth toward his mistress, with all these things simultaneously evident in my demeanor, I greeted her—she was my first cousin—and demanded what she had come for. Raising her beautifully aligned eyelashes, she smiled up at me as if looking at the sun. I have a message, she answered. It was always a message. In brief, she was a messenger. A messenger from whom? A messenger from the emperor, she said. To the prince. M liked to compare me to a prince. That was so she could compare herself to the princess who loved that prince. An order from that man? I barely managed to say, my tongue stiffened with shame. Or is it from that woman? Shaking her head, M merely pointed behind her at the direction she had come from, indicating the streets, the companies, the schools. In short, M had come from there and, under the pretext of bringing news of what was happening there, was doubling as a spy. But it was clear that most likely nothing was happening. For instance, that man and that woman—what other way is there of referring to them?—had already begun divorce proceedings by the time I was an adolescent. Their dispute had continued into that summer. But in the form of that woman absolutely refusing that man's request for a divorce, it would doubtless go on forever. Cooperating in their joint passion of hatred, they were building an indestructible tower. I was growing up crawling around inside it. I was the child of neither, drinking milk that came from myself and feeding only on my own flesh. After I'd passed my childhood as a member of that tribe of monsters known as "child prodigies," like all such prodigies I had turned into the most inoffensive youth in the world. Into a fiend of intelligence that had a soul like a globular cactus. Although I steeped myself in an incredible amount of reading material, it merely expanded the void, fattened the darkness inside the cactus. Nothing was born from there. I had a hatred of revealing myself in any form to another person. The instinct of self-expression was innately lacking in me. Despite that, I read more and more, growing endlessly fatter of soul until I could not move because of my weight. Just as the mouth takes in food, my eyes avidly devoured everything. No doubt my brain was swelling up from its morbid, chronic hunger. Even after I came to that cottage, my daily task (more even than studying for the university exams) was to continually browse among books like a crazed sheep.

No doubt the spy, observing me this way, had taken back reports. I was getting a steady stream of phone calls from that man and that woman. That man wanted me to concentrate on studying for exams, while that woman wanted me not to study so hard and instead get lots of exercise. What on earth was the point of getting lots of exercise? It was not as if I would ever do anything with myself. Please put on weight, M said, relaying that woman's message. Your mother has gotten terribly fat. At the hospital. It was a bizarre business. That woman had entered the hospital for treatment of insomnia. According to M, however, while undergoing a sleep-cure routine of sleeping for several days, waking up, gorging herself, and going back to sleep, she was growing unbelievably fat. Meanwhile, that man had evidently taken up with another woman. Recently he's been afraid that he has cancer, M said. He often goes to the hospital himself. How I longed to hear, from the lips of this messenger, news of absolute disaster! Of that woman's insanity and gangrene, of that man's death by strangulation, the explosion of his testicles scattering radioactive sperm, of the end of the world . . . But nothing had happened. Nothing at all.

M came out more and more regularly, bringing with her the collie, like a formal envoy. At some time or other, that large collie had completely become M's creature. By now he would not take food from anyone's hand but M's. Toward me, he merely turned courteously his pointed face from amid his ruff of thick fur. His tail was no longer wagged for me. It's my belief that M converted him into her faithful attendant by her technique of manipulating the direction arrow concealed under the belly of that male dog. When M understood by my silence that I would not let her stay, after taking care of the dog and the car stained by the salt wind and sand, she drove off, trailing behind her the dry sound of the engine and three stagy barks by the dog.

Probably I should try to write as fairly as I can about M. In her sixteenth year that summer, M was a truly well-brought-up girl. In brief, one could say that she was an extremely refined, alluring young woman, brought up on the milk of beauty and virtue, such as was peculiar to our class. What I first liked about her were her eyes. In their shape they were clearly eyes of the cat family, while in their color they were after all eyes of the dog family. But that is an inadequate description of them. They were more than that . . .

Before that summer, I'd had many conversations with M. I talked constantly about the universe inside my head—and where else should a universe be?—about its unnumbered nebulae, its exploding nebulae, its radio galaxies and its quasars, about their retreat, in other words, about the terrifying expansion of my universe. Whereupon M, against the concept of an expanding universe, a universe gone mad, would propose the idea of an eternally stable universe. Certainly in my universe nothingness was the aim of existence. But according to M, nothing always gave birth to existence and so the universe preserved its stationary condition.

Always in opposition over this point, we would stare at each other's faces. At such times I would look into M's eyes, but there was not a shadow of a star reflected in them. They were a sort of pure substance, the source of existence, a lake that gave off its own light. When I stared too long at them, those eyes would secrete a faintly salty liquid. But when I tasted it with the tip of my tongue, I felt a hunger for M that was close to sadness. At first, in my arms, M was like a mermaid. That was because I had made up my mind that the lower half of the body of this long-haired maiden was covered with fish scales of virtue, that it was closed in a perfect spindle shape and nowhere possessed any sign of sex. Actually, however, her legs parted easily at my touch. M completely opened up to me. Rather than disgust, fear impelled me . . . In this manner, I became M's creature. This is no slip of the tongue. I did not make M mine, she made me hers.

Wrapping the sheet around her torso, M stepped quietly toward the window. Even to the way her mass of hair trembled, M's whole bearing, gestures, and movements were those of a young woman who knew well that she was being watched by me. Stretching out both her arms, M pushed open the window to right and left, flooding the room with moonlight. Of course, with this action, the sheet slipped down from her torso, so that "naturally"—it was the kind of "naturally" that one sees in the theater—her apricot-colored body was revealed.

M showed that off to me. I don't know where she got this idea of displaying herself. M was following her own script. It was clear now that I should discard my arbitrary notion that M could not have such a thing. Crossing her arms so that they supported her breasts, M stood before me. More precisely, it was like an enactment of the phrase "rooted to the ground." Probably, in ordinary circumstances, this staring match would have ended in my defeat. That was because while I was looking at her with my eyes, M was looking back at me with the whole nude statue of her body. Taking advantage the moment my eyes let down their guard, melted in tears, M would attack her prey like a fierce animal. Outwardly, it would seem as if she had recognized her defeat and leapt of her own free will into the hunter's arms. And then the explosion of sighs for all the world as if her heart was broken, the stormy embraces, the exchange of delirious words of "love". . . But on this occasion I did not allow the scene to progress according to the script. It had occurred to me to position myself in the dark so as to observe M as a spectator. If I did that, M was not likely to flap her arms and throw herself onto the chest of the spectator. From a safe distance, I watched M. The tide of my awareness (or my interest, one might also say) was drawn up by M's gravitational pull. It was not long before my desolate sea bottom was exposed. I saw all. At this, I gave her a burst of applause that from a single, solitary onlooker seemed slightly excessive for a practical joke. In short, I uttered the words "I love you." I now plunged those words, like a spear of perfect irony, into M's bosom. The curtain immediately came down. Covering her face, M made her exit . . .

But M came back on stage and stood before me any number of times. Without the appearance of the least disturbance in her love, with the most innocent face in the world. It was my miscalculation not to watch out for that innocence and purity. By the time I realized this, she had turned the spearhead that I had plunged into her bosom into a pendant around her neck. As a decoration of my "love." In short, because I'd said "I love you," M could play the role of "one who is loved." This, for her, meant that she "loved" me, I believe. At times when, together with M, I was having lunch at the cottage—at such times that collie, sitting obediently at M's side, showed his white face above the edge of the table like a witness faithful to M alone—I tried to cut up with my knife and fork this word "love" that was formed from just one syllable. But it is a first-class kind of evil birdlime, and in the spell of this "love" that resembled the sticky properties of the vowel itself, all attempts at first simply brought on an even worse state of affairs. For instance, so that M would not be able to act like a girl "who is loved," I tried changing the signals, tried hoisting a flag that signified "I don't love you." Whereupon M read that as a sort of code. In short, she misread its true significance as meaning nothing other than "I love you." She thereby gave herself the right to act on the firm basis of that misinterpretation. I turned my eyes of hatred from M to her collie. Quickly reading my eyes, M gave up her habit of feeding the collie bits of cheese from her mouth. That was a truly crafty maneuver of the eyes. M clearly acted as if she had read their expression as jealousy.

One morning when M came out, her face was tinted red by the sunrise colors of the sky that burned and festered as if from some curse. The black birds that nested in the sides of the headland noisily flocked and

wheeled in the sky. The blast on the horn that announced M's arrival was unusually drawn out, sounding like a warning alert. M got out of the car wearing a
dress the color of fire. Where's the dog, I asked. He
went away, M answered in a meaning voice, and twin-
ing her arm in mine invited me to go for a walk. As,
barefoot, we walked along the narrow beach at the base
of the cliff, it seemed as if the rocks there, the size of
babies' skulls, had increased by giving birth to themselves in heaps. M, like a bobbing buoy, was in strangely
good spirits.

M was, if one is to describe her, a quiet girl who
rarely smiled. When she did smile, her face lit up as if
the sun had suddenly come out at dead of night. But on
our walk that morning, M raised her voice in laughter
many times. Whenever she lost her footing on the
rocks, she made me hold her wrist. It burned coldly in
my hand. They say a typhoon's on the way, M said, and
put her lips up for a kiss. When she lifted her face, the
sunrise colors had faded away. The wind had completely died down. It was as though the world had been
asphyxiated.

Shortly before noon, we decided to go for a swim in
the bay. As we walked along the level, shelly sand, we
met some fishermen's wives and old men drawing a
dragnet. In unison they shouted out something in
obscene-sounding voices to "the lovers." Or perhaps it
was a friendly warning about the typhoon that was
approaching. The bay, however, was glassily calm, as if
it were anesthetized. In the sandy area behind the bay,
where scrawny weeds grew sparsely, where gravestones
whose epitaphs were almost illegible stood askew and
shacks that were nothing but roof and posts were half-

buried by the invasion of the sand, we took off our clothes.

The fishermen's children who usually jumped up and down around us with yells and screams were not to be seen that day. The only two bathers on this gloomy forenoon, we submerged our bodies in the lukewarm sea. A lead-colored membrane was stretched all around the sky, and it was not easy to tell just where the sun was. When I stuck my head out of the water, the sea, endlessly raising little waves like obtuse triangular pyramids, was all together rising and falling with a gentle, heaving motion that reminded me of riding a swing in a dream. The smoothness of the water's skin was clearly that of a living animal. The sea was not an inanimate existence. Wanting to tell my discovery to M, I looked about me on the water's surface. But M's yellow bathing-capped head was bobbing up and down far away across the numberless wrinkled waves. When I tried to shout to her, I gulped down what seemed like gallons of foul, fishy water. In brief, it was like swimming in amniotic fluid.

Lying down in the prow of a boat whose rotted timbers were buried in sand, I closed my eyes. All at once my mind grew heavy, the wings of sleep covered me, my head began to be flooded with something like mucus. At these times what was always in my half-paralyzed thoughts was that headland. What was on the other side of the headland? The headland stretched out infinitely far into the distance. As I approached the end of it, the waves grew rough and choppy, and my dream swim would be broken off in an excess of terror. But I knew that what must be on the other side of that headland could not possibly be there. M, letting sand sift down on my chest, was listening to my story. In answer to that despairing question of mine, her mouth was singing like a lullaby the refrain "There's nothing there, there's nothing there." Of course, this did not mean that literally there was no earth there and nothing at all. If there was no world on the other side of that headland, and birds who flew there never came back, how wonderful it would have been! But without being told by the map, I knew that it was a continuation of the world on this side. On that side of the headland, the same sand and waves were intermeshed more inevitably even than mediocre human lives. No doubt fishing boats, nets, reefs, driftwood, and the same kind of headlands were interminably repeated. Like the teeth of a saw. That, for me, was the worst possible landscape. M's refrain of "There's nothing there" was none other than the sound of the wind that was blowing there.

With heavy oars I was rowing on a dream sea. Enduring a fatigue of wasted effort each time I rounded a headland, a fatigue that made my body feel like mud slumping over, I kept endlessly advancing. This sea voyage into the "future," in which I was unable to round even one headland although I was rounding numberless headlands, this vertical descent of "time" at the end of the world, beyond which only the dead could go . . . Suddenly I became the bird of ecstasy, and taking flight I saw the other side of the headland. Why had I not been able to do such a simple thing? It was the scenery of a dead star that stretched out there. On this beach the burnt-out sun descended on the other side of the headland. Therefore, what I saw now was without doubt the corpse of that sun. A sun moored in darkness, an empty, pale skeleton of a sun! It was the castle of "nothingness" that I had long dreamed about. A castle of nothingness that towered up in a place that was nowhere, a false light that issued from an imaginary lamp, a wind with no reason for being . . . When I looked closely, the enormous dead star was slowly revolving, making glitter its thorns and spines of desolation. Like a waterwheel that made "time" turn backward. No doubt it turned everything as far back as I could remember into a dead star. But if that was so, what was the warm, everyday sun? Wasn't it, exactly, a false sun? It was no more than a sun of illusion, its arc through the sky described by the desires of each day.

The tongue of a cold serpent insinuated itself between my eyelashes. Amid a tangle of hair, a face with great eyes that stared at me and a prodigious number of warts of water drops came down on me. M clung to me with her wet mouth and then, in a foolish voice full of anxiety, asked the most asinine question. What were you thinking about? I was asleep, I answered. At that M, pressing her belly on top of my belly, and arching back the upper half of her body, looked down at me and said, What were you dreaming about? About the future, I said jokingly. M, happily puffing out her cheeks as if the word were a delicious, big morsel, repeated, The future? Ah, you mean our future . . .

The wind suddenly grew stronger. Laden with sand and salt, long, attacking waves of wind instantly clouded our eyes with their rough, raspy tongues, inflicting numberless tiny scratches on our cheeks. The typhoon's coming. Saying this, M squatted down and began to gather our things. Like a small girl playing house, tidying up her make-believe possessions. Her buttocks were those of a lovable young girl. And when she stood up, saying that we must go back quickly, the look on her face was that of a perfect wife.

A tidewater-control embankment ran along the edge of the sand like an upper lip. When one had gone through a cleft in it, there was a forest of low pines as far as one could see. From the porch of the cottage this seemed like the membrane of a bat's wing that spread out at the crotch of the headland. As one approached it, however, there appeared a maze of little paths like capillaries that ran all through the forest. The pines had been uniformly brushed back by the wind at the height of my shoulder. Suddenly M sprang onto one of the paths of the labyrinth, immersing her head in the sea of trees. When I pursued her, M, while trying to escape through the meshes of the labyrinth's net, pursued me. During this annoying game of tag, the wind twisted my head around and tore my voice to shreds. I soon lost sight of M. And then, on the sea of trees in which M had drowned, scattered raindrops the size of small stones started coming down. Like shot-down birds.

M had already returned. Wrapped in a bath towel and sipping hot coffee, she was waiting for me. Laying out cards like a fortuneteller, she predicted the advent of the storm and prognosticated the necessity of her spending the night at the cottage. It was extremely amusing. During the afternoon, the wind and rain continued intermittently. Occasionally the clouds would part and the bloodshot eye of the sun, from an unexpected place, would send down a baleful look. But we were already in the lungs of the typhoon. As night fell, the storm began to breathe forth ferocious, gusting sighs. The lights simply went out. M and myself, with the caretaker and his grandson, setting up long, festive-looking candles, had a supper that made one think of Christmas Eve. Immediately afterward, M shut herself up in her room. When, carrying the candlestick, I went up to see her, she was already curled up in a self-sufficient sleep in the midst of the uproar. After I'd made sure of that provokingly sound sleep of hers, my eyelids burning with expectation that the huge palms of the storm would buffet the world to pieces, ship-wreck it, I fell into a fitful sleep on the bed that rocked like a boat. But it was not that I harbored any great hopes. Come morning, no doubt, everything would be as peaceful as a dream. The white light of the sun would set about giving a new coat of paint to the world. The world would be smiling, like the face of a woman who has taken off her makeup. That was truly something to despair about!

At daybreak the wind went away. And in the light of the morning I was able to see everything that merited my despair. Face down on the bed, M displayed her apricot-colored limbs and her flanks. Why did they make me think of an arrogant tiger? In that instant I saw M sprawled out in this same posture of sleep even twenty years from now. Piercing her every pore with the needles of hatred, I gazed at M's whole body. I put my lips to the extraordinarily charmless desert of her back. Whereupon this animal uttered a groan of satiety.

We went for an early-morning walk along the beach from which the typhoon had departed, trailing its stormy tresses. Various fragments of things had been thrown up on the beach. All the sand having been washed away, the beach was nothing but shells. As we walked along it, M exclaimed each time as she pointed at the driftwood, the tin cans, and the seaweed that was like fallen-out strands of hair. According to her, the world was a little worse for wear but had not at all gone bad. I half expect to see a dead body washed up somewhere, she said with deliberate good humor. Intertwining her arm with mine, she raised her face like a saucer to receive the sunlight and closed her eyes. It was just as if she was determined not to spill a drop of my "love." It was a terribly seductive temptation. I pushed M down onto the sand and kissed her. I wanted to drain all the "love" out of her face. M's arms, without trying to put themselves around my neck, lay outspread like wings. From the wrists her hands dug into the sand as if taking root. In short, M held me fast with her lips alone. Like a bird flapping its wings, I struggled to get to my feet, but I could not escape from this powerful trap—M's eyes were opened wide all the while. A futile anger boiled up in me, impelling me to further useless resistance. I was a soldier who, before the outbreak of war, was already certain of defeat. With what disgust I set about each task of undoing her fasteners, disengaging her legs from her panties, and performing the operation of opening up her brassiere! Despite this, I was able to appear impassioned because I knew how absolutely hopeless it all was. To force even M to see this, I ordered her not to close her eyes. She put on her sunglasses. Otherwise naked as the day she was born, M sustained my assault.

We're being watched by someone, M said in a calm voice. In an instant the sky turned into a blue eye. My body still on top of M's, I raised my head and slowly raked the crest of the dunes with my line of sight. The boundary of sky and sand, making a golden-colored

zone, burned dazzlingly bright. Because of my fantasy
that dozens of toadstools would suddenly and simultaneously stick up their heads from there and shower us
with barbaric cries of derision, I was almost unable to
move. M, putting on her clothes, told me that there was
a reformatory on a terrace of the headland. I hadn't
known this. Is it nearby? I asked. You can't see it from
here, she answered. Maybe it was some boys from
there. Somebody was watching us. Wriggling her nose,
M sniffed for signs of people about. What happened to
that dog? I abruptly asked. Checking me with her hand,
however, M said, My nose is keener than a dog's. We
went along the edge of the dunes. And then we found it
—a corpse, washed up among the driftwood. A Negro!
M exclaimed. It was the body of a Negro (or perhaps a
mulatto) youth. Limply crumpled, like the larva of a
devil that the sea had coughed up, the body lay with its
yellowish palms and soles exposed to the sun. Where
could it have come from? I asked. M silently pointed in
the direction of the reformatory. If he's from there, he
must have escaped under the cover of the storm. Is he
alive? Try touching him, M said. I refused. It was the
same to me whether he was alive or dead. For me, this
body was nothing more than a fish in human form. Its
outside was black, a skin of darkness that sucked and
soaked up the light, but—my eye, like a dissector's
sharp knife, cut open the torso from the top down—its
inside was rose pink, a flesh of fruit like fire. Inserting a
broken oar under the Negro's stomach, M flipped him
over with the rudimentary lever. We both gave a small
cry. A rose-colored knife of flesh tremblingly pointed at
the sky . . .

From a wrecked rowboat at the water's edge and the

broken oar, I understood the Negro's reckless getaway. In the middle of the storm, rowing his boat, he had tried to round that headland. As I, in dreams, had done any number of times. What a fool! I exclaimed. I was deeply excited. What's even more absurd is that he seems to be still alive. M, picking up a wet shirt, showed me an initial that was sewn onto the breast pocket. One could read it as the Q of the Roman alphabet. It probably stands for Quincy or something like that, I said. M looked indifferent, however. We should go back and call the police . . .

The sun had already dissolved in a blaze of golden light that flooded the whole sky. This intense heat that scorched the sand was too strong, I thought. I was almost certain that the flesh of this black false image would melt away like a dew snail. The word "police" made me smile. The officer who had responded to the call would surely find nothing but a sort of sweat stain soaked into the sand. There's no need for that, I told M. Either that guy Q will be found by the people from the reformatory, or he'll go back there on his own. What if he escapes? M asked, apparently anxious. If he does, it won't be long before he's caught. I don't know whether M, at this time, was thinking of more than that. After lunch, I went out onto the veranda. Titillated by a gentle breeze from off the sea, I dozed. Until I was awakened by M's short, sharp cry, I dreamed about Q.

Q came to the house, and slipping his bare feet into the fluffy, inside-out skins of some animal, entered my bedroom. Like an image inside a picture frame, he sat down on my bed. He showed his white teeth in a meaningless smile. It all seemed like a continuation of the dream, but this was a reality much rarer and more diluted than any dream. Q seemed to have lost some of his Negro density, to have faded in color somewhat. You intend to tell the police about me, don't you? Q inquired, in an effeminate voice. (It had a lustrous shimmer, like that of chamois leather.) When I answered that I had no such intention, Q, without appearing particularly relieved, said that it was up to me whether I informed on him or not, and that anyway it didn't matter much. I asked him why. Because it doesn't matter much, Q repeated. After that, he went to sleep on my bed. M, loudly revving up her engine as if in protest, drove back to the city.

In this manner Q came to my place, pointing his rose-colored knife at me. However, it was not a dangerous weapon for the purpose of stabbing me, but rather a harmless sword of flesh meant to be seized, looked at, and caressed by me, and afterwards to limply melt away. I soon understood that it was the motor handle by which I was to steer and propel this Negro dugout canoe. The time when I understood this was also the time when I understood that Q was a counterfeit woman. I was in the bathroom, washing Q off. He was a hairless animal, a rubber doll that obscenely contracted and expanded, bright flesh wrapped in a skin of thin clay or chocolate. In short, the Negro Q had on the outside the sinister darkness that women (including M, of course) concealed inside their white skin. This thinly spread darkness that coated his outside had no more power to cast a spell over me. Thus, without incurring the risk of being absorbed by the darkness of the other, I was able to observe him. Without being intimidated by "love." That is what it was, I think: a ceremony of pure knowledge. A ceremony that Q taught me, and one in which, slitting the skin of darkness, I poured an awareness like burning sulfur into the flesh of the fruit. While continuing my caresses in which there was no "love," I was perfectly clearheaded. This was because I was able to observe simultaneously both my object and myself who was attacking it. Q's screams of pain guaranteed the clarity of my awareness . . .

While in this manner I spent several August days as sweet as a melon, the conversations I had with Q were merely as a few seeds in the fruit flesh of silence. What had Q done before being sent to the reformatory? I didn't do anything, Q kept repeating. Probably the extent of his juvenile delinquency was that he had lived without doing anything. Like me now, for instance. And, in fact, Q did not try to do anything except be this counterfeit woman whom I had created.

On a morning whose sunrise colors made the sky seem like the face of an evil spirit presaging the approach of a second typhoon, the arrival of M was heralded by an inordinately long blast on the car horn. During a gloomy swim in the bay, M and I were by ourselves, "with no water between us," as the saying has it. But for some reason M did not bring up the subject of Q, and for my part I had no reason to do so. Like an inconspicuous household pet, Q was hiding himself in a room in the cottage. Night fell, the storm attacked, and M stayed over. Struck by the wind, the roof began to groan and creak. I remembered that it had done this the first time. Holding up a candlestick in the low-pressure darkness in which uneasiness drifted like a medusa, I went up to M's room. Just then I felt as if a scream, emanating from I did not know where, had reached my ears. Quickening my step, I rushed into M's room. A beating of unseen wings somewhere in the room made the candle flame waver and flicker. M was not in the bed. But there were signs of something moving on the floor, and when I held the umbrella of the candle's light nearer, M's face, tumbled about in her hair, and her naked arms in the shape of a cross floated up. Astoundingly, a dense mass of darkness of almost indistinguishable form was leaning over her naked body. Rather than the Negro Q, it seemed like a personification of darkness that had come out from between M's thighs. Like the Negro genie that appeared from Aladdin's lamp. Now I feel as if all this was not some trouble that had broken out but a splendid drama. Doubtless that's because of M's eyes, which were glittering fiercely with a touch of phosphorescence. Like two full moons, they stared at me and commanded me to do a certain thing. Shifting my grip on the heavy candlestick, I struck out at the black ghost. The convulsion of the Negro was difficult to tell from the convulsion of the whole darkness. Twice, three times, it may have been four times that I struck at a thing that was like a broken eggshell.

It was on that night, in those circumstances, that I realized that in due course I would have to call M, who was hanging on my neck and trembling like jelly, by the name of "wife." M, succeeding in exorcising the ghost Q, more than anything frightened me by her determination to possess me by any means. Wasn't M's endless trembling, then, not because of fear but because of joy? I had fallen into the bottomless well of a feeling of defeat and so could not read M's face at that time. And even now I can't. For twenty years now, we have been the happiest-seeming, the most exemplary man and wife in the world, but . . .

Nothing happened, M said that night. Nothing is happening. In this world. This was M's magic formula. And it was as she had said. The next day the morning sun gave a fresh coat of paint to the world. We took walks along the seashore. In a succession of days that were difficult to tell apart from each other, the summer wound down. One afternoon at the end of summer, like a couple that had already been married for twenty years—I was seventeen and M had just turned seventeen that day—we were sitting on the sand beneath the headland. M, while looking at the rough sea and as if playfully digging into the sand, uncovered something frightening. Under her hand, there appeared two pointed ears and two front paws. I have no doubt that they belonged to that collie of hers that had disappeared.

Bamboo Flowers

竹の花

水上　勉

MIZUKAMI TSUTOMU

It wasn't until I was seven years old that I learned for the first time that flowers bloom even on bamboo. The hamlet where I was raised, in the village district of Natanosho in the mountains of the Omi border up from the Wakasa seacoast, was called Uchikoshi. It was known as a foster-child hamlet. A place of many bamboo groves, it had barely fifty households. But the mountain ravines, rich in game, flourished densely with groves and thickets of long-jointed and speckled bamboo. From the back of any house you could see the groves. When you opened the windows, there were only the groves, their leaf-blades rustling in the wind.

In this hamlet of Uchikoshi the custom of taking in orphans dated from the old days. In roughly half the houses there were children who either had only one parent or had become separated from their parents.

Actually, I was one of those foster children. Nowadays there is the Child Welfare Law, and the authorities appropriate a budget for a foster-parent system that is officially encouraged. If you go to Nara Prefecture or Kyoto Prefecture, I hear, there are villages where every single household is raising somebody else's children. But this system came into existence only in the twenty-third year of Showa and so is not all that old.

There is a network of foster-child villages that take in children sent to them by child referral agencies in the cities and urban prefectures. A grant called a consignment fee, of 5,500 yen a month from the Ministry of Welfare, comes with each child. Separate monies are paid out for compulsory grade school and middle school education, so that even though you are raising somebody else's children, it comes to ten thousand yen or so per child each month. Among households that are fond of children there are cases of farm families that take in three or four children from the referral agency and raise them under a single roof as if they were their own. Even if the foster parents have their own children, they continue to take in foster children and bring them up together as brothers and sisters under the same roof. Uchikoshi, where I was brought up, might also be called one of these foster-parent villages. But this hamlet had been known for taking in orphans from far back in the past. I've heard that the custom dates from the beginning of Taisho. In Uchikoshi there is a Zen temple called the Sainen-ji. It's said that the head priest, when he was serving as a prison chaplain, adopted the child of a miserable convict. His having his wife bring up the child was the start of the foster-parent tradition in the hamlet. Inspired by the priest's example, households throughout the hamlet, applying to referral agencies in the city and the prefecture, took in children that were society's pathetic discards.

In the old days there were institutions called orphanages. They were operated by private charitable organizations and individuals. Gathering unfortunate children under one roof, they would bring them up there. But these orphanages, dependent on endowments and donations, often could not meet expenses. Occasionally the older orphans were sent out into the mountain villages to sell lead pencils and rubber bands. "These unhappy children should not be made to go out and sell things," the priest declared. After a discussion with prefectural officials, I've heard, the hamlet of Uchikoshi decided to become a foster-parent village. By doing so, it was a foster-parent village before the present system came into existence. That was, in effect, the start of the foster-child-care system.

At the age of three I was adopted by the family of a farmer called Yagoro in Uchikoshi. Already, though, the memories of when I was little are fading. Now there remain only memories from the time when I began to go to school. Later, however, from a chance occurrence I came to suspect that I was the child of a criminal.

But no one has been kind enough to tell me who it was that carried the three-year-old baby that I was on their back and brought me to this hamlet in the mountain fastnesses of Wakasa. Thus, I know neither the father nor the mother who brought me into this world. The parents I know are my foster parents. But even those foster parents have not told me the names of my real father and mother.

When I was old enough to use my head, I realized

that I was a foster child by the fact that my name was not the family name of Kareyama but Takarasu. My name was Takarasu Shohachi. That must mean that I already had the name when I was three years old and taken in by the Kareyama family.

I also have the feeling that some hazy memories do remain from when I was three years old. One is of a shadowy bamboo grove. From above the green bamboos, reaching up toward the sky like the teeth of a comb, numberless arrows of sunshine showered down like a rainfall into the grove. I was in the arms of a big, tall man. Perhaps because it was dark underneath me, the arrows of light that hung suspended from the sky seemed to glitter a golden color. Another memory is of the whitely flashing waters of a stream, long and narrow like a sash. In a bamboo basket I was being carried on somebody's back on a road alongside that stream. In the bamboo basket was a cushion with the cotton stuffing coming out, placed just right so that I sat nice and comfortable. But reaching up as high as I could, I'd grabbed hold of the edge of the basket and was trying to see around me. Who was the person carrying me? When I'd begun to go to school, I asked Auntie Ume, my foster mother, about those two memories.

"Most likely it's of a time when I went to cut bamboo with you on my back. The light coming down like rain sounds like it was morning. Back then I would go out to cut bamboo before the dew was fallen. That road along the white stream too was on the way to the bamboo grove . . . you were such an intelligent child. Even though I was carrying you in a basket, you kept reaching up and grabbing the edge. You were always getting splinters in your fingers."

That was what my foster mother told me, but people's memories, as time goes by, become blurred and vague. Only that memory of arrows of light in the bamboo grove and the one of the road along the white stream had already become scenes that I would never forget. If you journey south from the Omi border, there is the great lake of Biwa. If you go north, there are the stormy waves of the Sea of Japan. In Wakasa, wedged between the great lake and the great sea, even though you're sleeping deep in the mountains, in the middle of the night you can hear the sound of the distant, towering waves. In my foster mother's arms in the bedroom with the heavy cold-weather shutters, I have heard the reverberations of the billows assaulting the sheer cliffs of the promontories mingled with the rustling of the bamboo groves.

Yagoro, my foster father, was a man fond of doing fine work in bamboo. In the winter, sitting by the edge of the sunken hearth, he would make bamboo flutes. The village was plentiful in bamboo for use as laundry drying poles and for the framework of thatched roofs. I would see bamboo buyers from the city buying up bundles and loading them onto ox-drawn carts. At bamboo-cutting time both my foster parents would work hard from early in the morning. No doubt that road along which I was carried led to a bamboo grove where my foster parents were working one day.

My foster father was a swarthy, taciturn man with big hands and broad fingertips. We called him Father. When I say we, I mean that in Yagoro's house there were two other children being raised then, a girl called Min and a boy called Teiji. In short, there were three of us foster children. Min was three years older than I was, and Teiji three years younger. Teiji had been adopted when I was six. I remember that this child was short like myself, slight, and something of a crybaby. Min, a delicate-looking child with a white, classically oval face, often took care of us. But as soon as she graduated from grade school, she went to work in Kyoto as a maid. I only have scanty memories of Min after she left home. I remember one day, carried on Min's back, standing amidst the colors of the sunset over the Uchikoshi River until late in the evening. The sun, hidden by the peak of the mountain across from us, was reflected in the clouds. The leaves of the bamboo groves that surrounded the hamlet shone redly, fused into the vermilion of the sky. As I watched the wavelike rippling of the bamboo leaves astir in the wind, I all but mistook it for the fine, crinkled waves, like crepe silk, of an ocean of liquefied crimson.

My foster mother was a person with a white, round face. Her name was Ume. "Ume, Ume," my foster father, Yagoro, was always saying. This Auntie Ume was my only mother in this life, whom I will never forget. From my foster father having taught me how to work in bamboo, I became a bamboo handicraftsman. Living on the outskirts of this town of Tsuruga, I have managed to eke out a livelihood as a maker of fishing creels. But from my thoughts of my taciturn, sternly painstaking foster father, there are only strangely cold memories. In my memories of my Auntie Ume there are many warm things. On cold winter days, stirring up the fire in the sunken hearth, she would roast sweet potatoes for us. She would also toast rice cakes. Teiji, Min, and I grew up in the arms of this foster mother of ours.

The border of Omi was a region where the snow was

deep. Every year the snow that slipped from the edge of the eaves accumulated until it was higher than the sliding doors and shutters of the house. Inside the house it was very dark. When our family of five warmed ourselves at the fire, the heat would collect and hang heavy under the ancient straw thatch of the hip-gable roof. By the hearthside we watched Uncle Yagoro make his bamboo flutes.

Apparently for a bamboo flute, old bamboo is the best. When the bamboo is cut, one must look carefully at the joints and check the depth of the roots. My foster father, ruthlessly cutting a bamboo halfway up its stem and bringing it back roots and all, put it to dry in the attic storeroom under the triangular roof. From the smoke of the sunken hearth coming up through slats of the removable bamboo floor, it became smoked bamboo, dried out naturally. Selecting from these lengths of bamboo, my foster father would begin his winter work of making the bamboo flutes called shakuhachi. The shakuhachi has only five holes, four in the front and one at the back. Unless the distance between the joints and the spacing of the holes is skillfully harmonized, the tone quality will not be beautiful. The mouthpiece is a thin piece of inlaid seashell or tortoise shell. After sealing the compartments of the bamboo airtight, one must carefully polish the flute with scouring rush. Seen from behind as he assiduously polished the shakuhachi under the lamplight, my foster father's square-shouldered figure, unlike the carefree-seeming farmer in the rice paddies of summer, had the look of a craftsman fanatically absorbed in the art of flute-making. In later days I set up as a maker of bamboo fishing creels. Even now at forty-eight years of age, when I am cutting lengths of bamboo sheath in my shack on the beach, I suddenly remember my foster father hard at work on his flutes, and telling myself I must put energy into it, make an extra effort.

One time my foster father and foster mother were sitting alone at the sunken hearth, with me wedged in between them. It must have been when I was five or six years old. Since neither Min nor Teiji was there, I made bold to ask, "Father, Mother, my name isn't Kareyama. It's Takarasu . . . where are my father and mother? Please tell me."

For a moment my foster father and mother looked at each other and were silent. Then my foster father replied desultorily, "You came from Echigo . . . both your father and mother died young . . . the chief priest of the temple brought you to us . . . I don't know what village you're from myself . . . anyway . . . you're the child of an intelligent father. You're good at writing characters, and you remember things well."

My foster mother, sniffing back tears, added, "Your mother was a gentle person . . ."

I remember sadly that these answers of my foster parents echoed emptily in my ears, in my child's heart.

Since there were many foster children in the village, not knowing the names of one's parents was nothing to be all that ashamed of. And there were other orphans like myself. Teiji, the same as me, had merely been told that he came from Echigo. He neither knew the names of his parents nor had ever seen their faces.

It was when I was in my first year of elementary school that I began to have a fearful premonition that my real parents were living in this world. Our school was not in Uchikoshi but at the main school building in inner Nata, a walk of two and a half miles. It was in going to that school that we foster children were first exposed to the winds of what is called society. In the foster-child hamlet of Uchikoshi, children without parents were not unusual, and one could live without feeling inferior to anyone. But when we went to the main school, a mob of students teased and tormented us. In my first year, I had this said to me by a mischievous upper-class student called Yukichi: "Your father's a murderer . . . there's a fiendish criminal called Takarasu . . . it was in the newspaper."

I was dumbfounded. I felt as if my head had been cleft open. Glaring at Yukichi's face, I said, "That's not so. That's not so."

But in back of Yukichi more than ten children clapped their hands and laughed. Their laughing voices floored me after a while. I knew that the surname Takarasu was indeed an unusual name, but it took me a long time after that, twenty years, to find out the name of a man called Takarasu Yoshitaro, who had committed a murder. This crime had occurred in the town of Murakami in Niigata Prefecture. By the time I had finished my search, after the criminal had died in the prison at Abashiri, by going through newspaper articles of the day and court records, I'd pretty well possessed myself of the facts of the case. But whether or not the man Takarasu Yoshitaro was my father or not, I still do not know. The proof no longer exists. My surname was later changed and entered in the family register of the Kareyamas, and afterward I took the name of the family I married into, the Tamuras, so I cannot draw on the original family register for any knowledge of a relationship with the Takarasu of the town of Murakami. The incident was an atrocious murder, as follows:

One snowy evening in February of the eleventh year of Taisho, a brutal crime was perpetrated on the household of a tobacconist in the town of Murakami. Five people were either killed or injured. The motive was said not to be robbery but a grudge. The murderer, crawling in through the window late at night with a hatchet, hacked two people to death and inflicted grievous injuries on three others before making his getaway. Ten days later the Niigata police, making a sweep of a mountain outside the town where there was a mine, arrested the man, Takarasu Yoshitaro, who had holed up in the miners' barracks. The criminal made a full confession, and the judge sentenced him to a life term of penal servitude. This man, in July of the fourteenth year of Taisho, died of natural causes in the prison at Abashiri. Unfortunately I could find no record anywhere that he had a wife and child. If there was no mention of them in the court records, it perhaps meant that the man was single. At this point, thinking that even if my surname was the same as his, it was dubious whether I was the son of that criminal, I felt a little as if I had been saved, and broke off my investigation. But why, when I was in first grade, did Yukichi and those other malicious children say that I was the son of a murderer? Since Yukichi said he'd read about it in the newspaper, although several years had passed since the incident, perhaps it was that fourteenth year of Taisho when Takarasu Yoshitaro died at Abashiri. I would have turned seven at the time. That age would agree with my being in the first grade, which was for students seven years old. At this thought I am unable to avoid a deepening certainty that that brutal criminal was my father.

One other memory, also from my first year, is of a summer's day when I was walking back after school to Uchikoshi. When I came to the edge of the village, on the slope road that ascended in a series of terraces, twirling a white parasol, a woman was coming down toward me. In a pretty white summer kimono with a red sash, about twenty-seven or twenty-eight and carrying a kerchief bundle, she made her way down the narrow road between the bamboo groves. When she saw me, she abruptly stopped. Casually I looked at that person's face. With her white, beautiful features, she looked like a person from the city. Standing there as if she'd planted her legs, the lady looked at me. Then suddenly she called, "Sho. Sho."

I was startled. How did this person know my name? It was strange. She must be coming away from Uncle Yagoro's place. Why was she calling my name? Just then I saw that the lady's face had all of a sudden turned dead pale. Her mouth working, she abruptly covered her face with the kerchief bundle. It all happened in an instant. As if fleeing, she went down the road between the bamboo groves.

"Mother . . ." I called after her. Why did it seem to me that this was my real mother? Swallowing back the words that had leaped to my lips, I stood like a stick in the roadway. The woman's form, growing small with distance along the road through the rice paddies, became a speck, only the white parasol twirling round and round. Running home, as soon as I was in the house, I said to Uncle Yagoro, "Father, I just met my mother now."

For a moment my foster father's temples twitched with surprise. Then opening his big mouth, he burst out laughing. "Sho. It's not likely your mother would come here. Your mother died in Echigo."

All at once I became sad. Running out to the fields at the edge of the village to where my foster mother was digging up sweet potatoes, I said to her, "Mother, just now, when I was coming back from school, I met my mother . . . she's a person with a white face. She called me Sho, twice. She knew my name. She must be my mother . . . it must be so. My mother came to see me."

Taking my foster mother's hand, I asked her to please tell me the truth, and started to cry. For an instant my mother seemed to give me a lonely look. Then she said, "Perhaps today is the day that your mother came . . . Sho. I don't know, but if that kind of person came to the village and called you by your name, maybe she was your real mother . . . but . . . Sho . . . it's your dream . . . look. The bamboos are in flower, all over the village. In Jizo Valley, in Butsu Valley, the bamboos are flowering this year. The bamboos are singing . . . don't you see them? It's like a sea of yellow flowers . . . a year when the bamboo flowers bloom comes around only once every so often . . . Sho. That person you saw, she was a lady who came from the land of dreams . . . your mother died a long time ago, in Echigo."

As my mother spoke, the tears coursed down her cheeks in several lines from her sun-crinkled eyes. Drawing me close to her, she held me hard.

"Sho . . . it was a dream you saw . . . some person who came out to see the bamboo flowers, you thought in your dream she was your mother."

Rubbing my nose against the sweat-smelling skin of

my foster mother, I sobbed and sobbed for what seemed like forever.

Indeed, when at my foster mother's words I looked at the bamboo grove in Jizo Valley by the side of the field, all the green leaves had fallen off. From between the trunks and branches, yellow flowers like heads of rice were blooming everywhere in profusion.

Bamboo flowers. Rather than flowers, it seemed to me that the bamboos were shedding their yellow, dried-out leaves. From then on, with each day that passed, the bamboo groves grew yellower and yellower. Some groves, when you looked at them from a distance, seemed as yellow as a field of rape blossoms. The whole village was surrounded by flowering bamboos.

One could say that it was an unusual year. It was the first time in my life that I had seen bamboo flowers. Since then, in all the long time that I have been a bamboo craftsman, I have never seen all the bamboo groves in flower like that, as if the mountainside had been colored yellow. Even if at times I had seen one or two bamboos put out their dried-looking flowers at the base of their branches as if blooming out of season, I'd never seen anything like that beautiful sea of bamboo flowers.

The bamboo is a strange plant. It is said to put out flowers only once every fifty years. If that is so, the bamboos that bloomed in Uchikoshi must have been very old. Even now I remember that those groves I saw in a profusion of flowers when I was seven years old first began to wither that winter. Those groves of speckled bamboo and long-jointed bamboo, which made a canopy over the village, shed all their leaves and dried and withered away, just as if they were being devoured by worms. Because the bamboos had flowered, the villagers had been in a panic, thinking that some untoward event would occur. But nothing happened. The village merely entered winter environed by dried-out and decayed bamboo groves. When I looked at those desiccated groves and thickets, I would suddenly recall that lady who had visited the village, twirling her parasol around and around, on that summer day when the bamboo flowers were at the height of full bloom.

My foster mother said I'd had a dream. But I wasn't napping or anything like that as I walked back from school. I'm sure I saw, with these eyes, on that narrow road between the bamboo groves, a lady with a twirling parasol come down toward me. And that person, stopping and standing still, called out to me, "Sho. Sho."

And then covering her face as if she were suddenly afraid, she ran past me. I can still hear her voice.

She must have been my real mother. This conviction deepened in me later, when I was trying to find out about that dreadful murder in Niigata Prefecture. I now believe that the forsaken wife of the itinerant miner Takarasu Yoshitaro, namely my mother, weary from searching for me, came to the village.

I have almost never seen a bamboo grove in full bloom since leaving the hamlet of Uchikoshi. But among my memories of that foster-parent village, where I lived and was taken care of until I graduated from grade school, I always cherish the memory of the face of the lady with the parasol.

Was it, after all, a vision of my mother that I saw?

No matter whom I might ask, there is no one in this world who can tell me.

Some years ago my foster mother and foster father

died one after the other. At their two funeral ceremonies, there were five foster children. Teiji of Echigo and Min of Kyoto, grown to adulthood, saw to the funerals of our foster parents. The hamlet of Uchikoshi, surrounded as ever by the beautiful groves of long-jointed bamboo and speckled bamboo, seemed asleep in a deep, peaceful slumber in its ravine.

I still do not know the name of my father or the name of my mother.

自
殺
の
す
す
め

Invitation to Suicide

渡 辺 淳 一

WATANABE JUN'ICHI

◆ **ONE**

There are various ways to kill oneself, but the face of the suicide is most beautiful after death by inhaling gas or by freezing to death in the snow.

In the case of death by gas, the cheeks are suffused with a faintly rosy pink. This is due to the high level of carbon monoxide in the blood. When an innocent young girl has died by this method, she is especially beautiful. Delicately tinged with vermilion, the eyebrows contracted in a slight frown, the face seems somehow out of breath, dewy with sweat. It is like the face of a virgin who has been taught the pains of sex and a certain transitory joy by the lust of a middle-aged man. But such beauty does not last. It will not keep for two hours. Only someone who has discovered it soon after the event may see that beauty. Therefore, this mode of death is recommended only when one is sure of being found within the hour by a man whom one loves.

In my third year of medical practice there was a girl who took this way out with brilliant success. I don't clearly remember her age, but she must have been twenty-four or twenty-five. A business girl, she was in love with a man three years older than herself who worked at the same company. There had been sexual relations, but since that time the man had fallen in love with another girl and become formally engaged to her. After a few scenes of passionate accusation and reproach, the first girl seemed to resign herself to losing him. Otherwise tactfully avoiding her, the man continued to have her assist him with his office work. The day before her suicide, the girl (although knowing it would not change things between them) promised to go through some sales receipts for him at home. The next morning the man stopped off at her apartment on his way to the office. The woman had made it a condition when she accepted the work that he come by for it in the morning.

When the man entered her room, the gas was on and the woman was dead. The work he had given her lay neatly done on a small table by the window. The woman had taken sleeping pills late at night and then turned on the gas. She was rushed to the hospital. Her face was alluringly flushed, as if she'd made herself up to die. There was no sign of a pulse or respiration; both were perfectly extinguished in death. This woman in her midtwenties looked no older than a girl of nineteen. Weeping, the young man stroked her cheeks repeatedly and cradled them in both hands. Before the arrival of her family, he kissed her on her gorgeous red mouth.

This seemed in no way strange to the nurses who were standing by.

There was very little for me to do, as the girl was already dead. After giving the nurses their instructions, I made out the death certificate. The cause of death, one would have to say, was suffocation, which in turn had been caused by carbon-monoxide poisoning. The time of death could only be estimated. It was then eight o'clock. It seemed reasonable to assume that she had stopped breathing at about seven.

"I'll just die if you don't come early in the morning."

The young man, in a broken voice, recalled that she had said this to him when they parted the previous evening. By his side, the girl's slender face was demurely composed. As one looked at her, she seemed almost proud of her death.

"How beautiful she is," the nurse said as she dabbed at the girl's mouth.

Certainly, as everyone agreed, it was a beautiful face. But somehow I could not bring myself to calmly accept its beauty. In a little while it would begin to decompose. The lovely arrogance of the young suicide's face inspired me with no good feelings.

When one freezes to death in snow, the beauty of one's face is no less than if one had inhaled gas. In a way it is superior. As long as the face is covered with snow, its beauty will last. It is a form of refrigeration that, other circumstances being favorable, may be continued indefinitely.

In the winter of my third year of senior high school, I had a classmate who chose this way to die. We had been in the same class since second year, but even before then Kuniko had been locally noted for her talent. A member of the Girls' Arts Society, she painted in the abstract manner. Whether it was because she went around with artists from an early age or whether it was in her nature, Kuniko, despite a strict upbringing by her school-principal father, led a rather fast life of cigarette smoking and drinking.

Kuniko had an unusually fair complexion, even for a girl of northern Japan, and great dark eyes. At that time she had already dyed her hair red, and was wearing a red beret and a red jacket. She smoked the Hikari brand of cigarettes, which came in a red box.

"I want to die," Kuniko would always say to me. When I asked girls who had known her for a long time, they told me that she had already attempted suicide twice.

"I'd like to die." In her young beauty that had just begun to put out its buds, Kuniko spoke as if she were singing. She made death sound like something really pleasant to look forward to.

"If you want to die that much, why not go ahead and do it."

I liked Kuniko, but there was something affected about her that annoyed me. Never thinking she would do it, I ridiculed her.

Midway in December of that year, however, she suddenly vanished. It was known that she had gone from Abashiri to the shores of Lake Akan. Where she had gone from there was a complete mystery. By the end of December the snow on the lake front was more than seven feet deep. Kuniko's corpse was discovered late the following March by lumberjacks from the Kushiro Forestry Service. It lay partially buried by the snow, in the neighborhood of a lookout station about two miles up from the lake. If it had been summer, one would have had a view of the dark-blue waters of Lake Akan between Greater Mount Akan and Lesser Mount Akan. In winter the lake appeared as a white plain framed by ground pine and snowy mountainside.

Kuniko lay face up, her head pointed at a slight angle down into the valley, her feet pointing back up the mountain. The snow near the road had melted, and the body was exposed from the thighs down. The spring sun had evidently had several days to work on it. When the men peeled off Kuniko's stockings, the skin also came away wetly. But the rest of the body from the abdomen was still covered by a good foot and a half of snow. Its surface had been granulated by melting and then freezing again at night, but underneath the snow was packed firm and hard. The men removed it carefully with their shovels. First the stomach emerged, then the breasts, and then the throat. Finally the face was uncovered.

Packed in snow, with a white cloth around her cheeks, Kuniko had the face of a snow maiden. Rather than white, the face of this seventeen-year-old girl was of a bluish translucent pallor. The veins of her temples showed through the skin a delicate purple. Rather than beautiful, her face was unearthly and frightening. As if transfixed, the men stood over the dead girl and stared at it.

There was nothing objectionable about the snow having melted from the legs down. But if this had been reversed, if Kuniko's face had festered in the sun, no doubt it would have been an unbearable sight. But perhaps Kuniko had taken the factor of the spring thaws into account and died so positioned as to preserve her face the longest. If that were the case, how impudent of her, I thought. I even felt a certain anger toward her.

That day Kuniko's body was taken by sled down to the lake. There it was put into a coffin and sent by train to her hometown. Along with recalling her beauty, I felt the guilt of having incited her to her death. This also was a suicide that I would not easily forget.

◆ TWO

There is one other suicide that I shall never forget. In this case I did not see the body, but happened to have met the deceased once during his life. I cannot dissociate this suicide from Mr Y, my anatomy teacher.

At that time, which was fifteen years ago, Mr Y was already sixty-five. Five years before that, having given up his post at H University, he came to my university as a lecturer emeritus in anatomy.

Mr Y was unusually tall and erect for his age. Under a thatch of snow-white hair, his slender figure seemed almost buoyantly withered. Perhaps this was why stories of a legendary nature attached themselves to him.

The first story I heard about Mr Y was that upon graduation with honors from T University he had been presented with a silver watch by the emperor. Of course, he was not a man who would tell this sort of story about himself. It must have been handed down from one generation of students to the next, starting from his first year at H University. Although approaching seventy, he showed no traces of senility, being in fact exceptionally clearheaded and intelligent. On the other hand, he was somewhat eccentric. His class in first-year anatomy was attended by only four or five students. This was an unusually low number even for a course in basic medicine. He gave his lectures without notes in an unconcerned, dry voice. But their content and cogency was such that they compelled one's interest and acquiescence in their truth.

For those students who were with him all day, life under Mr Y was an ordeal. "It's too much—the man knows everything," they would say. By the end of the first year or early into the second year, most students gave up going to his classes even occasionally. For his part Mr Y repelled everyone with his peculiar inaccessibility. This was one reason why, although admiring his splendid qualities of scholarship, people wanted nothing to do with him. Dwindling yearly, his classes stood at their then low size. Mr Y gave no sign that he was bothered by his decline in popularity. "Those who wish to may come. Those who do not may stay away." Although not saying this in so many words, he conveyed it perfectly by his calm manner.

Another reason why young doctors-to-be kept clear of him was that he was neither a doctor nor a Ph.D. This in fact may have been the most important reason.

Students go into basic medicine unconnected with clinical work because they can get a degree quicker that way. In other words, they wish to live the easy life of the Ph.D. A degree adds luster to their calling cards, and if they do decide to open a practice, they will have no trouble getting patients. But when the teacher to whom they look for guidance is not even a doctor, much less a Ph.D., they cannot but hesitate to go to him. It is unavoidably awkward and embarrassing to say to such a teacher "I want a degree."

When Mr Y graduated from medical school in the early teens, there were no national medical exams as there are today. The mere fact of having graduated enabled one to receive a doctor's certificate from the Welfare Ministry for the sum of one yen, fifty sen. All one had to do was go there and get it. Yet Mr Y did not appear at the ministry within the prescribed six months' period. He could have sent a proxy, of course, but he did not even do that. His eligibility having expired, he forfeited the right to become a doctor. One could say that this didn't matter, since a dissector, unlike a clinical doctor, does not see patients but merely works with dead bodies and therefore needs no license. But one would think that Mr Y, having trained himself to be a doctor, might at least have taken his certificate. Be that as it may, Mr Y, eschewing all contact with the clinical side of medicine, went straight into the classroom as an anatomy instructor. Herein he differed from the average medical student. Was it because he didn't want to spend the money, or didn't have time to go to the ministry, or because he forgot to? Or was it that he disdained anything that could be gotten so easily? He never gave his reasons, so we could only guess at them. All we knew for certain was that Mr Y of the medical department was not a doctor.

And evidently it was the same story with his failure to take a Ph.D. Mr Y published many extremely original articles on the bones of the Ainu, which in number and quality were in no way inferior to the work of professors in other areas of medical study. And yet, not in his five years at T University after graduation, nor in his two years of study in Germany, nor since he had taught at H University had Mr Y written a doctoral thesis. He did not go after a degree, so he was not given one. It was as simple as that. Perhaps he was averse to such things from the start, having seen through the trend of our times in which Ph.D.'s are as numerous as pebbles on a beach. What difference does it make, you may ask, if, with neither a doctor's license nor a degree, he was named at thirty-six as lecturer at Tokyo Imperial University? But not many are capable of that kind of bold negligence. It is usual even for those with a good deal of self-confidence to obtain at least a doctor's license as a precaution.

Such being the case, students hesitated to commit the vulgarity of going to Mr Y with the intention of acquiring a degree. Somehow nothing is more embarrassing and shameful than to work for a Ph.D. under a teacher who is greatly superior to oneself and yet a mere instructor. Besides, Mr Y's doctoral coaching had grown stern and harsh of late. Most students did not even think of going to him.

Mr Y always accompanied his hour-long lectures with three or four drawings on the blackboard. These facilitated one's understanding immeasurably better than explanations from a book. Mr Y drew his pictures with swift, easy strokes. There was no hesitation, no correction or addition. Whatever part of the body was portrayed, it was startlingly lifelike. When Mr Y drew bones, they were magnificently bonelike. Even students specializing in medical draftsmanship could not compete with his skill. And it was not due simply to experience, for the drawings of the other anatomy teacher were totally inept.

"That strength of design is unusual. He must have studied drawing in the past." This was said by a man from the anatomical-charts department as he looked intently at the drawing of a leg that had been left behind on the blackboard. From the middle of the thigh, the biceps was gathered at the knee. Directly beneath, the "flatfish" muscle widened and narrowed again like a spindle as it neared the Achilles' tendon. The leg looked as if it would come to life at any minute.

System-dissection courses generally end with the first year of medical school. During winter recess I went out for a drink with Yoshimoto, an upperclassman and member of the mountain-climbing club. He told me a curious story.

"Mr Y was a member of the Pan Society, it seems."

"'The Pan Society'?" I'd heard the name but could not recall where.

"A couple of members of the White Birch Society were in it—Kitahara Hakushu, for one, and Kinoshita Mokutaro."

"Ah, *that* Pan Society," I said, still in the dark. Something I had learned in high school now came back to me. Wasn't the Pan Society a group of artists, poets, and novelists that flourished from the late Meiji era into the early years of Taisho? Advocates of a Western-style aestheticism, its members put out such clique magazines as *Viewpoint*, *Roof Garden*, *Pleiades*, and *Three Fields*, and used to meet at a downtown restaurant.

"You're sure of this?"

"Absolutely. Mr O told me." Mr O was a professor of Japanese literature at our university. Evidently it was true.

"This was after he'd left T University?"

"No. While he was a student."

Mr Y's having left the university in the early teens would fit the story exactly.

"What sort of things did he write?"

"He didn't. He was a painter."

"Oh, really?" That was why he drew so well. When I'd had this thought, I had another. "Mr Y can't have gone into medicine to study drawing . . . ?"

"'To study drawing'?"

"There's no better way to learn how to draw the human body than by studying anatomy. Why even Michelangelo . . ."

"No. It can't be."

"But it is. That's why he never took a doctor's license." My spur-of-the-moment idea, as I thought about it, seemed completely plausible.

"So why did he become a university lecturer?"

"Well . . ." This question had me stumped for a moment. But then I said, "Probably because he was too talented."

"'Too talented'?" Yoshimoto looked at me dubiously.

"Yes." I spoke with confidence.

Surely that was what had happened. Drawn into the workings of the medical department, Mr Y had been sent to Germany for two years' study. Recommended as an instructor, he'd been transferred to H University on the northernmost island of Hokkaido. He had lost contact with the Tokyo-based Pan Society, but his desire to be an artist had persisted. I was satisfied with my newfound theory. It explained everything. Mr Y the lecturer in anatomy was the ghost of Mr Y the artist. I thought of the old teacher in the classroom, his dry voice droning on and on.

◆ THREE

About a week after my chat with Yoshimoto, Mr Y brought up the subject of suicide in one of his lectures.

His lecture that day was on local dissection of the neck. With his customary skill, Mr Y did a drawing of the neck on the blackboard. Above the neck, the line of the jaw seemed to turn upward lightly.

"From the mastoid at the back of the jaw, there is a sinew that extends obliquely to the front part of the collarbone and the outer part of the breastbone. It is particularly visible at times of high excitement when the neck is twisted to one side. In long-necked young women, for example, it is particularly beautiful. There is a special German word for it: *konich*. In other words, it is the sinew that supports the neck."

Shading it in lightly with white chalk, Mr Y drew a full-length picture of the sinew.

"Traversing this sinew in front along the jaw and in back by the collarbone, the carotid artery and the jugular vein run parallel to each other. At this point the carotid is extremely close to the surface. If you place your finger beneath your jaw, you will feel a fairly strong pulse."

As if listening for a sound of distant footsteps, Mr Y put his finger to his neck. A few of the students did likewise.

"Of these two great conduits of the blood, the jugular vein is here," Mr Y said, drawing it in with blue chalk, "and the carotid is here." This one he drew in with red chalk. As the students were taking notes, he waited for them on the rostrum with a slightly bored expression. It was a tiered classroom, and a few students in the upper rows were asleep.

"There once was a medical student who contemplated suicide. Whether or not he had any reason to kill himself—I rather doubt that he did—he took a razor to himself, here." Mr Y laid a long, wrinkled index finger along his jaw. "The blood gushed out and he collapsed on the spot. When a friend found him in his apartment, he was lying face down in a pool of blood. But when the friend shook him and spoke to him, he answered."

The ghost of a smile hovered on Mr Y's lips.

"The student had severed not the carotid artery but the jugular vein. When one opens this vein, it will bleed copiously for a while. Once a certain amount of blood has been lost, however, it will naturally stanch itself. Even more unfortunate was the fact that the student had fallen face down. If one is to die, one must neatly cut the carotid artery and lie flat on one's back."

Even the students who had been asleep opened their eyes at this joke of the teacher's.

"If one has taken the trouble to go to medical school, one might at least learn where the carotid artery is."

The students began to laugh. One of those who had been dozing scratched his head sheepishly.

"When a medical student makes this kind of elementary mistake, it is indeed laughable."

A month later I got together again with Yoshimoto. After some talk of winter sports, I remembered the lecture and told him about it.

"He was referring to U," Yoshimoto said, pouring his own saké.

"'U'?"

"Yes. I believe you met him."

"I did?"

"It was after we'd gotten back from Mount Tokachi. I

had a sukiyaki party in my room, remember? He was that quiet fellow in the corner."

"Oh, and short, with a funny sort of striped shirt?" A few details came back to me.

"That's the one."

"Was he in your mountain-climbing club?"

"No. He never went near mountains. He was two years ahead of me. But for a while we lived on the same floor."

"Which room was his?"

"The last one down the hallway."

"Ah, was that the room . . ."

"No, I'm wrong. He'd already moved out when he tried suicide. He was something of an oddball. I never could understand those paintings he did."

If I remembered correctly, U had sat by himself with his arms around his knees and not said a word. He drank off five or six glasses of saké and was gone by the time the party began to get noisy.

"Where is he now?"

"U? He's dead."

"'Dead'?" Despite myself, I put my raised glass down on the counter. "Suicide?"

"Mm. He tried again. This time he cut through the carotid."

"On the same side?" I looked up at Yoshimoto. He nodded.

"But didn't he know that Mr Y made a joke of it to the class?"

"He must have. I think someone told him."

"Then why did he do it?"

"Who knows? Anyway, the second time was a splendid success."

I tried to remember if I'd seen a scar on U's neck. But memory failed me.

"Those who saw the body say it was done with a neat lateral incision, just like in the book."

"'The book'?"

"The textbook on dissection, where it talks about the carotid."

I could not speak.

"The blood had drained from the face. It was as white as a candle, they say. As beautiful as the face of someone who has frozen to death."

I had no clear memory of U's face in life. But I could imagine its pallor in death.

"Does Mr Y know about this?"

"Yes, he does. U was in his second year of medical school when he died. That would make him around twenty-two."

"And Mr Y, when he heard about it . . .?"

"Well, I don't know, but he didn't seem too impressed when he talked with the students."

"'Impressed'?"

"He said something like not having botched it the second time."

"He actually said that?"

"Because the second time U had done it the way he'd been taught."

I remembered the slight smile I had seen when the old teacher began to talk of suicide.

"He must have really hated him."

"Oh, no. He was old enough to be his grandfather." As he spoke, Yoshimoto ordered another bottle of saké.

In the suicides by inhaling gas and by freezing to

death, and in U's case as well, the face of the dead person was beautiful. But had they, at the moment of death, been thinking of how their face would look afterward? Was there vanity even in death? I felt a twinge of envy. At the same time I wanted to be angry with them.

Translator's Notes

Nagai Kafu was born on December 3, 1879, in Tokyo, in what is now Bunkyo-ku, then a secluded residential district of former daimyo estates. "The Fox," published in January 1909, is notable as the first of his works to draw on Japanese materials. Since his return from an extended tour of the West, Kafu had written only of his travels. Although a short piece, "The Fox" is justly ranked among his best work. More of a childhood memory piece than a story, it records exactly his ambivalence toward his authoritarian father and his feeling for his mother. And like Turgenev's childhood tale of the snake and the frog that led him to doubt the mercy of God, Kafu's story of the fox does nothing less than bring all notions of human justice into question. It also strikes the fundamental note of Kafu's work, that of nostalgia. Kafu died on April 30, 1959.

Satomi Ton was born on July 14, 1888, in Yokohama.

The youngest brother of Arishima Takeo, who went on to become a famous writer in his own right, Satomi was adopted by his mother's family at birth. He was a founding member of *Shirakaba (White Birch)* literary magazine at Peers' School. In contrast to the pronouncements of other members, Satomi commented that he was "moved by nothing more than a vague desire to try his hand at writing." On the strength of his early work he was acclaimed by the eminent critic Watsuji Tetsuro as Japan's foremost psychological writer. One of the most brilliant examples of Satomi's psychological acuity is "Flash Storm," first published in 1916. A precise description of the effect that light and dark exert on the human psyche, it has been praised by Satomi's contemporary Katsuoka Yoshikazu as all but conveying the actual personal scents of the man and woman secluded in a shuttered room during a thunderstorm and the beating of their hearts. Satomi died in 1983.

Okamoto Kanoko was born on March 1, 1889, in the Akasaka district of Tokyo, now Minato-ku. Both her father, who had been a purveyor to the Tokugawa shogunate, and her mother, descended from a famous old family of Kanagawa Prefecture and skilled in the ballad drama known as *tokiwazu*, were persons of artistic taste. "Ivy Gates" belongs to a group of stories about ordinary Tokyo people written during the last years of Okamoto's life. It preserves the atmosphere of the Meiji and Taisho eras that lingered on in the low-lying *shitamachi* district east of the Sumida River and the hilly district to the west until the late thirties. Her writing was much admired by Kawabata Yasunari, and more recently has served as an inspiration for the artist Oda

Mayumi. Her major work is the long novel *Shojoruten* (*The Vicissitudes of Life*). On January 31, 1939, on a trip to the Ginza with a young friend, Okamoto Kanoko was stricken by a cerebral hemorrhage as she got off the bus. She died eighteen days later.

Akutagawa Ryunosuke was born on March 1, 1892, in the Kyobashi district of Tokyo. His father was a milk dealer who owned farms in Kyobashi and Shinjuku. When his mother lost her sanity nine months after the baby's birth, he was adopted by her elder brother in Honjo, taking the latter's family name. The family was an old, cultured one, with a record of service as tea-ceremony masters under generations of the Tokugawa shogunate. "The Garden" is said to describe the boy-hood circumstances of Akutagawa's friend Koana Ryuichi. Akutagawa, who committed suicide early on the morning of July 24, 1927, with an overdose of Veronal at his home in Tabata, left one of the world's most famous farewell notes. It begins "No one has yet exactly described the feelings of the suicide himself." Despite this promising beginning, however, the note casts little light on the matter, mentioning only a "certain uneasiness."

Juichiya Gisaburo was born in Kobe on October 14, 1897. Although sickly from infancy, he learned to read two years before he entered grade school. His father died when he was twelve years old. During his middle school years he worked as a houseboy for a local brewer, studying in adversity. Before his graduation he had read his way through most of the volumes of Japanese, Chinese, and Western literature in his neighborhood library. After graduation he became a clerk in a pharmacy. His domestic circumstances were unhappy. While at Kyoto Third Upper School he published with a friend a literary magazine called *Heresy* and at Tokyo University another called *Journey*. His major was English literature, an interest that was to lead to his translation in 1931 of *Jane Eyre*, surely one of the unlikelier literary feats of its time and place. "Grass" is one of a handful of short stories he left. Juichiya Gisaburo died on April 2, 1937.

Yokomitsu Riichi was born on March 17, 1898, at a mountain hot-spring inn in Fukushima Prefecture. The peripatetic nature of his father's profession, that of engineering contractor, has been credited with Yokomitsu's later dislike for the dominant "I-novel," with its stress on origins, although, as Donald Keene has commented, his best stories ironically enough were those that made use of material most commonly drawn on by such novels. It might also be added that Yokomitsu's most successful work tends to employ methods more traditional than those espoused by the "new sensationalism," a mélange of perhaps not very clearly understood theoretical borrowings from modern Western literature with which Yokomitsu and a few other writers sought to underpin their work. "Mount Hiei" is one such story, first published in 1935. Yokomitsu Riichi died on December 30, 1947.

Kawabata Yasunari, Japan's sole winner of the Nobel Prize in literature, whose work is so well known abroad that his name is often written in Western order, hardly requires a biographical note. He was born on June 11,

1899, in Osaka. His father died when he was one, his mother when he was two. Orphaned thus early, he became known as "the master of funerals" for his authoritative demeanor on such occasions. The spiritual loneliness imparted by the loss of his parents in infancy informs all of Kawabata's mature writing. His single most famous work is *Snow Country*, the tale of a disaffected city intellectual who cannot fully respond to the love of a country hot-spring geisha, although Kawabata himself thought his work existed at its purest in *Palm of the Hand Stories*, a body of very short stories employing the insight and brevity of the haiku. Kawabata died, apparently by his own hand, in 1972.

Nakayama Gishu was born on October 5, 1900, in Fukushima Prefecture. In 1923, upon graduation from Waseda University, with the woman he had recently wed, Nakayama went to teach English at a middle school in Mie Prefecture. Finding it hard to reconcile his pedagogical duties with his literary ambitions, he quit two years later and returned to Tokyo. Later he taught for a spell at Narita Middle School, retaining his devotion to literature through all hardships. The year he lost his ailing wife, 1935, may have been the worst year of his life, mostly given over to drinking and drifting. Three years later, however, with his winning of a major literary prize for "Atsumonozaki," a short story about a successful seventy-year-old chrysanthemum grower and enthusiast, Nakayama began to see his way clear to a life as a writer. Leaving his two children with his parents in the country, he lived alone in Tokyo for two years writing. By 1941 he was able to have his family rejoin him. During the Pacific War he took a pleasure trip through the South Seas. After the war and the marriage of his daughter, he remarried and lived out the rest of his life in uneventfulness. "Autumn Wind," a tale of the old days that reveals the author's fondness for the past, was published in 1939. Nakayama died in 1969.

Sakaguchi Ango was born in the city of Niigata on October 20, 1906, the son of a high-level local administrator. Sakaguchi, like Dazai Osamu, is a writer primarily associated with the postwar period, a brief flowering amid the prostration and confusion of defeat. His essay "Discourse on Defeat," with its words "We do not fall because we have lost the war; we fall because we are human beings; we fall because we live . . . live, and fall," and his story "The Idiot," a tale of life if not love among the ruins, brought Sakaguchi immediately to the forefront of the postwar literary scene. Critics have commented on the strangely lighthearted note Sakaguchi manages to strike in such stories as "One Woman and the War," as if at the heart of human aloneness and the vulgarity of the world, beyond all depression and despair, a sane and healthy brightness might be found. Sakaguchi is, again like Dazai, an essentially youthful writer, much read and loved by young people. And like Dazai he died when he was fairly young, on February 17, 1955.

Hayashi Fumiko was born on the last day of 1909 on the second floor of a tin-roofed shack in Shimonoseki, the daughter of an itinerant peddler and a hot-spring-inn chambermaid. Her *Diary of a Vagrant*, which was just that, brought her instant popularity when it was published in June 1930. Perhaps her most important work is *Floating Clouds,* the story of a woman faithful to her lover from the idyllic days of their meeting in occupied French Indochina to the sad, deprived days after their return to defeated Japan, his abandonment of her, and her death. There is a roadside shrine to Hayashi outside the inn in Sakurajima where her mother worked. A tourist bus stops there regularly, and the girl guide sings a song from Hayashi's work, a song about love of family and home. On the literary marker, this poem by Hayashi is engraved: "The life of a flower is short; only bitter things are many" *(Hana no inochi wa mijikakute nigashiki koto nomi ōkariki).* Hayashi Fumiko died of a heart attack on June 28, 1951, after an evening on the Ginza. Kawabata was the chief mourner at her funeral service, held in her home.

Mizukami Tsutomu was born in 1919 in Fukui Prefecture. He lived in a temple of the Rinzai sect of Zen from the age of nine until his graduation from middle school. He was obliged to withdraw from college midway because of financial difficulties. Thereafter, he went through a succession of some thirty jobs, such as grade school teacher and vagrant peddler, studying literature and writing all the while. In 1948 he published *Song of the Frying Pan.* This was followed by ten years' silence due to personal circumstances. Then in 1959, inspired by a reading of Matsumoto Seicho's *Points and Lines,* he made a literary comeback with *Mist and Shadow.* In 1961 he won the important Naoki Prize for *Wild Goose Temple,* and since then has been at the forefront of popular Japanese fiction, which tends (or has tended) to have folk themes.

Kita Morio was born on May 1, 1927, in Tokyo, the son of the poet Saito Mokichi. From his fifth year in grade school Kita was a passionate insect collector and, with the intention of becoming an entomologist, read almost no literature. However, shortly before entering Tokyo University, he had begun to write poetry. During his university sojourn Kita abruptly embarked on what was to be a two-thousand-page novel, but having left off at about page 400, was obliged to boil it down to a ten-page story, which was never published. Graduating with a medical degree, Kita interned as a nerve specialist at Keio University Hospital. However, he began to find his way as a writer, publishing such stories as "Along the Mountain Ridge." Since then, he has gone on to become a very successful writer on the light side, known especially for his Doctor Mambo series of children's books.

Kurahashi Yumiko, a writer born in 1935 who made her debut in the sixties, streaked like a meteor through that decade with her daring experimentalism. In the world of her stories she absolutely barred the intrusion of realistic truths. By so doing, she was able to create a world whose characters, unhampered by reality, could commit the most purely outrageous actions in following their spiritually flamboyant life (and death) styles. "Ugly Demons" has as its protagonists the young lovers M and the narrator (from other stories tentatively identified as S) and the sexually as well as otherwise ambiguous Q, a Negro of dubious provenance who is found washed up on the beach one day near the lovers' seaside villa. They exemplify Kurahashi's world, in which nothing happens except in the mind. Having fallen largely silent since the sixties, Kurahashi is by way of being a mystery figure of the Japanese literary world.

Watanabe Jun'ichi, a contemporary author born in 1933, is known as a prolific writer of romantic novels. In some of his earlier work, however, he draws on his experience as a medical student. Notable among these is "Invitation to Suicide," a story woven of pathos and paradox. The narrator affects indignation at the girl who has used gas to achieve the most beautiful after-death look, arranging to be discovered by her lover within the two-hour period during which the alluring, gas-induced flush remains in her cheeks. Later in the story, rather than the indignation and envy he has displayed at such earlier suicides, the narrator shows no interest in the bedridden demise, from cerebral hemorrhage and proctoparalysis, of the elderly medical lecturer who has egged on one of his students to kill himself. In this and other stories Watanabe seems to be getting back at his scientific training.

Glossary

-chan: a suffix often attached to a child's name or nick-name

haori: a kind of short jacket worn over a kimono

I-novel: a form of modern fiction that is largely autobio-graphical

kae-uta style: a type of singing in which the words of one song are sung to the melody of another

Kansai: the west central area of Japan, in particular around the cities of Kyoto, Kobe, and Osaka

kotatsu: a foot warmer consisting of a low table, a coverlet, and an electric (or charcoal) heating unit

Meiji Restoration: the coup in which antishogunate forces seized the Imperial Palace in Kyoto and announced the return of political power from the shogunate to the emperor *monpe:* baggy peasant trousers that women were expected to wear during World War II

obi: a kimono sash

rōnin: a samurai who lost his master and thus was forced to wander

shitamachi: the old downtown, traditional area of Tokyo

tabi: a kind of sock, with the space for the big toe divided from the space for the other toes

yukata: a light, cotton kimono commonly worn in summer

Other New Releases in the TUTTLE CLASSICS

ELLERY QUEEN

Japanese Detective Stories   ISBN 4-8053-0851-6

Japan, with its cacophony of humming factories, boisterous night-spots, and silent, sober tea rooms, temples, and gardens, is one of the most crime-free societies in the world today—hardly fertile soil for the well-tuned tale of murder and mystery—yet the stories in this volume, written by award-winning Japanese writers, are as entertaining, perplexing, and homicidal as those of the best Western writers. Although malice and murder are inescapably international, motives often differ from East to West, and many of the stories in this book explore a criminal psychology that is uniquely Japanese. Here we have crimes provoked by shame or pride, by an avenging or sacrificial spirit, by fierce loyalty or fear of betrayal. In this first major attempt to introduce mystery writers and readers throughout the world to a completely new and provocative collection of styles, motives and victims, compiler Ellery Queen selected a dozen first-rate mysteries from among 2500 detective-crime-mystery stories published in Japan in the 1970s that are sure to delight and befuddle the devotee.

SAKAE TSUBOI

Twenty-four Eyes   ISBN 4-8053-0772-2

Twenty-four Eyes is a deeply pacifist novel based on the perversion and inhumanity of modern war. Set on Shodoshima, a small island in the Inland Sea, and covering a twenty-year period embracing prewar, war-time, and early postwar Japan, it centers on the relationship between a primary school teacher, Miss Oishi, and the twelve island children (the twenty-four eyes of the title) in her first class. In the course of the novel, Miss Oishi faces problems of acceptance by the children and their parents, then ideological criticism from the educational authorities, then wartime privations and losses in her family and among her pupils. The book concludes with a tearful graduation reunion between the bereaved teacher and her original pupils, whose ranks are sadly depleted by the suffering of the past decade. Differences of class, gender and political opinion are finally rendered less important than a common experience of suffering.

Twenty-four Eyes, first published in Japanese as *Nijushi no Hitomi* in 1952, immediately became a bestseller. It was made into a film two years later by Keisuke Kinoshita, a leading director, winning Best Film of the year. In 1987, it was filmed for a second time.

IHARA SAIKAKU

Comrade Loves of The Samurai   ISBN 4-8053-0771-4

First published privately in London in 1928 for subscribers to a set entitled *Eastern Love*, this volume comprises two separate books in one. The first, *Comrade Loves of the Samurai*, is a selection of stories from the works of the Japanese novelist Ihara Saikaku on the theme of homosexual love: of samurai for samurai or samurai for court boy bent on becoming samurai. To the old Japanese, such love was quite permissible. The sons of samurai families were urged to form homosexual liaisons while youth lasted, and often these loves matured into lifelong companionships. Ihara describes Japanese love scenes of all kinds with a frankness that has made him a favorite of expurgators, but he treats the subject of normal and abnormal love with tenderness.

The second book is an anthology entitled *Songs of the Geisha*, selected and translated by E. Powys Mather. The folk songs, composed to be sung to the accompaniment of the *shamisen*, are intimately personal, expressing the feelings of the geisha toward their sympathetic listeners. Love, frustration and the futility of hope are their main themes. The lyrics, for all their erotic symbolism, are restrained and tactful and have a charmingly nostalgic quality suitable to the times.

JIRO OSARAGI

Homecoming   ISBN 4-8053-0649-1

Jiro Osaragi's *Homecoming*, originally published in 1950 as Kikyo, was the first contemporary Japanese novel to be translated into English after World War II. Against a background of often confrontational and coincidental meetings and partings, fleeting joys and regrets, initially in Singapore and then in Japan, it describes the author's anger at the trivial attitudes that surfaced after the war through a gallery of magnificent contemporary portraits: Kyogo, whose exile and Europeanization have made him yearn for old-fashioned ways; Professor Oki, an opportunistic and hypocritical bureaucrat shaped by war and its aftermath; Saeko, the adventuress, and her husband, the ineffectual son of an aristocratic family; Otane, his passive mistress, the prototype of the geisha; Admiral Ushigi, who represents the attitudes of former officers toward new times in Japan; Toshi, the slick undergraduate who justifies his "democratic" egotism with glib argument; and Yukichi, the repository of Japan's hope. The novel is an honest portrayal of postwar Japanese feelings and characteristics from a purely internal point of view.

KENKŌ

Essays in Idleness   ISBN 4-8053-0631-9

Between 1330 and 1332 the Buddhist priest Kenkō having, as he put it, "nothing better to do", turned to his inkstone and brushes. He jotted down his thoughts, observations and opinions; anecdotes that he found interesting, amusing or instructive; accounts of customs and ceremonies—everything that seemed to him worthy of preservation. Donald Keene's complete translation admirably presents this extraordinarily influential Japanese classic.

The little essays—none of them more than a few pages in length, and some consisting of but two or three sentences—give us the self-portrait of a most engaging gentleman. He loves the past: every scrap of tradition is precious to him. He is haunted by transience, by the vanity of human desires and ambitions, by the inevitable approach of death. He values modesty and simplicity, even as he appreciates subtlety and formality. Sometimes he contradicts himself, as a journal keeper may so easily do, but these lapses are in themselves endearing.

However, Kenkō is consistent in his statement of the peculiarly Japanese aesthetic principle: beauty is intrinsically bound to its perishability. The imperfect, the irregular, the understated, beginnings and endings—these have a charm of their own which surpasses that of completion.

Essays in Idleness has been, writes Professor Keene, "a central work in the development of Japanese taste. Though Kenkō's argument . . . often consists merely in a brief statement of perceptions, he succeeded in defining with great sensitivity aesthetic preferences that have been true of Japan ever since."

SHUGORO YAMAMOTO

The Flower Mat   ISBN 0-8048-3333-8

First published as *Hanamushiro* in 1948, the setting for *The Flower Mat* is eighteenth-century Japan, a time when families were bound together by a rigid code of honor and individual lives were of necessity valued far less than the interests of the group. It tells of a young bride, Ichi, born into such a tradition, groomed in the virtues of ideal womanhood, and finally tempered by tragedy. Her life and fate are bound up inexorably with the fortunes of her in-laws, high-ranking officials. She soon becomes aware that something is dreadfully wrong, that something is threatening her home and her peaceful way of life. Uneasy and frightened, she tries to put clues together, but her questions go unanswered. Political intrigue and sudden tragedy force her into a new and unfamiliar world. We follow Ichi as she grows from passive observer—a wife suppressing her own passions—to active agent—a woman who will risk anything for justice. Struggling for truth and justice, Ichi finds that her only weapons are her own strength and the lovely mats, decorated with delicate flowers, that she designs.

MURASAKI SHIKIBU

The Tale of Genji   ISBN 0-8048-3823-2

Not speaking is the wiser part,
And words are sometimes vain,
But to completely close the heart
In silence, gives me pain.

— Prince Genji, in *The Tale of Genji*

Written centuries before the time of Shakespeare and even Chaucer, *The Tale of Genji* marks the birth of the novel—and after more than a millenium, this seminal work continues to enchant readers throughout the world. Lady Murasaki Shikibu and her tale's hero, Prince Genji, have had an unmatched influence on Japanese culture. Prince Genji manifests what was to become an image of the ideal Heian-era courtier: gentle and passionate. Genji is also a master poet, dancer, musician and painter. *The Tale of Genji* follows Prince Genji through his many loves, and varied passions. This book has influenced not only generations of courtiers and samurai of the distant past, but artists and painters even in modern times—episodes in the tale have been incorporated into the design of kimonos and handicrafts, and the four-line poems called *waka* which dance throughout this work have earned it a place as a classic text in the study of poetry.

JOHN ALLYN

The 47 Ronin Story   ISBN 0-8048-3827-5

The 47 Ronin Story is the unforgettable saga of a band of samurai who defied the Emperor's laws and faced certain destruction to avenge the disgrace and death of their master.
The story begins in 1701, when Lord Asano is goaded into lashing out at a corrupt court official. Although the wound Asano inflicts is minimal, the Emperor's punishment is harsh—Lord Asano is ordered to commit seppuku, or ritual suicide. His lands are confiscated and his family dishonored and exiled. His samurai now become ronin, or masterless, and are dispersed.
The ronin are not trusted by their enemies, and live under the watchful eyes of spies for months. They seem to be adapting to their new circumstances, some more gracefully than others, by taking on the roles of simple tradesmen and teachers. Their leader, Oishi, appears to have lost his path in life, and become a hapless drunk.

In fact, the ronin only appear to accept their fate. They are making careful plans for revenge, and counting the minutes until the moment is right to strike. Their acts are the source for Japan's most celebrated story of bravery, cunning and loyalty. It has been told and retold in plays, in print, in books, in movies and on television—ever since the news first swept through feudal Japan.

While many of the historical details are lost to time, John Allyn does a masterful job of presenting *The 47 Ronin Story* as a compelling and suspenseful tale—one that remains true to the spirit of an age when the samurai was an icon and honor and loyalty were worth dying for.

TUTTLE CLASSICS

HEARN, Lafcadio　ラフカディオ・ハーン

In Ghostly Japan　霊の日本　0-8048-3361-2 (4-8053-0749-8 for sale
　in Japan only)

Kokoro　心　0-8048-3660-4 (4-8053-0748-X for sale in Japan only)

Kwaidan　怪談　0-8048-3662-0 (4-8053-0750-1 for sale in Japan only)

INOUE, Yasushi　井上靖

The Counterfeiter and Other Stories　ある偽作家の生涯、他
　0-8048-3252-8

The Hunting Gun　猟銃　0-8048-0257-2

ISHIKAWA, Takuboku　石川啄木

Romaji Diary and Sad Toys　ローマ字日記、悲しき玩具
　0-8048-3253-6

KAIKO, Takeshi　開高健

Darkness in Summer　夏の闇　0-8048-3325-7 (4-8053-0644-0
　for sale in Japan only)

KAWABATA, Yasunari　川端康成

Beauty and Sadness　美しさと哀しみと　4-8053-0394-8

The Izu Dancer and Other Stories　伊豆の踊り子　0-8048-1141-5
　(4-8053-0744-7 for sale in Japan only)

The Master of Go　名人　4-8053-0673-4

The Old Capital　古都　4-8053-0610-6

Snow Country　雪国　4-8053-0635-1

The Sound of the Mountain　山の音　4-8053-0663-7

Thousand Cranes　千羽鶴　4-8053-0667-X

MISHIMA, Yukio　三島由紀夫

After the Banquet　宴のあと　4-8053-0628-9

Confessions of a Mask　仮面の告白　4-8053-0232-1

Death in Midsummer and Other Stories　真夏の死　4-8053-0617-3

The Decay of the Angel　天人五衰　4-8053-0385-9

Forbidden Colors　禁色　4-8053-0630-0

Runaway Horses　奔馬　4-8053-0354-9

The Sailor Who Fell from Grace with the Sea　午後の曳航
　4-8053-0629-7

The Samurai Ethics and Modern Japan　葉隠入門　4-8053-0645-9

The Sound of Waves　潮騒　4-8053-0636-X

TUTTLE CLASSICS

TUTTLE CLASSICS